ANGELA M. SANDERS

Secret of the Blue Lily

WIDOW'S KISS

Printed in the United States of America.

First Printing, 2020

ISBN 978-1-7349675-0-0

Widow's Kiss
P.O. Box 82488
Portland, OR 97282

www.WidowsKissBooks.com

Book design: Eric Lancaster

For Denyse and Jicky

Secret of the Blue Lily

Chapter 1

Pallbearers lowered the casket into the freshly cut earth. Inside lay Pearl Littlewood. Joanna couldn't have said what she looked like, since they'd never met. Pearl's mother hadn't even been able to produce a photo.

Lilies of the valley and yellow roses quivered as the casket descended. The August sky above the Montparnasse cemetery had thickened to a woolly gray. The marble crypt's lid, littered with a lacy blanket of yellow acacia blossoms, rested beside the grave, already a few caskets deep. It was carved with the family name LE GALL.

Joanna glanced across the grave to Philippe Le Gall, the man Pearl's mother said would be her contact in Paris. She and Philippe had met briefly at the funeral before he'd been absorbed into the crowd of mourners. Despite the heat, he wore a sober wool suit the same shade of charcoal as his hair. Grief lined his thin face.

After the priest muttered his final benediction over the casket, Philippe led Joanna to the cemetery's gate. "If you don't mind, I'll leave you here. My driver will take you to the apartment."

"Thank you for managing Pearl's service," Joanna said. "I'm so sorry for your loss. I hope they find the driver who hit her."

"Pearl was special to me." Philippe pronounced her name as "Pairell," but his English was smooth with a hint of a British accent. "I'm sorry her family wasn't able to make it."

"Her mother is very grateful," Joanna said, hoping the words came off as genuine.

"I had the linens changed and a few things put in the refrigerator for you. I hope you'll be comfortable." He seemed about to say something else, but changed his mind. "I'll see you at dinner tomorrow. We'll go over the paperwork then. Oh, and" —he handed her a red leather book, the funeral's guestbook— "please give this to Mrs. Littlewood."

"Thank you. I will." Joanna had a vague idea that Philippe, Pearl on his mind, would return to a small apartment, open a can of pâté, and listen to opera on the radio.

As Joanna slipped into the sedan's backseat, thunder grumbled in the distance. Her eyes burned with fatigue. She absently slid the funeral's guestbook to her lap, but left it closed in favor of watching toast-colored buildings stream by the windows.

At Pearl's apartment—Joanna's for the next two weeks—she rolled in her suitcase and tossed the guestbook on a coffee table. She pulled open a French window to relieve the room's stuffiness. A few fat drops of rain splattered to the sidewalk five stories below.

Joanna turned to face the apartment. Open French doors separated the front into two modest rooms, each anchored by a marble fireplace and filled with furniture and decorations seemingly gathered from flea markets and antiques shops.

Across the entry hall was a small kitchen. Joanna opened the refrigerator. As Philippe had promised, a plate wrapped with a linen napkin held slices of ham and cheese and three purple figs. She popped a fig in her mouth, then realized she was ravenous. Standing at the kitchen counter, she rolled up three slices of ham with Gruyère cheese and devoured them. As she wiped her fingers with the napkin, she spotted a water dish and food bowl in the corner. A bag of cat food sat on the counter.

"Kitty," she called gently. No cat trotted in. Too bad. She was already missing Pepper, back home. Maybe Philippe had found a home for Pearl's cat.

Down the hall beyond the kitchen was a tiny room with only a toilet, and past that a larger room with a bathtub and sink. At the apartment's rear were two bedrooms. One was now an office, but the bedroom on the apartment's courtyard side had been Pearl's.

Joanna rolled her suitcase next to the carved walnut bureau and a mirror-fronted wardrobe. Exhausted, she plopped onto the bed, then instantly sprang to her feet. A Siamese cat slinked from beneath the bed and hissed at her. The hiss subsided to a low growl.

For a moment, they stared at each other. "Hi, baby," Joanna said finally, sweetening her voice. She dangled her fingers toward the floor. The cat's growl climbed in pitch, and Joanna snatched up her hand. "We're going to have to be practical, you and I. You put up with me for two weeks, and I'll find you a nice new mama."

The cat hunched in the corner and watched her with cornflower eyes.

Lord, she was tired. Some kid had kicked at the back of her seat during the entire last leg of the flight to Paris. It was hard to believe she'd arrived only this morning—although "this morning" French time had been the middle of the night in Oregon.

The ring of Joanna's phone startled her. She still wasn't used to having a cell phone. She rummaged through her purse and glanced at the phone's screen. Paul. She hesitated only a moment before answering.

"I was just going to call." She plopped back onto the bed, drawing her feet under her.

"Hi, Jo. How was the funeral?"

She relaxed. This was safe ground. "Fine. I think the man who's been arranging everything—Philippe Le Gall—was Pearl Littlewood's lover. Isn't that interesting? Pearl's buried in his family's crypt. She seemed popular, too. You should have seen the turnout at the church. After listening to Mrs. Littlewood, I was expecting it to be just me and a wilted floral tribute from the Ungrateful Daughter Society."

"You sound good, anyway. I still wish I could have come with you—"

"Someone has to take care of Gemma and Pepper," Joanna said, referring to their dog and cat. "Besides, you don't have two weeks to lose on your job."

An even more important "besides," she acknowledged, was that she needed some time alone. To think. With the tension they'd lived with over the past month, Joanna would never be able to make a decision. She turned her wedding ring on her finger. It was only a matter of time before Paul would give her an ultimatum. This trip—this quick side job—had come at the right time.

"Have you seen anything of Paris yet?" he asked.

"Only from the taxi's window. And the church and cemetery."

"You must be exhausted. Get some rest." His voice lowered. "And, Joanna, I miss you."

She sank against the pillows. "I miss you, too."

Joanna set the phone on the nightstand. She hadn't realized how dim the afternoon had become until lightning slashed the dark. Rain rattled the bedroom window.

With one eye on the cat, she slipped off her shoes and rested her head back in her palms. All she needed was a moment to rest.

*
**

Where was she? Joanna rubbed her eyes. That's right. Paris. Pearl Littlewood's apartment. She'd fallen asleep. The sky through the bedroom window was blacker than a Victorian mourning jacket.

Something had woken her. What was it? The wood-on-wood scrape of a cabinet closing sounded inside the apartment. Her fogginess vanished. She fumbled for the bedside lamp.

"Who's there?" she said.

Nothing.

Holding her breath, she crept from the bed and looked down the hall. All was quiet. And cool. The storm had swept away every trace of the day's mugginess. She latched the living room's windows and double-checked the front door's lock.

She must have been dreaming. She'd heard the old building settling, that's all.

Reassured, she went to the kitchen for a drink of water. The digital clock on the microwave read four in the morning. A tickle of air caused her to turn, and she saw a door ajar beside the refrigerator. Funny—she hadn't noticed it earlier. It opened onto an interior staircase. She pondered the door a full minute before shutting and bolting it and returning to bed.

Chapter 2

When Joanna awoke the second time, sun washed the apartment's windows. She glanced toward the foot of the bed and saw a cat-shaped indentation, but no cat. She yawned and stretched.

Step one, get dressed.

Travel books advise travelers to Paris to focus on black—black separates, black dresses, and black jackets—and good shoes. Joanna agreed with the good shoes part, but, as the owner of the vintage clothing store Tallulah's Closet, she wasn't going to limit herself to black. Not with so many gorgeous prints from past decades at hand.

She had packed one black dress, a 1940s rayon number with a peplum and a sweetheart neckline. It's what she'd worn to Pearl's funeral. The rest of the suitcase was filled with 1950s cotton dresses—three with full skirts and two with trimmer silhouettes—two cashmere cardigans, and three pairs of sandals that could see lots of walking, if need be.

But she hadn't packed a robe. The door to Pearl's wardrobe creaked as Joanna opened it. *Yes.* A knee-length silk kimono dangled from a hook inside the door. She fingered the hanger, then lifted her eyes. "Pearl, do you mind if I borrow this?" A pigeon cooed from the balcony. "I'll take that as a yes." A hint of violet and sandalwood wafted around her as she slipped it on.

She opened the door wider. What the heck. Everything here would soon be on its way to France's version of the Salvation Army, anyway.

Within a few seconds, Joanna's expert eye determined that Pearl was a little shorter and bustier than she, but about the same waist size. Judging from the profusion of blues and reds, plus smaller patterns, Joanna thought Pearl had probably been a brunette with fine features. Pearl had a good eye. Her clothing skewed feminine with a slightly nostalgic feel, which Joanna liked. And—bingo!—she had a few vintage pieces, too: a strong-shouldered jacket from the 1940s, a prom-style sleeveless gown with rhinestones sprinkled over its tulle skirt, and a few early 1960s cashmere coats. Joanna was beginning to think she and Pearl would have gotten along well.

Barefoot, Joanna went to the living room and opened a window. She grasped the iron balustrade and leaned out. She was in Paris, she reminded herself. Paris, France. And the day was clear and bright and glorious.

A noise on the street below caught her attention. A tall black woman in full African dress, including a head wrap printed with—could it be?—*roosters* emerged from the building's entrance, her hips swaying. A gentleman greeted her, and she nodded toward him but didn't break stride. Another slim-hipped man leaning against a doorway shouted something Joanna couldn't understand, but it didn't sound friendly. The woman ignored him and picked up her pace.

Joanna closed the window and crossed to the kitchen. Despite the clink of kibble on porcelain, the cat refused to appear. As she filled the coffeepot, her gaze wandered to the door she'd found ajar. What was on the other side? If someone had tried to break in, maybe she'd find a scrape on the doorjamb or muddy footprints.

No. She had to get to work. She took her cup of coffee to the couch, along with a notepad and pen. Philippe said she could have today to relax from the flight, but she had the gut feeling the one thing she could expect was the unexpected. Yes, the notaire would manage Pearl Littlewood's estate, but until Joanna returned to Oregon, she was, with Mrs. Littlewood's authorization, the executor. It was Joanna's job to inventory Pearl's assets, including the apartment, her shop, and any investments she might have owned. Joanna was to make sure the shop's finances were in order, and—this part of the job gave her pause—tell the shop's employees they'd be let go with a modest separation payment. She was also charged with finding a trustworthy real estate agent and estate sale manager. Yes, she'd have a lot to do, but it was a small price to pay for the mental and emotional space she so desperately needed.

Joanna's first order of business would be to visit Pearl's perfume shop, Parfum d'Antan. She'd need to see what the store's finances were like and whether it had a thorough inventory. She glanced at the mantel clock. It was Sunday, and Parfum d'Antan wasn't open. She had a key. No rush about visiting.

She set down the coffee cup and slid the funeral's guestbook toward her. Its red leather cover was cool on her lap. With her limited French, she made out some of the messages. "I will miss you" and "with deepest condolences" came up more than once. One person had simply drawn a perfume bottle framed with hearts. Despite what Mrs. Littlewood might have said, her daughter had clearly been loved.

Joanna began to close the book, then stopped. Something was scrawled on the last page. The crabbed handwriting was distinct, wider than it was tall. She squinted. "Lys Bleu." Blue Lily. Had she read that right? Her French wasn't perfect.

However, the next words were unmistakable. "*Mme Littlewood n'est pas morte d'un accident.*" Madame Littlewood did not die in an accident.

"Not an accident." "Lys Bleu." Ruth Littlewood had told her Pearl had been struck down by a car while crossing the street, a random hit and run.

Joanna sat back. Skin prickled along her neck and arms. She knew this feeling. It could simply be a joke, she told herself as she slowly returned the book to the coffee table. Then again…

She wandered to the kitchen and deposited her empty cup in the sink. Hands on hips, she looked again at the kitchen exit and remembered the noises she'd heard so early that morning. Could someone have picked its lock? There was one way to tell.

Twenty minutes later, showered and dressed, Joanna lifted the bolt and pulled the door. It opened to a dark stairwell with a twisting staircase. She rummaged through kitchen drawers until she found a flashlight, and then stepped onto the landing. She ran the light around the doorway and examined the door handle. It hadn't been obviously messed with.

Now for the stairs. The flashlight's yellow beam shed feeble light. From the track worn into the dust, someone had been up the stairs before her, and not long ago. Joanna took a steadying breath and continued her climb. If someone had broken into Pearl's apartment—*if*, she reminded herself—he wouldn't still be here so many hours later.

On the next floor, she found another door—the apartment just above Pearl's. A few steps up, she halted. A cigarette butt lay near the wall. She knelt to examine it more closely. Its edges were crisp, undamaged by the stairwell's damp.

At the top of the stairs, a landing ran the building's length, with doors letting onto it. One of the doors was ajar, casting a slice of sunlight into the hall.

"Hello?" Joanna said, her voice quavering a little. No response.

She clicked off the flashlight and crept forward. Peering through the door into a nearly empty room, she saw a tuna can stuffed with cigarette butts and a half-full bottle of wine. And a ladder under an open hatch in the ceiling.

"Hello," she tried again. Maybe it would work better in French. "Âllo?" No reply.

She slipped through the door. She might poke her head up to the roof and have a look. It wasn't as if a burglar would leave the door open and scatter evidence up the stairwell. Likely, it was workmen. These old buildings needed a lot of upkeep. Probably.

Joanna tested the stepladder with a hand. If she didn't go up—just for a quick look, that's all, she wouldn't even leave the ladder—she'd always wonder. If she saw anything suspicious, she'd simply yank the ladder away and run downstairs. She mounted one step, then two, then reached the top.

Joanna popped her head above the roof into bright sunshine. Face-down and lifeless, a few yards from the roof hatch, was a half-naked woman. Joanna clutched the stepladder and gasped.

The supposedly dead woman shot up, yelped, and held a shirt over her bare chest. She looked to be in her mid-forties, a good ten years older than Joanna, although her skin, cooked to the gray of a well-done steak, tilted the estimate higher. But her youthful makeup—frosted eyeshadow lining each eye—and burgundy hair brought it down again.

Well, this was awkward. As her pulse slowed, Joanna forced a smile. "*Pardon, Madame.*"

"You are the girl in Madame Littlewood's apartment, *n'est-ce pas?*"

Now the stranger was all sweetness. In a quick motion, she slipped her shirt over her head. "Just some sunbathing. Sorry to alarm you. Quite a storm last night, no?" She pulled a pack of cigarettes from her nearby purse and shielded her mouth to light one. "*Désirez?*" She offered the pack to Joanna. The same brand as the cigarette butt in the stairwell.

"No, thank you. Your English is terrific."

"English teacher." She blew a stream of smoke to her side. "Come and sit down. You and I, we're neighbors. I live across the landing. I saw you come in yesterday afternoon."

Joanna stepped onto the roof and lowered herself cross-legged near the woman. A row of clay chimneys punctuated the metal strip of roof, sloping to slate tiles behind her. They were seven stories above the street. Joanna focused her attention on the neighbor and not on the sheer drop to the pavement.

"Excuse my manners," the woman said and extended a hand. "Amandine Chomette. My husband needs his sleep during the day, so I come up here sometimes to get away."

"Joanna Hayworth. Pearl's mother sent me to take care of her estate."

"I'm sorry for your loss. Madame Littlewood was a lovely woman. We were all shocked—and upset—at the accident."

"Thank you." A "lovely woman." Who was Pearl Littlewood, anyway? "Did you know her well?"

Madame Chomette shrugged. "She was friendly. Chic for an American." The Frenchwoman's gimlet eye grazed Joanna head to toe. "Like you."

This morning Joanna had chosen a sundress sprigged with lilies of the valley that reminded her of a Dior but bore the label of a local department store. Its skirt moved with the wind. She turned to the expanse of chimney pots and television satellite dishes dotting the roofs around them. The sky was the blue of a Delft china vase. "I found the rear stairwell and followed it up here. Where are we?"

"That's the maid's staircase. The top floor is for the *chambres de bonne*, the maids' rooms. Before the war, lots of families had maids who lived in-house." She pulled a drag on her cigarette and took in the view. "You have been to Paris before?"

"Once, but it's been a few years."

"Such a beautiful city. Stand up. Look over my shoulder."

Joanna braced herself and stood. The breeze rustled her hair. Rising beyond the slate rooftops stretched the lacy point of the Eiffel Tower. "It's so close."

Madame Chomette chuckled and ground out her cigarette. "Just a few blocks away. Is that awful cat still at the apartment?"

"You mean the Siamese?" Joanna sat again. The first chance she had, she'd go see the Eiffel Tower up close. "I haven't spent much time with her yet."

"Jicky. That's her name. Madame Littlewood adored her, but she's sour tempered. Have you met anyone in the building?"

"Not yet. I'm only staying a few weeks. Just long enough to take stock of Pearl's home and business and sign a few papers on her mother's behalf."

"Then the only people you'll need to know are Madame Dédé who lives above you, and Monsieur Saunier, who lives below. Madame Dédé will be the difficult one. She probably stamps all over, making a lot of noise. If she doesn't have rugs, you won't get a minute of sleep. My husband would never stand for that." She grimaced a moment, seeming to imagine her husband's reaction. "She acts like she was a member of the Senegalese royal family instead of just a *femme de ménage* who married the boss."

Joanna remembered the woman she'd seen leaving the building that morning. "Does she wear African dress?"

"That's her. *Par contre*, Monsieur Saunier—Martin, below you—is very quiet. Keeps his curtains shut and sleeps during the day. We barely see him. He won't be a bother. You might bother him more."

"I'll try to be quiet."

"Hmm." Madame Chomette reached for her purse. "I had better go downstairs and see if Monsieur Chomette needs anything. It's been a pleasure to meet you."

"Thank you. I'm sorry for startling you. It's just—" should she say anything? "—just that I thought someone might have come into the apartment last night. The kitchen door was ajar, so this morning I followed the back stairs up here. You didn't hear any strange noises, did you?"

Madame Chomette's hand flew to her chest. "Someone in the apartment? Are you sure?"

"Honestly, no. I was so tired."

"My husband would have mentioned it had he heard anything." She shook her head. "Someone breaking into the building. No. It's not possible."

"You're probably right." Joanna brushed her rear end as she stood. "One more thing. Have you ever heard the words 'Lys Bleu'?"

Madame Chomette examined her, her frosted-plum-rimmed eyes screwing closer together. "Blue lily, it means."

"Does it stand for anything else? Some kind of slang term, maybe?"

She clicked her tongue once against the roof of her mouth. "No. Never heard of it."

Chapter 3

Parfum d'Antan was on the grassy Place du Commerce, sandwiched between a bookshop and a florist. Here, Joanna had expertise. She might not know the particulars of settling an estate, but she knew how to run a shop—and how to tell if a shop was run well.

To her surprise, the shop's night gate was already partially rolled up. She pushed open its door, and a bell jingled. An elegant woman emerged from the back and smiled, then recalculated. She quickly smiled again, this time with her eyes, too. Joanna recognized her as the impeccably turned-out brunette at the funeral. Today she wore a crisp white blouse styled on a men's shirt that emphasized her delicacy. Her gaze, though, was pure steel.

"You've come about Pearl, haven't you? I saw you yesterday." The woman closed a laptop and pushed it toward the back of the counter. She extended her hand. "Elise Noiret, manager. I worked with Pearl practically since the store opened."

"Madame Noiret—"

"Elise."

"Elise, it's nice to meet you. I'm Joanna Hayworth. I thought the shop was closed on Sunday."

"Just taking care of some paperwork. I was on my way to visit my father. He's in a special care home outside of town."

If it were her boutique, Joanna would have come in early on a weekday rather than spend a weekend morning here, but no matter. "Pearl's mother wasn't able to make it. I'm here in her place to help settle her estate."

"Oh, I see. To sell it, you mean?"

This woman's livelihood might depend on the shop. "Probably," Joanna admitted. "I'll need to talk to you about arrangements."

Elise didn't appear bothered by the news. "Do you know very much about the boutique? Or about perfume?"

"I wear it, but I'm not an expert." In fact, Joanna probably knew more about classic fragrances than most people, thanks to her many years of trolling estate sales. Her profession in vintage was one mark in her favor for Ruth Littlewood, she knew. She had a modest collection of old perfumes—Arpège, Je Reviens, old Miss Dior, L'Heure Bleue, and a bottle of Bandit extrait with, sadly, only a few drops left.

"Parfum d'Antan sells vintage perfume. Most of our fragrances aren't even made today. Or, if they are, they aren't made with the same beautiful materials."

Joanna turned toward the boutique's interior. Persian carpets covered the floor. Wooden shelves neatly stacked with perfume boxes lined the walls. The top shelf appeared reserved for intricately faceted perfume bottles, some with fringed atomizers. The boutique felt like Jean Harlow's boudoir—if she'd had a fragrance obsession, that is.

"So that's why there aren't any testers out," Joanna said.

"No. This is like a fine wine shop. No testers." A sly smile crossed Elise's lips. "Although like many wine shops, we do have a few special bottles open in the back for good customers."

"Like what?" Joanna was still absorbed by the rows of bottles. A factice shaped like a dressmaker's dummy sprigged with flowers stood out from the rest. Schiaparelli's Shocking.

Elise disappeared behind the blue velvet curtain hiding the back of the shop and brought out a black rectangular bottle with a tall, chiseled top.

"That's gorgeous." Joanna reached for it.

Elise pulled back the bottle. "Baccarat crystal. Show me your wrist." Joanna extended her hand, and Elise dabbed a drop of amber liquid from the bottle's stopper. "Wait a moment, then smell."

Joanna lifted her wrist to her nose, and a chill vibrated through her body. The perfume was pure tuberose, rich and buttery and carnal. She met Elise's eyes but couldn't respond.

Elise's smile widened. "Fracas by Piguet. I knew it would suit you." She stoppered the bottle and set it on the wood-framed glass counter. "It's still made, but this is an older formulation with materials too expensive to use today." She seemed particularly satisfied as she straightened a pile of invoices. "Now, let me show you around."

Joanna followed Elise to the back room. "Where do you get your stock?"

Elise clicked on the overhead light. "We are known all over the world. Sometimes we buy perfume at auction, but mostly people come to us. From time to time a pharmacy will find forgotten stock in storage. Plus, Pearl loved to search for old bottles at flea markets."

"The perfume doesn't turn bad?"

"Not if it's stored away from light and heat." She pointed toward a wooden cabinet. "That's why we don't keep much upstairs. Just bottles with higher turnover. And the empty flacons."

"And a place to take a break, it looks like." A small gate-legged table with an electric kettle and tea tin was pushed against the wall. Next to it sat a low, plush armchair. Joanna did a double take. The garbage can was stuffed with fast food hamburger wrappers.

Elise lifted her regal chin. "What? I get hungry dealing with customers all day." She pointed to another doorway, this one with its
door ajar showing a tidy desk and laptop computer. "That's the office."
She turned toward another doorway, also swagged with a velvet curtain. "Follow me. We'll go down to the basement. Watch your step."

The dip in the stone stairs told of decades of feet traveling up
and down. The basement ran the shop's length, and metal shelves
perpendicular to the wall maximized storage. Hundreds of cello-
phane-wrapped boxes of different sizes and colors crowded the shelves.
A dehumidifier hummed in the corner.

Elise continued the tour. "Down here, the perfumes are stored by
house, alphabetically, from 4711 here" —starting from the right, her
finger swept the room— "all the way to Yves Saint Laurent."

"Are they valuable? I'm familiar with vintage clothing, but not
vintage perfume as much."

"Most, no. Not particularly. We have bottles that have recently
gone out of production—for instance, Fendi—but that are still
some women's signature scent. They aren't especially expensive. We
also have some common but popular older fragrances, like My Sin
by Lanvin. If you know where to look, you can buy them for a
song." Elise reached for a bottle labeled Scandal. "Other bottles are
much more valuable, this one, for instance—" The jangling doorbell
upstairs interrupted them. "Just a moment. We're closed. I don't
know who this could be."

Joanna followed Elise back up to the boutique. A tall man with
a worn leather satchel over his shoulder stood just inside the door.

"*Bonjour, mesdames,*" he said. "*Je suis prof d'histoire à la Sorbonne,
et—*"

Leaning on the counter, Joanna nearly knocked over a bottle of perfume. She caught it before it tumbled. Both Elise and the man turned to stare at her. "Sorry," she said.

"Madame is American," the man said. "Let me apologize. Shall we speak English?"

"You don't have to," Joanna started, "I just—"

"English is fine," Elise said. "We're closed today, but if you return tomorrow—"

"I know. When I saw the gate partway up, I couldn't resist stopping in." He flashed an earnest smile. "You see, I'm teaching a course about Paris and the Occupation, and I want to include some information about a particular perfume. The perfumer was a hero in the Resistance. I've researched him, but" —here his grin widened, and Joanna couldn't help smiling in return— "I haven't smelled it. I was hoping I could purchase a bottle."

Something about this man mesmerized her. He wasn't particularly good looking—he could use a haircut and shave, and he clearly didn't spend much time at the ironing board. Maybe it was his long fingers, or the way his eyes seemed to laugh. At the same time, he was serious.

"And that perfume is?" Elise asked.

"Lys Bleu."

This time Joanna did knock over the perfume bottle. In a second, both the man and Elise were at her side, and the air smelled of roses and sandalwood. "I'm so sorry."

"*Oh, là là*," Elise said. "The Magie Noire. It's not serious. The top notes were going off anyway."

"Lys Bleu?" Joanna said.

"Yes," the professor replied. He stared at her a second too long before taking from the roll of paper towels to help Elise mop up the spilled perfume. "Released by Fath."

"Almost released by Fath, you mean. I'm sorry, monsieur. There's only one bottle of that fragrance, and it's promised to the Osmothèque." For Joanna's benefit, she added, "A national perfume archive. Pearl was working with a fragrance historian to arrange it."

"I see." The man straightened and set a wad of crumpled paper towels on the counter. "Maybe I could simply smell it?"

"Impossible. The bottle is sealed."

"Oh." The man's smile vanished, and with it the light in his expression. "Well, I won't bother you further. If you change your mind, I hope you'll call me." He pulled a business card from his satchel. Elise reached for it, but he handed it to Joanna.

"*Bonne journée,*" he said on his way out.

"*Au revoir,*" Elise said to his retreating back. She waited until the door closed. "Now that one was a charmer. I wouldn't trust him if he came with a hundred euro guarantee."

Joanna slipped the card into her purse. "Lys Bleu."

Elise tossed the perfume-soaked paper towels into a bin under the cash register. "It's a special fragrance. A legend. This year would have been its seventy-fifth anniversary."

"You said it was almost produced, but not quite."

"Before the fragrance was to be turned over to Fath, the Nazis killed Lys Bleu's nose, Ernest Beaulieu, as the professor said."

"But the shop has a bottle."

"Oh, yes. *The* bottle. From the original concentrate. It's in a flacon the perfumer had specially manufactured. We keep it locked up."

Amazing. Lys Bleu was perfume history. More than that, it was mentioned next to the claim that Pearl Littlewood had been killed deliberately. "Have you smelled it?"

"No. No one has. It was supposed to have been Beaulieu's greatest creation."

Joanna opened her mouth to ask more, but Elise turned toward the basement stairs. "You want to see it, don't you?"

"Yes. Yes, I do."

"Follow me." She crossed the storage room and drew her key ring from a pocket. She unbolted a heavy door. "We've had so many inquiries about it lately. Pearl was very particular. We could have paid the rent for three months with our Lys Bleu, but she insisted it go to the archive." Now inside a dark walk-in vault, Elise flicked on a light switch.

"What kind of inquiries?"

"Oh, someone is doing a documentary. People like that professor. Some cosmetics conglomerate." Elise turned and pointed to a shelf. "There it is."

A cream-colored box with Lys Bleu in swirled gold lettering stood front and center on the shelf. The box was tall and thin, about a foot high. Its lid was made to lift off, essentially leaving the bottle standing on a squat platform.

"May I?" Joanna asked.

"If you'd like. It won't hurt to look at it. The bottle's still sealed."

Joanna carefully lifted the box from its bottom. Puzzled, she turned to Elise. "Something's wrong."

"What do you mean?"

She pulled off the lid. "It's empty."

Chapter 4

"Let me see." Elise snatched the box from Joanna's hand.

"There's nothing in it," Joanna said.

"Can't be." Elise turned the box in her hand, then peered into the gap it had left on the shelf. "Maybe Pearl took the bottle out, set it somewhere else."

They searched the closet top to bottom. Two breathtaking crystal bottles topped with vining gold flowers—Diorissimo and Miss Dior—held pride of place at the top of the cabinet, and a sealed box of Iris Gris sat on the shelf the Lys Bleu box had occupied. But no Lys Bleu.

"It can't be," Elise repeated. "No."

"Is there anywhere else in the shop that Pearl might have put the bottle? You said a lot of people have been asking about it. Maybe she brought it out to show someone."

"Maybe." She seemed to take hope in Joanna's suggestion, but just as soon as her voice had lifted, it fell again. "No. No, I would have seen it by now." She shook her head. "Let's go upstairs."

Joanna squinted at the boutique's sunlight after the dim basement. "Is there a chance Pearl had the bottle with her when she died?"

Elise faced Joanna. "It was a large bottle. Two hundred-fifty milliliters." She placed her hands far enough apart to have held a submarine sandwich.

"Maybe it was in her purse."

Elise squeezed her eyes shut. "I don't think so." She opened them. "I saw her leave the shop that evening. She had her usual tote and no other bag. Besides, she would have told me if she'd taken the bottle. It was too important." She collapsed into the blue armchair behind the counter.

"How valuable was this bottle of Lys Bleu, anyway?"

"Very. We locked it up every night downstairs. You saw."

Joanna fidgeted with a pen on the counter, then tossed it to the side. "Elise, yesterday I was thumbing through the guestbook from the funeral. Someone left a strange note."

Elise stared at her. "Yes?"

"It said that Pearl's death wasn't an accident. Then it said, 'Lys Bleu.' I didn't know what it meant at the time."

Any composure Elise had regained evaporated. "Not an accident? What does that mean?"

"I don't know," Joanna said. "Maybe it wasn't serious. But the bottle is gone. I have to wonder. Was it worth enough to kill for?"

"Kill for? You mean, murder Pearl?" Her voice climbed in pitch.

"You have to admit, it's a strange note. Plus, why mention the perfume?"

Elise wandered to the front of the boutique and stared past a prop flacon with frosted doves on its crystal stopper. When she turned around, her expression was determined. And calmer. "It was just a bottle of perfume. The Diors downstairs—they're worth almost as much, and more as a set. No one would have killed Pearl over the bottle. Impossible."

The way she said the words left little room for argument. "You did say Lys Bleu might have paid three months of the shop's rent."

Joanna knew collectors could chase the price of a Lili Ann princess coat, say, through the roof, when a nearly identical coat without the Lili Ann label could be had at a fraction of the price. Maybe Lys Bleu was like that.

"True. But that's hardly the price of murder." Despite her tone, her voice quavered at the last word. "The note in the guestbook was a joke."

Joanna took in the rows of perfume bottles, the cash register, the invoices Elise had set aside earlier. All of this belonged to Ruth Littlewood now, including the missing bottle of Lys Bleu.

"Maybe it was worth stealing, if not killing for," Joanna said. "We should report it to the police."

"We don't know for certain that it was stolen," Elise said.

"You're sure it's not somewhere in the shop?"

"Positive. Like I said, I would have seen it."

"I'm assuming Pearl wouldn't have sold it without its box," Joanna added.

"No." Elise fingered her pearl necklace and sighed. "No, you're right. It must have been stolen. I'll call the police."

"I'm sorry," Joanna said. "Thank you for reporting it missing. As Mrs. Littlewood's representative, I feel responsible. And, Elise?"

"Hmm?" She avoided looking at Joanna.

"It's almost lunch time. I passed a fast food place on the way here. Want me to get you a cheeseburger?"

On her way home, Joanna stopped at Café de l'Espérance, the corner café she'd passed that morning. Fast food hamburgers and fries might be fine for Elise, but Joanna was in Paris, and she wanted a real Parisian meal. Elise had told her she and Pearl used to lunch there. It had been one of their favorites.

She took a seat out front, with her back to the glassed-in veranda and a view of the metro station under the elevated tracks. She relaxed into her chair. An elderly man browsed at the newsstand. A woman who looked far too thin to have given birth to the baby in her stroller trotted by. A moped putt-putted at the stoplight, behind it a tall white delivery van. Thinking of Pearl, Joanna eyed the van's grille.

She wondered how Pearl had seen Paris. This café was no rural Oregon diner, like in Pearl's hometown. No pickup trucks within miles. Not a single Blazers baseball cap. No speculations on the start of this year's hunting season.

"Madame?" A waiter in a knee-length black apron and black vest materialized at her table, his pen hovering above a pad.

She hadn't even been offered a menu. The waiter pointed at a chalkboard on an easel just out of range of easy reading. He returned his pen to its upright position.

"*Le plat du jour*," she said confidently. "*S'il vous plaît*." Let it be a surprise.

The waiter paused only a second, then smiled. He returned straight away with a carafe of water, silverware rolled in a linen napkin, and a tripod rack with salt, pepper, and a pot of mustard with a spoon in it.

It was almost one in the afternoon now—way early morning Wilfred time. She'd have to wait until tonight, after dinner with Philippe, to call Mrs. Littlewood if she didn't want to wake her. What should she report?

Once again, Joanna reflected on the strange turns life could take. It had only been five days since she'd run into—literally run into—Ruth

Littlewood at an estate sale in Wilfred where she'd gone to search for stock. Normally, Joanna wouldn't drive as far out of Portland as Wilfred, but she'd felt the need to be somewhere other than home. She'd have time during the hour-and-a-half drive to consider her life with Paul, she'd thought. To consider her future. They'd had a good year together since Gene, his uncle, had moved out, but Paul's expectations were growing. Joanna didn't know if she could meet them.

At the estate sale, arms weighed down by old Pendleton shirts, Joanna turned a corner and collided with Ruth Littlewood, who clutched an old framed Audubon print of nesting Vermilion Flycatchers.

"What are you doing here?" Ruth Littlewood asked, an accusatory tone to her voice. "I haven't seen you before."

"That's because I haven't been here before," Joanna said, setting the shirts on the chair next to her and smoothing her skirt. Why was this lady so hostile? "I go to estate sales all over."

"Why?" Ruth Littlewood said.

"It's my job. That's what I do. I run a vintage clothing boutique in Portland."

Ruth Littlewood eyed her up and down. A smile unexpectedly spread over her face. "I suppose you know quite a bit about estates?"

Joanna felt the need to defend herself. "More than most. I've probably been to thousands of sales over the years and assisted at quite a few, too." "Assisting" being helping to price vintage clothing for a first shot at the best of the lot.

"Surely, though, there are better estates to pillage closer to Portland. All we have out here are a lot of retired millworkers and farmhands."

"It's nice to get out of town sometimes," Joanna said.

The older woman stuck out her hand. "Ruth Littlewood. How'd you like to have lunch?"

Over soup and salad, Mrs. Littlewood asked her about the shop and explained that her daughter Pearl also owned a vintage shop overseas, but hers specialized in fragrance. Unfortunately, Pearl had recently died. As she talked, she put her fork down and watched Joanna. Joanna felt something was expected of her, but she didn't know what. She made the usual remarks—how sorry she was for Mrs. Littlewood's loss, how she'd certainly have lots to take care of with the estate—and the older woman nodded.

"You ever been to Paris?"

Now this was an unexpected turn of conversation. "Yes, a few years back. Why?"

"Just a question," she replied.

The next day, Mrs. Littlewood appeared in Tallulah's Closet's doorway, looking like a house sparrow among peacocks next to the shop's vivid colors and patterns. Joanna put down the bias-cut nightgown she was mending and greeted her.

"I've done some checking up on you," Mrs. Littlewood said, "and you seem legit."

It was hard to know how to answer that, so Joanna said, "How can I help you?"

Mrs. Littlewood proposed that Joanna should fly to Paris to be her eyes and ears for liquidating Pearl's estate. She wanted to make sure she wasn't getting ripped off, but she refused to go herself.

"This is sudden. You don't really know me," Joanna said.

"I'm a successful businesswoman, Joanna. I've made more money on my cannery than I'll ever be able to reinvest, and my most important business decisions have always come from my gut. My gut tells me you're the right one for the job."

"Why don't you go yourself?"

"That's none of your business."

Their staring match ended when Joanna spoke. "What's the catch? There's got to be a catch."

"You'll have to leave the day after tomorrow. I want you to go to the funeral and pay my respects."

And that had been that. Paul hadn't liked the idea, but instinctively he must have known he was on the verge of losing her if he pushed harder. As she'd reminded him, it was only two weeks. Two weeks to figure out her future. She sighed. Children, or not? Yet the issue felt even larger than that.

If she couldn't sort out her own life, at least she could work on Pearl's. She'd be able to report to Mrs. Littlewood that she'd start an inventory of Parfum d'Antan's stock right away, and Elise would show her how they tracked sales and expenses. Joanna could easily list the store's furnishings. Elise was calling the police about the missing bottle of Lys Bleu, so there'd be that, too, if Mrs. Littlewood wanted to file an insurance claim.

The waiter returned with a small glass of red wine and a plate with three thin leeks, halved and sprinkled with chives. He left before she could even thank him. The leeks were tender enough to cut with a fork.

A brown mutt with short legs and wiry fur crept onto the café's terrace, sticking close to the wall. He made eye contact with Joanna and slinked toward her table. He wasn't wearing a collar.

Just as Joanna was opening her mouth to greet him, the waiter nudged the dog away with a foot. "Cassoulet! *Vas-y!*" he said. Then, to Joanna, "Don't encourage him. The confit de canard will be out in a moment. House specialty."

"Where's his owner?"

"He doesn't have an owner. We feed him scraps from the kitchen door. The cook calls him Cassoulet since he loves it so much." The waiter added, "Cassoulet. A casserole of beans and meat."

Joanna knew what a cassoulet was. She didn't think beans and dogs were a great match. "Where does he sleep?"

"Don't worry about it, madame. He does all right."

Chapter 5

That evening at seven o'clock on the dot, Joanna heard a knock on the door. Philippe. All afternoon she had ignored the city's lure and focused on making an inventory of the apartment. She'd wanted something to report to Ruth Littlewood later. She'd also hoped that putting her hands into Pearl's life would give her some insight into her death and its connection to Lys Bleu.

Philippe stood in the hall holding a wicker hamper. He wore khakis and a polo shirt—less dressy than the suit at the funeral, but not exactly casual.

"*Bonsoir*, Joanna. I hope you don't mind that I came straight up."

Of course he knew the codes to enter. He probably had a key, too. "I'm glad you did."

"How was your first full day in Paris?"

A floorboard creaked at the other end of the short hall. Madame Chomette, no doubt, ear pressed to the door.

"Come in."

Philippe stood a moment in the hall, taking in the apartment. Maybe he was thinking of Pearl. Maybe he wondered if this would be the last time he'd be in her apartment. Joanna's chest tightened. Talking about Pearl with him would be hard enough. Suggesting she might have been murdered seemed downright cruel.

"Let me take that." Joanna lifted the basket from his hands and set it in the kitchen. When she returned to the living room, she found Philippe holding the silver-framed photo of Pearl that had been on the mantel. He touched a finger to the glass.

"I'm sorry," Joanna said. "I didn't think about the memories you have here. Would you rather not eat in?"

"No." He crossed to the kitchen. "Let's stay here this evening. My memories are good ones. Besides, I see you've prepared."

Earlier that afternoon, Joanna had taken a break from making an inventory of the apartment's furnishings by setting the table. She'd found pine green ceramic dinner plates with a glossy glaze and satisfying heft. No two of Pearl's wineglasses matched exactly, but they were old with hand-cut stems. A drawer had yielded a stack of soft linen napkins. Finally, Joanna had set a silver candelabra with three arms holding half-burnt beeswax candles at the table's center.

He picked up one of the plates and cradled it. "We bought these dishes on a trip to Provence a few years ago."

Philippe looked to be about sixty, slightly younger than Joanna's father, but the two men couldn't be more different. Joanna's father had been a logger. He'd risen at dawn and spent his days in the woods. She didn't know if she'd ever seen him without dirt under his fingernails. Philippe's hands were elegantly shaped and had probably never had to deal with anything more troublesome than a sticky briefcase latch.

"How did you meet her? Pearl, I mean?" Joanna asked.

"Over perfume, of course. My mother wears Joy. She says it doesn't smell like it used to, so I wanted to find an older bottle for her birthday. I went to Parfum d'Antan." He slipped his hands in his pockets. His gaze softened. "Pearl was on a stepping stool trying to set a gigantic crystal flacon on the top shelf. I helped."

"Did you know her long?"

"It would have been eleven years in October."

"You managed to see her outside of the boutique."

"I stretched out our conversation—let me tell you, now I know everything about Joy there is to know—then asked if she might want to share an apéro." His smile widened. "She said no, even after I explained that the perfume was for my mother."

"You still got together."

"I left my business card. She called a week later to say she had some Joy bath powder I might be interested in." He settled on the couch. "I was very happy with Pearl."

"But you never married."

"No." His smile dimmed. "I almost had her convinced, and then…"

Joanna got it. For all the advantages of marriage—and there were many, she knew this firsthand—it also came with drawbacks. Your life wasn't completely your own. The big decisions you shared with someone else. Their expectations.

She took the photo from the fireplace mantel. "I think you should have this." In case he hesitated to take it, she added, "I'm the estate's executor by proxy. It's perfectly all right for me to give it to you." It wasn't as if Mrs. Littlewood wanted it.

Philippe looked at the photo one more time and then set it on a side table. "Thank you."

Joanna stood awkwardly, playing with the fringe on a throw pillow. "There's something else I want to talk to you about. It has to do with Pearl."

"Let's wait until after dinner to talk business. Are you hungry? I stopped by the Bon Marché for a few things. Nothing elaborate. Roast chicken and a salad."

"We'll have an indoor picnic," Joanna said with relief at putting off the talk.

She brought the plates to the kitchen, where Philippe heaped them with golden chicken legs on watercress and a salad of grated vegetables. From the bottom of the basket he took a bottle of wine.

They brought their plates to the dining room. The French windows were open, and a slight breeze rippled the lace panels. Pearl's cat emerged from the balcony and stretched her front legs, then padded to Philippe and rubbed her cheek against his legs.

He reached down to scratch her ears. "Jicky. You miss your mama, don't you?"

Whether it was travel, the time change, or the emotions swirling around Pearl's death and Joanna's own situation, she found a lump forming in her throat. "Well, she certainly doesn't seem to get along with me."

"She's shy, that's all." They settled at the table, Jicky at Philippe's feet.

"Maybe you'd like to take her with you. She'll need a home," Joanna said.

"I'd like to, but my" —he seemed to search for the words— "my housemate's dog wouldn't appreciate it."

Joanna raised an eyebrow. Philippe didn't wear a ring. It didn't mean he didn't already have a wife, despite his talk of marrying Pearl. Was it normal for the French to bury their mistresses in the family crypt? "I see. I suppose there's some equivalent of the Humane Society in Paris?"

"An organization that helps pets find homes? Yes. Don't worry about it. Jicky will be my responsibility." He filled her wineglass, then his. "*Bon appétit.*"

An hour later, demitasses of coffee in hand, they were in the living room. Philippe sat on the couch, Jicky at his side. Joanna took the armchair that had clearly been Pearl's favorite spot for reading. A pair of her reading glasses still rested on a folded-over issue of *The New Yorker*.

"I suppose we should get down to business," Philippe said. "Tomorrow I'll introduce you to the notaire responsible for sorting out Pearl's estate. His English is excellent. I've also contacted a real estate agent who specializes in apartments in this neighborhood. She has a good record, and she's reliable." His gaze swept through the living room. "She might be able to recommend someone who sells estates, too. Joanna?"

Her attention was fastened on the funeral guestbook. "Sorry. Before we get into too much detail, there's something I want to show you."

"Everything was in order at the perfume shop today?"

She set the demitasse and saucer on the side table. "It's a wonderful shop. No, that's not it." She pushed the funeral guestbook toward Philippe. "Tell me what you think of this. Last page."

Philippe flipped through the pages. "Yes, many notes of condolence, but—oh." He held the book open, and a muscle tightened in his jaw. "I see."

Joanna scooted forward. "Is it possible? Could Pearl have been pushed into the street?"

Philippe took two full breaths before responding. "Her death was an accident. The police were on the scene shortly after it happened. No one reported seeing her pushed." He shook his head. "No, it can't be." The words came out as a whisper. "And yet…"

"The other part, the part about Lys Bleu."

"A perfume, yes? Pearl told me about it." His brows furrowed.

"It's been stolen. Elise and I went to the locked closet in the basement to look for it, and it was gone. Elise says she has no idea where it is." Joanna shook her head. "It's valuable, so I asked Elise to file a police report. But what about the guestbook? It's too much of a coincidence."

Philippe absently tapped his coffee spoon against his thigh. The spoon clattered on the saucer as he tossed it aside. "Something had been bothering Pearl the week before she died. I asked her about it, but she wouldn't tell me. Said she'd take care of it herself."

"That's all she said?"

"The morning when—the same day she died, she said she wanted to talk, get my advice about something. I planned to stop by when she closed the shop, but she called again later that afternoon and told me she needed to postpone our date. She had something else she needed to do right away."

"Then she was killed." Joanna and Philippe stared at each other. "Should we take the guestbook to the police?"

Philippe stood and, hands in pockets, paced in front of the French windows. "We could. I doubt it would do much good. One offhand remark in a guestbook may not be enough evidence to open an investigation. The police will tell us it's a joke, some kid wrote it."

"If the perfume hadn't been stolen, I wouldn't give it another thought. But what kid would know about a rare old perfume like Lys Bleu? My gut tells me something is seriously wrong."

Philippe pulled the photo of Pearl to his knee. "Lys Bleu." He shook his head. "You have a point. There is maybe one thing I can do. I know a few people in the Sûreté. I'll make some calls and get back to you."

*
**

Philippe gone, dishes done, it was time to call Ruth Littlewood.

Joanna blew out the beeswax tapers and watched the smoke curl like ghosts in the draft from the open windows. The night air felt good. She stepped outside and clutched the iron rail. Across the street, a window went dark. Bedtime. Another window was yellow with light, and the flickering from just beyond her view told of a television. Many of the windows were shuttered, the residents probably on vacation for the month.

She picked up her phone. Ruth answered at the first ring.

"Finally," she said before Joanna had the chance to say hello. "What have you got?"

In Wilfred, Ruth was clearly known for taking care of business. She'd told Joanna that after her husband had died, she'd stepped into managing his vegetable canning operation and tripled profits. Before leaving for Paris, Joanna had made a flurry of phone calls to check on Ruth and learned that if a house burned down, Ruth spearheaded a fundraising campaign that had the family in new digs within a month. Major decisions in Wilfred weren't made without touching base with Ruth. When she wasn't at the office, she was birdwatching or raising money for one of her favorite environmental nonprofits.

When Ruth had made Joanna the offer, she'd said, "I want someone onsite to make sure I don't get rooked. You're the one to help me. " She'd withdrawn her wallet from her purse. "You'll fly coach, of course, and stay at Pearl's to save money. I expect to hear from you every day."

Now it was time for Joanna to prove her worth. "The funeral was very nice, and Pearl is buried at the Montparnasse Cemetery in her boyfriend's family plot."

"That's the least he can do, seeing as he never married her," Ruth said promptly.

"It may have been Pearl's choice to remain single. He really loved her."

Ruth hesitated. "Tell me about him. Philippe."

Joanna took the phone to the window and gazed down at the dark streets. An older man walked a fox terrier on a leash. The tip of his cigarette glowed in the night.

"Well, he's tall and thin, probably sixty-ish. Seems he's from an old family. He has a refined way about him."

"Like what? What do you mean by 'refined'?"

"Oh, I don't know. I wouldn't be surprised if he knows vintages of Bordeaux and things like that."

She took a moment to digest this. "Hmm. What else?"

"As I said, he really loved Pearl."

"I didn't mean that," Ruth said, her voice taking a sharp tone. "I mean, what else about Pearl's accounts? Or the shop?"

"Well…" Plunge in about the Lys Bleu, or stall?

"Well, what?"

Stall. "I've only been here a day, so I don't have much to report. I've been photographing Pearl's belongings. I also visited the perfume shop and met the manager. We're starting an inventory tomorrow. I'll look through Pearl's office for investment certificates or anything like that. Philippe gave me her accountant's phone number and set up an appointment with the notary responsible for sorting out her business."

"Good, good." A rustle came over the wire, then Ruth said, "No, not there. Put my coffee on the side table. Yes."

"What?"

"Not you. Go on."

"That's about it for now, except for two things." Joanna formed her words carefully. "Would you like me to set aside Pearl's photos or any of her personal things?" Joanna braced herself for a sharp rebuke. Instead of shouting, Joanna got silence. "Hello?" she said finally.

"I'll get back to you on that."

"Mrs. Littlewood—"

"Ruth. Get to it. This phone call is costing a fortune."

"It's probably nothing, but for the sake of being thorough, I thought you should know."

"Spit it out, honey."

"Your daughter's death was ruled an accident by the police."

"That's not news."

"In the guestbook, someone claimed her death was intentional. This person also mentioned a perfume called Lys Bleu. Blue Lily."

"I know what Lys Bleu means," she said sharply.

"Pearl's boutique had a bottle—the only bottle, actually—and it was valuable. People have been asking about it lately."

"What do you mean by 'had'?"

"It's gone missing." Again, silence. Joanna lowered herself into Pearl's reading chair, which was fast becoming her favorite seat. Jicky stared at her from beneath an end table. "We filed a report, so you may be able to recoup some of its value. Plus, Philippe is following up with the police."

"I want to know more about this perfume and the people who've been after it. If someone killed my daughter, I ought to know."

"It might slow down my work—even put a hold on the estate altogether if Pearl's death is ruled a homicide." Joanna squeezed her eyes shut as she said the words.

"You didn't understand me? I thought I was quite clear. A few questions won't slow anything down."

Joanna was willing to bet this was the most concern Mrs. Littlewood had shown for Pearl in years. "Then I'll ask around."

"After all, that bottle might be worth money."

Chapter 6

Joanna arrived at Parfum d'Antan early the next morning ready to work. Except for the tabac and the boulangerie, few of the businesses along the rue du Commerce were open. The shop's night gate was halfway rolled up, and warm light shone from the store's depths.

Elise greeted her with a smile. Instead of the bourgeois Parisienne's summer uniform of white linen and pearls, she wore denim and a man's worn chambray shirt. The shop's subtle miasma of amber and wood carried a new note, coffee.

"It smells delicious in here," Joanna said.

"I made a pot of coffee. And Christophe brought croissants. Christophe, this is Joanna Hayworth. Pearl's mother sent her from Oregon to help take care of things."

A short, muscular man in his twenties in jeans and a Fats Domino T-shirt offered his hand. "Christophe Selicier."

"Christophe helps out at the shop from time to time," Elise said. "He really knows perfume. I thought it would be good to have him today, so I took the liberty of hiring him for a few hours. We have a lot of work ahead of us." She handed Joanna a mug of coffee with Jicky's photo on it. "Cream is on the counter."

Joanna gratefully took the mug. "Nice to meet you. How do you know so much about perfume?"

"I write about vintage fragrance." Christophe's voice was surprisingly deep and rich for such a small man. "Their style was so much more sophisticated and less obvious than so many of today's perfumes."

"Christophe studied at perfume school. He used to come to draw samples from our testers for projects. Plus, he blogs about perfume. He's quite knowledgeable."

"I've learned more here than I could at ISIPCA."

"Yesterday, Elise mentioned a perfume historian who'd worked with Pearl to have Lys Bleu donated to the national perfume archive." Joanna grimaced. "I'm sorry, I can't remember the name."

"The Osmothèque. Yes, that was me." His face lit up. "You agree, then? It's a wonderful gift to France's patrimony. You might donate it, *non*?"

"You haven't told him, then?" Joanna asked.

"About what?" Christophe said.

"I'm afraid we won't be able to donate the bottle of Lys Bleu. You see—"

Christophe's easygoing expression tightened. "But it's a work of art! You can't simply sell it to someone who will never appreciate just—"

Elisa laid a hand on his shoulder. "No, Christophe. It's not that. You see, the bottle was stolen. Joanna and I just discovered it yesterday."

"Did you get the police report?" Joanna said.

Elisa tapped a folder next to the credit card machine. "Right here."

Christophe didn't seem to hear any of it. "It was stolen? How?"

"Someone broke in. A professional, apparently. The police said the locks weren't damaged, and whoever it was knew how to circumvent the alarm. It had to be someone who wanted the Lys Bleu and nothing else."

Or someone who had a key and the code to the alarm, Joanna

thought, looking from Elise to Christophe.

Christophe couldn't speak. He circled the boutique's small showroom. "It can't be. Someone stole it." His expression hardened. "CosmeCorp. They did it."

"Who's that?" Joanna asked.

"You know the luxury goods conglomerate I told you about? Cosmetics? That's them," Elise said.

"Only the biggest bunch of crooks in business," Christophe said. "They buy up perfumes, cheapen them, then sell them at department stores. No, thank you. This is a tragedy."

"I'm just as heartbroken as you, Christophe," Elise said.

"I understand the Lys Bleu was valuable. But" —Joanna looked Christophe in the eye, then Elise— "it's simply a bottle of perfume."

"And La Joconde is simply a painting!"

Joanna's eyes widened at the force in his voice.

"I'm sorry." Christophe ran a hand over his short hair. "I take this very personally. Ernest Beaulieu, the perfumer, is my idol. He was brilliant."

Lys Bleu inspired strong emotion. If Christophe felt this strongly, others might, too. Definitely strongly enough to steal the bottle. But to kill Pearl?

"The police didn't have any leads on the theft, Elise?" Joanna asked. "No fingerprints or anything like that?"

"No. Nothing." She poured herself a cup of coffee. "Honestly, I don't think they cared. As you said" —Elise glanced at Christophe, who stared sullenly at the rug— "it's just a bottle of perfume to them."

"Who else wanted the Lys Bleu?" Joanna asked.

Christophe let out a long breath. "Any number of collectors. They aren't thieves, though." He nodded. "Yes. This is the approach to take. Be logical." He was beginning to calm down. He pulled the end of a croissant and stuck it in his mouth.

"Probably, whoever stole the bottle tried to buy it first," Joanna said. "Who has come in asking about it?"

Elise fidgeted with the edge of the police report. "I didn't work every day, so I wouldn't have talked with everyone interested in the bottle. Pearl worked the first part of the week."

"It's a specialized item," Joanna said. "Not everyone would have known about it."

"That's true," Christophe said. The entire croissant was gone now. Joanna couldn't think of an American guy who'd down a croissant like that, what with all the concern about carbs. "True perfume lovers would know."

"How?" Joanna's gaze took in the boutique from the front windows to the blue velvet curtain. "You don't advertise the bottle, I assume."

"Word gets around in fragrance circles," Elise said.

"Online, for instance," Christophe said. "Social media. Aficionados know each other, mostly through blogs and social media. Those of us who revere Beaulieu know that it's here. Was here," he amended.

"And yet no one has smelled Lys Bleu," Joanna said.

"No," Christophe said. The word came out almost as a groan. "I've studied Beaulieu's papers and have an idea of its composition. He wrote that he wanted to express both sides of a lily—the innocence and the darkness. He said he wanted it to smell like sapphires."

"Sapphires. How curious—and fascinating. Where did the shop get the bottle?" Joanna asked.

"It was a tremendous find. Pearl bought it at the flea market about a year ago. Porte de Vanves," Elise said. "You should have seen her when she brought it in. I was selling bottles of Patou's 1000 to some vacationing Argentines when she came in with a huge smile on her face, cradling Lys Bleu's box like she was holding a baby."

Christophe apparently hadn't heard this story. He listened so intently that Joanna wondered if he was even breathing. "Then what?"

"The box was sealed. It felt heavy, but we didn't know if the weight was from the perfume or from the flacon. So we peeled off the cellophane."

"And the bottle was full," Christophe said.

"Right up to its neck. The fragrance had probably darkened a bit—"

"Jasmine can do that with time," Christophe said.

"—but it looked perfect. For a moment or two, we thought about opening the bottle to smell it, but we decided to leave the stopper tied on and keep the seal intact."

"To smell it," Christophe said simply. "Oh."

"Hmm." This was all good information to report to Ruth. Joanna absently sipped her cooling coffee and wondered what the perfume smelled like. All she could imagine was visual: stems of lilies the blue of stained glass. "So, let's go back to the first question. Who has been asking about the Lys Bleu?"

"Well," Elise said, "collectors have come by. Maybe half a dozen. They left when I told them it wasn't for sale. Frankly, they probably couldn't afford it, anyway. There was the professor who stopped in yesterday."

Joanna remembered him. That smile. If he were a criminal, it would probably be from charming and defrauding rich widows instead of breaking and entering.

"Then there was the baron," Elise said.

Christophe's head snapped up. "The baron. What did he want?"

"He offered Pearl twice what she paid for the Lys Bleu, and when she said no, he upped the offer to a thousand euros."

"A baron?" Joanna said. "Tell me more."

Christophe reached to a shelf behind the cash register and plunked a telephone directory-sized volume on the counter. "This is him."

Joanna pulled the book toward her. "*The Everything Guide to Perfume*," it read. "An expert's guide to what to wear and when. Baron Ellsworth Barking."

"'A guide to whoever gave me money to hype their perfume' is more like it," Christophe said. "It's outrageous. The man is all snark and no sensibility. CosmeCorp has him in its back pocket."

"Word is he bought the title on the Internet," Elise said.

"The book says it's a bestseller," Joanna pointed out.

"So is the Fat Jack hamburger," Christophe said.

Elise folded her arms. "No need to get personal."

"Sorry. But you see what I mean."

"Why would this baron be so interested in Lys Bleu?" Joanna asked.

"Prestige, likely. I'm sure he'd love to take his dirty money and add Lys Bleu to his collection. He'd never truly appreciate it," Christophe said. "Then he'd sell a sample to CosmeCorp to copy."

Maybe that "dirty money" would buy him an experienced thief to break into Parfum d'Antan. Could he truly want a perfume enough to kill for it, though? Joanna flipped the book over. "He lives in London."

"He has a flat here, too," Christophe said. "I'll ask around. If it's him, you can bet I'll find out."

As she was leaving Parfum d'Antan, Joanna's phone rang. She still wasn't used to carrying a cell phone, but it was coming in handy in

France, where she had business to take care of without a client who was hip to her quirks about avoiding new technology.

It was Philippe. She sat on a bench in the shade of a plane tree in the Place du Commerce to answer the call.

"We aren't due to meet for another half hour, are we?" Joanna said.

"You're right. I'll see you at the Denfert Rochereau metro station as we planned, but I wanted to tell you first that the police have found something."

"Your call to the Sûreté paid off." How strange to be talking about murder on a summer afternoon while children chased each other near the swing set and men clanked pétanque balls nearby.

"Not really. When I called, they told me they had nothing to show Pearl's death was anything but an accident. There are dozens of hit and runs each year, apparently. No, about an hour after I called, my friend called back saying the driver who hit Pearl had turned himself in."

"Who was he?"

"A delivery man for the—how do you say it?—hardware store. After mass yesterday, he went straight to the police station. Apparently the priest had delivered an especially moving sermon about forgiveness."

A small soccer ball in green and pink rolled to Joanna's feet. She lobbed it back toward a boy waving at her.

"So, it really was an accident," Joanna said. "The missing bottle of perfume is a coincidence."

"That's just it. The driver says Pearl leapt into his path as if she were pushed. One minute, the street was clear, and the next…"

"Yes." A few pigeons pecking the dirt dispersed all at once when the soccer ball landed among them. "Did he see who might have pushed her?"

"No. Not at all. But at least now the police will follow up. They'll interview the businesses at the intersection and look at surveillance tape."

"It's been nearly a week since the accident," Joanna said. Tapes would be erased, memories faulty. Still, at least one person knew what happened—the person who had written the note in the guestbook.

"They have to try. If Pearl was murdered, I must know who did it."

Joanna glanced back at Parfum d'Antan. "Maybe that starts with the 'why.' Lys Bleu."

Chapter 1

Still mulling over Philippe's news, Joanna keyed in the code to enter Pearl's building.

The meeting with the notaire had been uneventful. She and Philippe had sat in his office on the ground floor of a classic Parisian apartment building—nothing like the glass and steel office building back home that would have served a law office. As promised, the notaire's English was solid. He'd laid out the several-months-long process Pearl's estate would have to go through before it would be completely settled. Ruth wouldn't be thrilled, but Joanna had the feeling that French bureaucracy ground away more slowly than glaciers in the Arctic Ocean, and it was just about as malleable.

Joanna had raised the question of what would happen were Pearl's death ruled homicide. The notaire treated the question as if he'd answered it every day. Short answer: dissolving the estate would take even longer.

But now Joanna was almost home, and her thoughts slid from Pearl's death to perfume. All morning she had sniffed the sublime. As they'd inventoried Parfum d'Antan's shelves, Elise kept finding an open bottle of something Joanna really needed to sample—"What? You've never smelled Coty's original Chypre? You have to try this example from the 1950s"—and Christophe would egg Elise on with a comment about lively citrus or nitromusks or grandiflora jasmine.

It had been glorious, but she had an olfactory hangover.

As she started up the stairs to the apartment, she smelled something else, and it was seductive in a gut-stirring way, not like the dressing room scents from the shop. She smelled dinner. As she drew closer to her apartment, the aroma grew stronger: tomatoes, onions, and caramelized meat. It might have been a genie snaking down the stairwell's twisting iron balustrade and beckoning with a vaporous finger.

As she reached the third floor landing, the door opened of the apartment directly beneath her own. This was the apartment of the neighbor Madame Chomette had said slept during the day. A large man with a leonine puff of frizzy gray hair and a beard that would have made Santa jealous emerged holding a bin of spent wine bottles. With him wafted the scent of braising stew.

"Oh, excuse me," Joanna said. "*Pardon.* Are you…" The words froze in her throat. She didn't know if he spoke English, but her lame French wouldn't help the situation much.

"*Oui?*" his voice was rough, as if it hadn't been used that day. He tried again, "*Oui, madame?*"

She tried again. "*Bonjour, monsieur.* For *deux semaines*, I live there." She pointed up.

"In heaven?" he replied in English.

She stared at him.

"No," he said. "That's presumably where Madame Littlewood is now." The neighbor set down the recycling bin and extended a meaty palm. "Martin Saunier."

"Joanna Hayworth. Pleased to meet you. Pearl Littlewood's mother sent me to take care of her estate. Madame Chomette mentioned that you sleep during the day. I hope I'm not too loud upstairs?" Then she had another thought, about the night she arrived. "I suppose you hear everything up there?"

He shrugged. "You likely smell everything up there. Like my dinner."

"It does smell wonderful," she admitted. "A red wine reduction and maybe some rosemary?"

"With mushrooms. I marinated the beef all night. Well, all day. My night."

"Very nice," Joanna said. She was overdue for lunch.

Monsieur Saunier seemed to make a decision. "Madame Hayworth—"

"Joanna, please."

"Joanna, do you have dinner plans?"

"Well, no."

"If you can stand Sunday dinner with an old bachelor, I'd be delighted to have your company. I'm making boeuf bourgignon—my own version, with, as you remarked, rosemary. As for hearing you, no. I sleep with earplugs."

Joanna considered. She didn't want to impose, but if she continued upstairs, it would be to a baguette sandwich and a cat that hated her. And that mouthwatering smell...

"I always make too much." He cleared his throat. "The company would be nice."

"Then I'd love to stay. Thank you," Joanna said. "Shall I run out for a bottle of wine?"

"I'm sufficiently stocked," Monsieur Saunier said. "If you don't mind a simple Beaujolais. I like a lighter red in the summer, even with a heavy meal." He lifted the container of empty bottles. "I'll take this to the courtyard and meet you back here in, say, ten minutes?"

Joanna nodded and continued up the stairs. Beef burgundy. Plus, he might be able to tell her more about Pearl.

When Monsieur Saunier opened his door the second time, he'd smoothed his beard and put on a clean shirt. Now inside, it wasn't the smell that captured Joanna's attention, but how dark the apartment was. Velvet draperies with bobbled fringe were pulled tight across the French windows. A peek into the living room showed a minefield of stacked books and furniture and at least three easels with half-finished canvases on them. Through the doorway to the kitchen she saw an enameled iron Dutch oven with a drip of something red on its side. The dining room table was stacked with books and pots of paint. Now Joanna made out a trace of turpentine above the stew's aroma.

"May I help set the table?"

"Thank you."

As she laid white crockery plates on the table—Monsieur Saunier cleared away a history of Polish painting to make room—she told him about Tallulah's Closet and the unexpected offer to help Ruth Littlewood by going to Paris. He was easy to talk to, asking questions now and then and listening intently.

"It's funny," she said. "It's like Portland doesn't even exist right now."

"Travel is nourishing," he said. "You're lucky to do it. I don't get out very often."

This was the first he'd mentioned his odd hours. "That's too bad."

"I don't know what you call it in English, but, basically, I'm allergic to the sun. I'm an art restorer, so it means I have to take commissions I can complete here. Even the television hurts my eyes."

"Is it difficult to find work?"

"Surprisingly, no. Besides work I can do here, occasionally I have jobs restoring murals in churches when I can work at night."

Joanna imagined the incense-dank smell of a church full of rows of wooden chairs and the ghosts of Latin services. The stained glass windows would be dark. "Sounds eerie."

"You think that's eerie? Once I worked on a chapel in the streets below Paris."

"Did you say streets *below* Paris?"

"Oh, yes. In some parts of the city there's an entire network of underground caves. Catacombs. There's even a famous dance club for drag queens down there. 'Infamous' is the better word, I suppose."

"Disco?" she asked. "I can see you in a white suit, Travolta style."

He laughed. "It's called À la Folie. I don't know about the disco. Perhaps sometime I should check it out."

"It must be hard to keep up a social life if you can't go out during the day."

He lit a single taper, giving the room the feeling of a Flemish still life, then filled plates with tiny boiled potatoes sprinkled with parsley and a ladle of beef burgundy. For a moment, she thought he hadn't heard her.

"I don't get out much," he said. "I've always enjoyed my own company, anyway."

"But you're an artist. Don't you want the visual stimulation? You know, see the change of the seasons and all that?"

"I get it from books. And memory."

"There must be something you can do," Joanna said.

He had to be lonely. Look at how quickly he'd invited her to dinner. She didn't buy it that perusing books was enough visual stimulation. Joanna's own thirst for beauty required constant input, whether it was 1930s *Harper Bazaars* or stealing glances on her evening walks through lit windows before curtains were drawn. Apple—Joanna's best friend and Tallulah's Closet's manager—was an artist, too. She was always looking, always noticing. It wasn't just her hobby, it was the food her brain required.

"I have everything I need here," Monsieur Saunier said.

"I suppose there's a whole world right inside this building." Joanna sprinkled parsley on her stew. "Did you know Pearl Littlewood very well?"

"We didn't talk much, but over the years I got a sense for her personality."

"What do you mean?" The Beaujolais and heavy food were making her sleepy, but she still had accounts to go over upstairs.

"She liked Baroque music, for instance. Summer nights she opened her windows and serenaded me with Handel. Every once in a while she threw in some Janis Joplin." He rose to clear the plates and bring a bowl of salad to the table. "She kept gardenias on the balcony. They smelled wonderful."

Joanna remembered Jicky sitting among the pots of flowers in the dining room window. They probably needed a good watering. "Sounds peaceful. You never heard arguments, for instance?"

Even in the dim light, Joanna made out Monsieur Saunier's surprised expression. "No, why?"

Joanna toyed with her fork. Saunier was surprisingly easy to talk to. Despite their many differences—age, gender, and nationality being only a few—she felt a kinship. It was unlikely that Monsieur Saunier had anything to do with Pearl's death. She'd been pushed into traffic during an August afternoon when he'd have been indoors to avoid the sun. He should be a safe confidant.

"It might be nothing, but there's a possibility that Pearl's death wasn't an accident after all."

He didn't respond immediately but forked salad onto her plate. "Why do you say that?"

"I probably shouldn't say anything until I know more. It's just that—"

At the sound of shouts from the street, they both turned toward the window.

"What's that?" Joanna said.

"Go look. Please."

She edged behind the heavy velvet curtain, where the window was open to the late afternoon. The African woman Joanna had seen that morning was coming into the building, and the thin man in the tight jeans from across the street was shouting something and pointing. The African woman disappeared through the front door without saying a word.

Joanna emerged from behind the curtains and nearly bumped into Monsieur Saunier. "He was laughing at her! The man across the street was yelling at Madame Dédé—Madame Chomette told me her name. I saw him shouting at her this morning, too."

"It's getting worse. He's the gardienne's nephew from across the street. Doesn't seem to have a job."

"What is he saying?"

"I won't repeat it. He's a sexist jerk," he said.

"She obviously doesn't like it. Can't someone make him stop?"

"How? Sit and eat." Monsieur Saunier lowered himself into a sturdy bentwood chair, its dark brown curves melting into the room's dim shapes. "She's been dealing with this her whole life, I imagine. Many women do."

"It doesn't mean it's right."

"No, Joanna. It's certainly not right. But what can one do?"

Joanna reluctantly returned to the table. Distracting her, Monsieur

Saunier described a few of his recent commissions. He told her how he shopped at the twice-weekly farmers' market when the stalls were just opening—just as the sun was rising and before he went to bed for the day. He told her stories about growing up in Bergerac and about art school. It was clear he'd been craving an audience, and Joanna was more than happy to fill in.

As she rose to leave, she said, "You're sure you can't hear me upstairs? For instance, the night I arrived did you hear anything unusual?"

He shook his head. "The day before yesterday, no?"

"That's it. Late afternoon, after Pearl Littlewood's funeral."

"I didn't hear anything disturbing. It must have been jet lag that woke you in the middle of the night. I was surprised you'd roam the back stairwell at four in the morning."

Joanna faced him full on. "I only discovered that stairwell the next day."

He tilted his head. "I was drinking coffee and contemplating cleaning my brushes. It was a cool night after the storm, and my windows were open. Four o'clock. I remember it well. You weren't in the rear stairwell? You're sure?"

"Positive."

"Well, somebody was."

Chapter 8

Across Paris, families were slicing roast chicken, serving up plates of fish sautéed in butter and tarragon, and cutting into wedges of cheese for dessert. Church bells sounded the evening mass. The afternoon sun hadn't yet dropped behind the buildings across the street, which was good, because despite a full belly and a yen for a nap, Joanna's day wasn't finished yet.

Ruth Littlewood had been explicit. "Find out everything there is to know about this perfume." Now that the driver who'd killed Pearl had come forward and Monsieur Saunier had confirmed that someone had been in her apartment the night of the funeral, the call to learn more about Lys Bleu was even more urgent. Joanna's sole comfort came from knowing that whoever broke in was likely the same person who stole the shop's bottle. He wouldn't be breaking in again. He had what he wanted. And, yet, if that were true, why would someone try to break into the apartment the night Joanna had arrived? Two people couldn't be involved, could they?

Joanna dug through her purse for the professor's business card. What was his name? She found the card in a side pocket. "Luc Cazaubon," it read and listed a phone number and email address. Nothing else. She dialed.

The phone rang in a double ring. Strange how the everyday noises of life—telephone rings and busy signals, sirens—could sound just different enough to remind you that you were somewhere else entirely.

"Âllo?"

"Monsieur Caz—" she wasn't sure how to avoid mangling the rest of his name. "Luc? This is Joanna Hayworth. We met at Parfum d'Antan."

"Yes." He slid easily into English, and his voice softened. "You've changed your mind about selling your bottle of Lys Bleu?"

"No. I'm afraid it's not that. In fact, the bottle was stolen."

"What?"

If people had told her a week ago how shocking the disappearance of a bottle of perfume could be to so many people, she wouldn't have believed them. "Yes. We noticed it just after you left." A few seconds passed without a response. Jicky rounded the corner of the living room and stood uncertainly in the doorway. "Are you still there? I'm not interrupting your dinner, am I?"

"Yes, yes. I'm here." Despite his words, he sounded distracted. "What can I do for you?"

"I wondered if you could tell me more about Lys Bleu and why it's so important." When he didn't respond right away, she added, "You probably have a full schedule, with preparing your lessons and teaching. Maybe we could set a time for another call, if you're busy."

The cat had now crept closer. Joanna kept still and pretended not to notice. Jicky sniffed at Joanna's bare feet before backing away and settling under a side chair.

"Let's meet in person. What are you doing tonight?"

✳✳

Joanna and Luc met at Café de l'Espérance, the café Joanna had lunched at the day before. Daylight was fast disappearing, but they took seats on the terrace to enjoy the warmth radiating from the sidewalk.

At first, Joanna wasn't sure if she'd recognize Luc. She'd had a vague memory of a tall, gangly man with a lopsided smile. Although he was already seated when she arrived, she knew him at once, like seeing a cousin after years apart. She couldn't help smiling, but felt ridiculous for doing it.

"What are you drinking?" she said after an awkward hello.

He nudged the brandy glass of amber liquid in front of him. "Calvados."

Oregon had some terrific apple brandy, but it had been years since she'd had brandy from Normandy. "I'll have one, too."

Luc signaled the waiter. "*Un calva pour madame.*" He leaned forward. "Thank you for calling me."

"Pearl's mother, she wanted me to do it. Pearl Littlewood—she was the owner of the perfume boutique." Why was Joanna feeling so self-conscious?

"You say 'was.'"

Joanna nodded. "She died last week. A hit and run. Right over there." She nodded toward the intersection. "That's why I'm here. I'm helping her family."

Luc's gaze shot to the intersection. "Oh, that's awful. I'm so sorry."

"I didn't know her, actually. But thank you."

"So, Pearl's mother wants to know what happened to a valuable bottle of perfume?"

Joanna noticed how quickly he'd skipped by Pearl's death. "Yes." The calvados arrived in a small snifter on a saucer. "*Merci,*" she said to the waiter.

"I see. Did you talk with the police?"

"Elise—the store's manager—filed a report. I guess they didn't take it very seriously."

Luc nodded and rolled the stem of the snifter between his fingers. "I'll tell you what I know. Ernest Beaulieu is the perfumer who made Lys Bleu. I can't tell you very much about the perfume itself."

"From what I understand, Beaulieu was a talented nose."

"He was from a very old family with a house in the seventh arrondissement and a chateau in the Touraine. It was a scandal that he became a perfumer instead of following the family into politics, but he was a rebel. He told a magazine interviewer that he fell in love with his mother's L'Heure Bleue perfume and became obsessed with fragrance. He apprenticed with two perfumers in Grasse. Many perfumers work for a large perfume company or a particular brand. Beaulieu had family money. He didn't have to do that."

The calvados smelled like baked apples but burned her tongue like rubbing alcohol. As soon as she sipped, it seemed to vaporize into Golden Delicious warmth. "Then what did he do?"

"He took on projects that pleased him. And, ultimately, it gave him cachet. When the Jacques Fath fashion house came calling, they let him create whatever he wanted. World War II was brewing then. Eventually, the Nazis occupied Paris."

The brandy snifter lay still in Joanna's hand. She imagined rationing throughout the city, the convoys of German trucks, residents marked with yellow stars. "And that's when he was working on Lys Bleu?"

"Luc? *Chéri! Ça fait longtemps.*" A blonde in heels, with immaculate cat's-eye liner, approached the table. Luc rose, and they kissed each other on both cheeks. Musk and jasmine wafted over the table.

"Martine, meet Joanna Hayworth. Joanna, Martine."

Joanna offered a hand. "It's nice to meet you."

Martine glanced at Luc before taking her hand. "Nice to meet you, too," she said with a heavy accent.

Luc sat again, leaving Martine standing. When it became clear that Luc had nothing more to say, her smile dissolved, and she left for the metro station with a glance—a longing glance? Joanna wondered—back.

"Martine is a concierge at the Hotel Meurice. Very nice girl."

"I'm sure." Joanna hadn't missed Luc's hand on her hip.

When she didn't say more, Luc pointed to the café wall behind her. "You seem to have a friend."

Cassoulet, the stray dog she'd seen the day before, lay against the wall, his head nearly under Joanna's chair. He looked small compared to Gemma at home—larger than a Chihuahua, but not as big as a cocker spaniel. She dropped a hand for him to sniff, then scratched his ears. "Such a good boy." Then, to Luc, "Apparently the waiters here feed him. Anyway, you were telling me about Ernest Beaulieu."

He downed the rest of his apple brandy. "Yes. During the Occupation, Beaulieu became involved in the Resistance. He ferried money and information between Paris and Nice. Eventually, he was caught and killed."

"Oh."

"They say he was responsible for saving dozens of lives."

Now it was dark out. The streetlights had come on, their light dappled by the plane trees lining the boulevard. Strings of round bulbs garlanded the café terrace. As they talked, the terrace had filled with people, some with wine or brandy glasses, and others with small coffee cups. During the war, the scene might have been similar, but the mood different. Women would be wearing wide-shouldered dresses and shoes with wooden soles, thanks to the wartime leather shortage. To save fabric, hems would be barely at the knee.

"Lys Bleu was Beaulieu's crowning work," Luc continued. "That's what perfumers say, anyway."

"But you're interested in it as a historian," Joanna pointed out. People settled at the table next to them, and Cassoulet slinked away.

"Yes. The family has a long history, stretching back centuries. In fact, there's another link to blue lilies."

"What is that?" Luc could certainly tell a story.

"The Beaulieu family was supposed to have owned a reliquary containing the tibia of Saint Francis de Sales."

Joanna drew back. Now, this was a twist. "You say, 'supposed to have owned.'"

He nodded. A few strands of hair fell forward, and he tucked them behind an ear. "At this point, it's hearsay. The reliquary disappeared during the French Revolution. That's not so unusual—lots of aristocratic families hid their valuables."

"And the reliquary was valuable?"

"Very. They say it was encrusted with sapphires and painted in gold leaf. Painted with lilies."

Despite the warm night, a chill ran down Joanna's arms. "Blue lilies."

"Lys Bleu. Exactly." He nodded toward her empty glass. "Would you like another?"

"No, thank you." Between wine at dinner, the calvados, and the feeling of being in a grand movie that Paris and the evening inspired, she needed every wit she had. She hadn't felt so heady since she'd fallen in love with Paul. "Do you think—?"

"Think what?"

"Could the bottle's theft have something to do with the reliquary?"

Now that the words were out of her mouth, they sounded farfetched.

However, Luc seemed to take them seriously. He toyed with his glass again and stared at the table. "I've wondered the same thing. Beaulieu might have intended the reliquary to be found after his death and used the perfume as a signal that it was still out there. He was the last Beaulieu of that line. We couldn't know for sure unless we had the bottle." He pushed his glass away. "Just a thought. Probably ridiculous."

Jewels would be a greater motive for murder than perfume, she knew. "There's one more thing—" She stopped. No, she wouldn't tell him about the note in the funeral guestbook. She barely knew him. And yet, it was way too easy to talk to him.

"Yes?" One eyebrow rose barely perceptibly. He seemed to hold his breath.

She caught his gaze. Her face warmed. She was married, she reminded herself. "I need to use the ladies' room."

"It's inside, beyond the counter, I believe."

She took the tiny spiral staircase to the basement toilet. As she washed her hands, she noticed that her face was flushed. Must be the brandy.

On the way back to the terrace, she saw Luc reaching his hand out for Cassoulet, who had sneaked back around. She smiled. Then stopped short.

Near the door was the chalkboard of the café's daily specials. It wasn't the menu that startled Joanna, but the handwriting. It was distinct—wide and slanted to the left. Exactly like the writing in the funeral guestbook.

Chapter 6

Luc stood as soon as he saw Joanna. "What's wrong?"

"Sit down," she said. Should she tell him? Why not? He was a stranger to Pearl. "There's something about Lys Bleu I didn't tell you."

He pulled out her chair before taking his own. "Okay."

"Someone wrote in Pearl Littlewood's funeral guestbook that her death wasn't an accident. Next to that, the person wrote 'Lys Bleu.'"

"Okay," he repeated. "Not an accident. Meaning it was… intentional."

She nodded, still catching her breath. "Worse, the driver who hit Pearl came forward and said she had flown into his path like she'd been pushed."

"Why is this important now? Something happened in there," Luc said. "What was it?"

"From here, you can see the intersection where Pearl died."

Luc craned his head to follow Joanna's hand. A few stragglers filed out of the metro station, and a bus rumbled past. "On the boulevard de Grenelle."

"Exactly. Well, when I came out of the bathroom, I passed the chalkboard with the day's menu. The handwriting—it was exactly the same as the writing in the guestbook."

Luc's eyes widened. "One of the staff here saw Pearl killed."

Joanna nodded. "It's possible."

Luc pushed his chair back and strode into the café, Joanna on his heels. He slowed within a few feet of the counter, and a lazy smile filled his face as he engaged the man behind the bar in conversation. She couldn't understand them, but Luc pointed at the chalkboard, and the man shook his head. After a moment, the man disappeared into the kitchen.

"Olivier, one of the waiters, wrote the menu. He's gone home. The manager is checking when he'll be in next."

The manager emerged from the kitchen and traded a few more words with Luc. After a "*merci, au revoir*" and "*bonne soirée,*" Luc took Joanna's elbow and steered her to the sidewalk.

"He'll be in tomorrow afternoon," Luc said.

"What did you tell the manager about the chalkboard?"

"I told him you'd seen the waiter and had a crush on him and couldn't wait to see him again."

"You didn't!"

"You're right. I told him we were working on a design campaign and admired the waiter's unusual handwriting. We wanted to commission him to write out some of our slogans."

How easily he invented that, Joanna thought. "Clever."

He looked up and down the street. "The bottle of perfume is gone, so I don't imagine anyone else will get pushed into traffic, but the evening feels creepier somehow."

"I agree."

A group of American tourists crossed the street from the metro and narrowly avoided being hit by a man on a moped. In the distance, a siren cut the sound of traffic.

"Where are you staying?"

"At Pearl's apartment."

"If you don't mind, I'll walk you home. I'd feel better about it."

He turned in the direction of her street. It was only when Joanna was in the building that she realized she'd never told him where Pearl lived.

As she climbed the stairs to the apartment, Joanna considered what she'd learned. The waiter may have seen Pearl pushed into the path of the delivery van. The bottle of Lys Bleu had vanished. Why? It had to be about more than simply perfume. Luc suggested there was a link between the Beaulieu family's treasure and the perfume, although he didn't know what it was. Could the bottle have contained some clue to where the treasure was hidden?

Joanna unlocked the door. The clunk of the bolt reminded her of Monsieur Saunier below her. He'd heard someone in the apartment the night she arrived. The intruder must not have expected her and left, maybe to break into the perfume shop. If that's true, why would he have killed Pearl? Whether she was alive or dead didn't matter—unless she knew something.

Joanna picked up her phone. Her first instinct was to talk it through with Paul, but as soon as she'd tapped "phone," she wondered if it was a good idea. Maybe he'd be at Uncle Gene's digging into a midday meal of whatever Gene's girlfriend Melba had cooked up. Maybe he'd be enjoying time alone, puttering in the garage with Gemma. Maybe he'd be thinking of her...

"Jo? I was just thinking of you."

She smiled. They were still on the same wavelength. "Can you talk? Or are you at Gene's?"

"I'm home, but who cares where I am? I'm simply glad to hear your voice. Has it been a good trip so far?"

A slight sigh of relief escaped her. Paul wasn't going to push the matter. "I'm making headway, but something strange has come up. I wanted to talk to you about it."

"Lay it on me." Lefty Frizzell's guitar blared in the background. He must be enjoying not having her there to ask him to turn it down.

"Pearl may have been murdered."

Silence. Except for Lefty, that was. "What?"

"The driver who hit Pearl has finally come forward. He says Pearl flew in front of his truck like she'd been pushed."

Paul let out a breath. "Did he see anyone?"

"No, but—"

"Then it could have been an accident. Maybe she thought she could cross in time if she ran. Or, maybe she was pushed, but it was completely innocent."

"That's not all." Looking down at the street—a few pedestrians in fancy dress; a taxi's headlights streaking the dark—she told him about the note in the funeral guestbook and the missing bottle of Lys Bleu. She didn't mention Luc.

"Oh, no," Paul said. "You've got to be kidding."

"Not kidding."

"Can't you let the police deal with this?"

"I am," Joanna said. "They're handling it. All I'm doing is reporting what I know to Pearl's mother." When he didn't respond, she added, "Hello?"

"I'm here. I'm just wondering what it is you want me to do."

It was so hard when she couldn't see him, read his expression. The tone of his voice on the phone could have meant anything from frustration to simple puzzlement.

"I thought maybe you'd have some ideas about why Pearl was killed."

"I say, leave it to the police. That's my idea. If Pearl was killed because of a bottle of perfume, and the perfume is gone, then there's no threat to you. Do your job for Ruth Littlewood and come home."

Joanna turned toward the living room. She made a decision. "Someone may have tried to break in the first night I was here."

"No. No, Joanna. That's it. Tell Ruth Littlewood you're through. We'll reimburse her for plane fare and whatever else she fronted you."

"I'm okay. I don't feel threatened. I've made friends in the building, and they're keeping watch."

"Oh, Jo." His voice had tightened. He'd be working to control his breath, jaw clenched, she knew. "When we have kids, you won't be able to take these kinds of risks."

No, she told herself. Don't say anything. Let it lie for now. But she couldn't.

"I don't know if I want to have children," she said. There. It was out.

"But you said—"

"I don't know what I said or when or how." Joanna went to the chair in the corner of the bedroom. She felt like being somewhere small. "I'm simply not ready to commit to having children, that's all."

"We've been talking about it, though. We don't have a long time to waffle."

"You've been talking about it. Not me." He didn't need to remind her that at 34, her fertility was running out.

What would happen now? She'd wanted this time to think, to make a decision, to plan what she'd tell him. She'd never intended to blurt it out like this.

"This is big," Paul said, his voice scarily quiet.

"I know."

The Lefty album had finished. Silence filled the background.

"Do one thing for me, will you? Don't do anything until we've thought this through. I don't want you hurt, and, as for the question of kids, we can talk more when you get back."

Somewhere outside, a man shouted to a friend. Joanna closed the windows.

"And—" Paul's voice started tentative but picked up authority. "You'd better not bother Ruth Littlewood with your ideas. She has enough to digest, without having to consider that her daughter might have been killed when you're not even sure. Let the police deal with it."

Joanna's throat burned. She had so much to say, starting with, how dare you. But she didn't. Instead, she said, "Right."

Then she hung up and dialed Ruth Littlewood's number.

"I've been waiting for your call," Ruth Littlewood said. "It's already ten o'clock over there. I know. I set the living room clock to Paris time."

Joanna imagined the clock. It would be a mantel clock with wood so old it was practically black. Mrs. Littlewood likely wound it each Sunday before church. She'd claim it never lost a second. Mrs. Littlewood would demand the same kind of fidelity from her timepieces that she did from her staff.

"Was I wrong to tell you about the note in the guestbook and the missing bottle of Lys Bleu?" Joanna asked.

"You certainly get to the point."

"I thought you'd appreciate it."

"I do. But why not tell me? You didn't think I could take it?"

Joanna sank into the blue armchair. "It was my husband. He didn't think I should bother you with conjecture about the death of your daughter. He said I might be hurting you."

Someone in the building across the street was pulling her curtains closed. Behind her, other lives with other concerns unrolled. So many windows, so much potential drama.

"Honey," Ruth said, "I haven't spoken to Pearl in decades. Even if we'd been closer, I'd want to know the truth about her death."

"I understand," Joanna said quietly.

"Your husband, that's why you jumped on this job, isn't it? Thinking things through?"

"He wants to have children. I'm not sure. It feels bigger than that, though. He wants to rein me in."

"You're right to give children serious thought," Ruth said. "Maybe I should have given the matter more thought, myself."

"I shouldn't have brought it up—"

"Hush! I say you'll tell me everything. You're me while you're in Paris. Besides, who's paying the bills? Me, that's who. What I say goes."

Joanna relaxed. "Thank you."

"You're all right, honey. Now, let's have it. You went back to the perfume shop today, right?"

"It's been a wild day."

Joanna told her about the driver's revelation, meeting Christophe and learning about the baron, having dinner with the downstairs neighbor, and then coffee with Luc, including the chalkboard.

The second Joanna stopped to catch a breath, Ruth stepped in. "The driver, he was sure?"

"He didn't see anything unusual, he said. Just a group of people at the curb waiting for the light."

"Hmm. Tell me more about this professor," Ruth said. "This sounds like more than a lecture to him."

"I had that impression, too. Plus, he seemed to know where Pearl lived. When we left the café, he turned right for my street. Of course, he was at the café when I arrived."

"So, he might have seen the direction you came from."

"That's probably it." Joanna remembered how raptly he listened, how completely she felt listened to. Then he would suddenly smile, and his whole face was transformed.

"He's a looker, isn't he?"

"I wouldn't call him handsome, really, but there is something—"

"I knew it. I can tell from your voice. Your husband had better watch out."

Joanna sat up. "Oh, no. I love Paul. We're simply sorting a few things out, that's all."

"Hmph. Anyway, this professor, he's going to help you find the waiter, right?"

"He did say he'd check in at the café tomorrow afternoon."

"Good," she said before Joanna had even finished the sentence. "Maybe it's nothing, but we won't know until we ask. Now, tell me what you can about the shop's finances."

Chapter 10

The next morning promised more sun, more heat. Cole Porter's lyrics about Paris in the summer, when it sizzles, slipped into Joanna's head.

Yes, the day would be busy with finishing—hopefully—the perfume inventory at Parfum d'Antan, talking to the waiter, and, time permitting, digging into the shop's finances. But this was her fourth day in Paris, and she still hadn't ventured beyond Pearl's world.

Christophe and Elise weren't scheduled to arrive at the perfume shop until noon. Joanna stretched and reached for Pearl's kimono, which she was increasingly thinking of as her own. Jicky leapt from the bed and ran ahead of her to wait expectantly at her bowl. Joanna fed her, changed her water, and started a pot of coffee. The cat still wasn't friendly, but at least she no longer growled.

Today, Joanna would see a bit of Paris, starting with the fashion museum at the Palais Galliera. She'd walk by the Champ de Mars, gape at the Eiffel Tower, and take the metro on the other side. But she only had a few hours.

Hurrying down the winding staircase, she almost ran into Madame Dédé in the lobby checking her mailbox.

"*Bonjour, madame,*" Joanna said.

Madame Dédé raised an eyebrow. Today she wore a long skirt and puffy-sleeved blouse printed in blue and orange with wristwatches.

Her skin was a luminous purple-brown. "Bonjour." She then raised her eyes toward the ceiling and said something in French that Joanna couldn't understand.

Joanna smiled apologetically and shrugged. "*Pardon. Je ne parle qu'un peu de français.*" This was a sentence she'd be using a lot, she feared.

"*Ah, bon,*" Madame Dédé said. She snapped her mailbox shut, raised her chin and passed through the lobby door, then the front door. Joanna followed. On the street, Madame Dédé went one way, and she went the other.

Joanna hadn't walked a dozen steps when she heard the jeering man from across the street shouting insults. Madame Dédé didn't break stride, but Joanna whirled around, and, without thinking, shouted, "Shut up!"

Both the man and Madame Dédé turned to her, shocked. The man's startled face morphed into a jeer at her, too.

"Don't look at me like that," Joanna said. "And you might think about getting some pants that fit, moron. I'm surprised you can even sit in those."

Whether or not the man could understand her English, she didn't know, but the anger in her tone was unmistakable. The man went into the apartment across the street, slamming the door behind him. Madame Dédé stared at her a moment before continuing down the street.

Adrenaline fueling her, Joanna marched toward the Champ de Mars. She passed a rug store, a wine shop, and a restaurant. She waited at an intersection while cars—most of them much smaller than they would be in Oregon—whisked down the boulevard. Ahead, two tour buses idled in front of the École Militaire. Their rearview mirrors extended like an insect's antennae. Tourists streamed from one of the buses, already snapping photos.

What had gotten into her this morning? Yelling at a stranger like that. She wasn't usually so impulsive. She rubbed her eyes with her palms.

Last night, Paul had finally come out with it. He'd been hinting, but now he was clear. They were to have children, and she'd give up on her extracurricular activities like this. Or, if she did take on a job outside the shop, she'd stay far away from crime. She knew he thought it, even if he didn't say it. As his words sat in her mind, they soured.

Joanna reached the top of the Champ de Mars, in front of the tour buses. She'd purposefully kept her gaze straight ahead to heighten the drama. Now she turned to face the stretch of the park and raised her eyes. There it was. Chills ran down her arms. The Eiffel Tower was framed perfectly by rows of trees interspersed with gardens. She was grounded, now. Whatever drama surrounded Pearl's life—now hers—Paris was still here, as glorious as ever.

The world was full of story. Maybe Amandine was sunbathing right now with the tower in the background and worrying about Monsieur Chomette. Mrs. Littlewood would be asleep in her four-poster bed with her spaniels scattered on dog beds around her. Paul would be sleeping, too, hopefully not feeling as disturbed as she'd been by their conversation. Elise might be twisting her hair into a chignon. And Luc—

"Joanna." Luc turned from the tour bus driver he'd been talking to. "How are you? It's a fine morning for a walk."

"What are you doing here?"

"Taking care of business in the neighborhood. Ran into an old friend." He gestured toward the bus driver, who'd stomped out his cigarette and disappeared into the bus.

It was surely the surprise of seeing him that stole her breath for a moment. "I'm on my way to catch the Dior show at the Palais Galliera."

"Would you like company?"

She glanced down the Champ de Mars, its row of trees turning green then silver as the breeze rustled the leaves. "Not this morning, thank you."

"I see." He didn't seem offended at all. "How about later? You should take in more of the city. I'll show you the Luxembourg Gardens."

"I'm working at Parfum d'Antan this afternoon."

"Then you'll definitely need a break. Is five o'clock all right? I'll tell you what happened with the waiter. Will you be at the perfume shop, then?"

"Yes, that's good," she said. Was she making a mistake? The warm wind ruffled Luc's hair. She smiled. "That's perfect."

Chapter 11

Elise waved from the Parfum d'Antan's rear counter. "Come in. Christophe is already downstairs."

Joanna passed a wadded fast food wrapper on the counter and made her way down the stone steps to the basement. Christophe's phone was tipped into an empty tumbler, the better to amplify his jazz piano as he logged an entry into the laptop.

"Bonjour, Joanna. I've made it as far as Lanvin." He lifted a black sphere with a gold cap. "Arpège."

"I know that one," Joanna said. The bottle felt cool and heavy in her palm. "The vintage version, too." Christophe and Elise, they were her tribe. They appreciated the quality and elusiveness of old school things.

"Night and day from the new version." He turned down the phone's volume. "You don't mind, do you? It's an American." He smiled. "Miles Davis."

"I like it." It crossed her mind that Christophe and Paul might get along.

"Yes, Arpège changed quite a bit in the early 1980s. Lanvin first released it in the 1920s. It was a complex but light floral truly deserving its name. A real arpeggio of scent. Now it's much darker and heavier. A different fragrance altogether."

Christophe should teach fragrance, Joanna thought. He certainly enjoyed talking about it—not that she minded. Starting now, when she went to estate sales for stock for Tallulah's Closet, she'd be paying closer attention to perfume.

"I've smelled both versions. Since the old one was so good, why did they change it?" She lifted the bottle, which had already been opened. The testers stood at the front of each row. As she'd learned the day before, the fact that Arpège had a tester showed it had been popular. "May I?"

"Why are you asking me?" He barely smiled. "All of this belongs to Pearl's mother now."

A mist of fragrance settled onto her forearm. She lifted her arm to her nose. Images flew through her mind: bolts of watered silk; flutes of champagne; mirrored dressing tables. "It's—it's tender and sparkling at the same time."

Christophe's smile widened. "Nicely put. Unfortunately, it's also out of fashion and almost impossible for the modern consumer to understand."

"I get it, believe me." No way she'd have new furniture in her home when a 1930s club chair carried stories of the man who drank an Old Fashioned in it each evening. Old cotton linens washed up softer than a kitten's belly stocked her closet. Depression-era cocktail glasses were so much more glamorous—and prudently proportioned—than their modern counterparts from a big box store.

"Like Miles Davis." She gestured toward his phone.

"Exactly. Music lovers know how to listen. Today, perfume is driven by focus groups and marketing plans. People aren't educated to smell anymore." There was no hiding the disgust in his voice.

"You know so much about fragrance. Teach me something." She

pulled up a stool and closed the laptop. They could return to the inventory in a moment.

"How much do you know?"

"Not as much as I'd like. I regularly wear vintage perfume, but I really don't know a thing about perfumers or how a fragrance is made." She turned the bottle of Arpège in her hand and placed it back on the shelf. She sniffed her arm once again. Less champagne and more dressing table now, but still lovely.

"Well, I suppose the first thing to know is that perfume is categorized by its notes. We have floral, citrus, fougère, wood, leather, and chypre. Those categories can, in turn, be broken into subcategories."

"This is floral." Joanna held up her wrist.

"Yes. Floral."

"I think of the categories as people," Elise said.

Joanna turned. She hadn't realized Elise had come downstairs. "People? What are you?"

"Aldehydic floral," Christophe said.

Elise nodded in approval. "Very good. A grand one, too. Like a vintage champagne or picnic in a hot air balloon."

"Floral is easy to understand. But the others—"

"Ah, fougère and chypre," Christophe said. "Here." He pulled a bottle from further down the aisle. "Monsieur by Rochas. Fougère means 'fern,' but that could be confusing. Smell it, and you'll know." Christophe sprayed the tester on a strip of paper.

"A person?" Joanna asked. "If this were a person, he'd wear a suit and read the financial pages, but play polo on weekends. It smells masculine, but in a refined way."

"Now for chypre," Elise said. "Smell this. Another Rochas. Femme."

"Whoa," Joanna said. "Bombshell. Know and love this one. I have a bottle at home."

"Chypre is one of the most complex and beautiful categories of fragrance, a real symphony. But completely not understood by the perfume-buying public anymore," Christophe said. "A chypre has citrus top notes but is grounded in oak moss, cistus labdanum, and patchouli."

"Our customers who love chypres, though," Elise added, "they are rabid for them."

"I'm getting an education, thank you. What sort of person is a chypre?" Joanna asked, already forming the image of Marlene Dietrich in her mind.

Encouraged, Christophe continued. "They vary quite a bit, from the grande dame to a waif, depending on the middle notes. One thing they have in common is that they are completely themselves. They follow their own star, so to speak."

"Here's another one." He pointed nearby to a box with nested 'L's on it. "Lucien Lelong N. It's a sheer leather-floral chypre with tart top notes. No one would ever call it pretty."

The box was still wrapped in cellophane. "Too valuable for a tester?" Joanna asked.

"Definitely," Christophe said. "Lelong was an important couturier until he retired in the early 1950s. He had N made for his wife, Natalie Paley, a Romanov princess."

Joanna longed to smell it. "Why would he make his own wife a fragrance that wasn't beautiful?"

"I didn't say it wasn't beautiful," Christophe said. "I said it wasn't pretty. It was very beautiful, as was his wife, with her delicate features. She was also troubled. Rumor had it she was an opium addict. N reflects the push and pull of her beauty. It complemented her."

"I completely get it," Joanna said. It was such a pleasure to be with people who understood beauty as she did.

"Few modern perfumes do that," Elise said.

Christophe turned back to the shelves. Joanna couldn't see his face, but the disgust in his voice was clear. "It's a dying art form, perfume. The public doesn't have the patience to explore it anymore. Then you get people like Baron Barking touting himself as an expert, then selling his reviews to the highest bidder."

Joanna chilled from the ice in his voice.

Elise didn't seem to notice. She leaned back and squinted at Joanna. "You know the perfume I had you smell the first day? Fracas?"

Joanna nodded. Buttery tuberose.

"Now that I know you better, I wouldn't choose that one for you. In some ways, it's too obvious. No, I'd say you were a chypre. A fruity chypre. A special taste."

Joanna and Christophe were well into Yves Saint Laurent when Luc arrived.

Elise stood at the top of the stairs and shouted, "Joanna? Guest for you." She whispered "The professor," and gave her a curious look as Joanna brushed past, smoothing her hair with one hand.

"Luc," Joanna said, aware of Elise standing behind her.

"You have plans this afternoon?" Elise said.

"Well, yes. We're going to stop by the café—"

"And take a stroll at Luxembourg Gardens. Joanna has barely seen any of Paris," Luc finished.

"What café?" Christophe stood behind Elise at the top of the stairs.

"It has to do with Lys Bleu, actually. Luc was telling me about its history. There's a waiter—"

"Can you believe she's been here three days and hasn't even walked through the Latin Quarter?" Luc said.

Christophe looked perplexed, Elise slightly worried. Joanna already knew about Elise's reservations about Luc. Yes, he was a charmer. But he was helping her out.

"You know about Lys Bleu?" Christophe said.

"I'm a history professor, and the Resistance is one of my specialty areas. That's why I'm familiar with Beaulieu. The perfume, though— don't know it at all. I've never smelled it."

Something strange was going on here. Joanna looked from Luc, in full charm mode, to Elise, arms crossed in front of her chest, to Christophe, eager to talk more about the perfume.

"I wish I knew what happened to that bottle," Joanna said.

"Me, too." Christophe stepped forward. "I put the word out—I didn't want to tell you in case it came to nothing. Between us, we should know if any of the big fragrance collectors bought Parfum d'Antan's bottle. Someone will see something on a forum."

"Thank you, Christophe. And thanks for all the work you're doing here. I'll let Mrs. Littlewood know. Thank you, too, Elise. I'll see you tomorrow."

Elise didn't budge from behind the counter. She gave Luc another long look before turning to Joanna. "Be careful out there."

Chapter 12

At the Café de l'Espérance, Joanna and Luc went straight to the counter. Instead of the manager they'd talked to the night before, a petite white-haired woman counted money at the cash register.

"*Bonjour, madame,*" Luc said and continued in a rush of French with enough charm that the woman pushed in the register drawer, tilted her chin, and actually batted her lashes.

Even with Joanna's high school French, she could tell Luc was coming up dry. When they left the counter, she asked, "No dice?"

"Apparently his wife called him in sick today."

"But he'll be in tomorrow."

"Maybe." His thoughts seemed to be somewhere else.

Joanna stopped in front of the newsstand, a kiosk that opened with wings stacked with newspapers and magazines. "Look at that. I wish I could read them. *Le Monde*, *Le Figaro*—"

Luc grabbed Joanna's hand and pulled her to the metro station. His grip was firm and warm.

"Luc!"

"Why bother with a bunch of stuffy newspapers?" He dropped her hand, and that charming smile again spread over his face. "Come on. We'll take the metro to the Luxembourg Gardens. You'll love it." Before she could respond, he said, "I know you're here for business.

But, for this afternoon, you're a tourist."

It was hard not to compare Luc with Paul. Paul was better look-ing, but Luc had the edge on pure charm. Luc wanted her to relax, to have fun. Paul wanted her to knuckle down and start a family. In Joanna's experience, family was a landmine of trouble. Did she want to tie herself down that way? Did she want to let herself love someone else—a child—enough to be cut down by the inevitable disappointments? Or was that simply a story she told herself?

The train took them down canyons of apartment buildings, some with geraniums trailing off narrow balconies trimmed in wrought iron, some with blankets soaking up the sun, and one with a little girl bobbing a balloon.

Neither Luc nor Joanna talked as the train rumbled on. She felt as if she were leaving a dead woman's world behind and now truly seeing Paris.

At the Raspail stop, Luc stood. "If you don't mind a little bit of a walk, let's get out here."

They emerged onto a wide boulevard next to a tall stone wall.

"What's that?" Joanna asked.

"The Montparnasse cemetery," Luc said. "Isn't that where Pearl Littlewood was buried?"

Joanna stopped. "Yes. How did you know that?"

"You told me, didn't you? You must have."

Did she? Perhaps at the café she'd said something. She didn't remember.

"Did you know Pearl?" he asked.

"No. Not at all." They'd started walking again, down the boulevard Raspail to a narrow street, where they took a left. "I only met her mother last week."

"You work for her law firm?"

"No. Why are you so interested, anyway?" A tabby cat trotted down a building's steps to loll on his back in front of Joanna. She scratched him under the chin.

"You were telling me about your legal background," Luc said.

"And you're trying to change the subject," Joanna said.

The side street let onto a boulevard noisy with mopeds and buses.

"Touché. The boulevard du Montparnasse," Luc said. "We're a block from the tip of the Luxembourg Gardens."

"That's the Closerie des Lilas," Joanna said. "Where Hemingway used to go."

"The prices were more affordable back then. Here we are."

They'd come to a path of yellow stone crushed to dust flanking a wide strip of lawn. The lawn drew the eye down an alley of trees to a chateau with a clock on its central tower, the Sénat. As they drew closer, a circular pond with a single jet of water rising from it came into view.

"It's lovely," Joanna said. "Marvelous."

"Nothing like this in Wilfred?"

Joanna laughed. "I'm actually from Portland. A much larger town, but, no, nothing like this."

"Tell me more about Wilfred and Pearl."

Luc had a gift for drawing people out, Joanna thought as they walked under the old chestnut trees. At the back of her brain, a warning flickered. What could go wrong, though? She was simply seeing some of Paris with a native.

"I don't know much about Wilfred or the Littlewoods, really. Wilfred's an old timber town. The mill shut down years ago, and there's talk of building a new retreat center there, but it seems pretty depressed economically."

"And the Littlewood family?"

"Pearl's mother runs a cannery in the valley. She wasn't particularly close to Pearl. In fact, I have the impression they hadn't talked in years. Then Pearl died." Or was killed. The park now felt more melancholy than joyful, even in the full summer afternoon. "Why do you want to know, anyway?"

"I'm sorry, Joanna. I shouldn't be so nosy. An occupational hazard, I guess."

"Professors are nosy?"

"Of course. Look here—a tiny vineyard."

They were at the park's edge next to a plot of grapevines. "And fruit trees," Joanna said, taking in the apricot and cherry trees, all neatly pruned and labeled.

"And beehives just around the corner. Come on, I'll show you."

Luc was so easy to be with. She found herself watching for the dimple in his left cheek when he smiled. They naturally fell into a pace.

"I'm married, you know," she said all at once. Where had that come from?

He smiled. "Maybe I am, too."

"Are you? You haven't told me anything about yourself."

He shrugged. "What's to tell? I'm not very interesting. I grew up in northern Burgundy, near Chablis. It's flat there, not so scenic."

"Vineyards there, too."

"True. Look, the pétanque courts. The players are serious. Want to sit and watch for a while?"

An older woman in shorts and a bearded man picked up the metal balls with a magnet on a rope.

"If you don't mind, I'd like to keep walking."

"See as much as you can before returning to work, huh?"

They crossed by the big fountain in front of the Luxembourg Palace and Luc waved at the man renting toy wooden boats to children to float on the basin.

"I swear, you know everyone in Paris," she said. Plane trees framed a vista of a colonnaded building with a cupola a few blocks away. "The Pantheon. It's part of the Sorbonne, isn't it? Where you teach. Is your office there?"

"Not far." He led her away from the view. "You should see the Medici Fountain."

Joanna turned to face Luc. "Every time I ask about you, you change the subject. Why is that?"

For a moment, he stiffened. Then the familiar smile returned. "All right. What do you want to know?"

She let her fingers brush a tree's smooth trunk as they passed. "Tell me about your best friend when you were in grade school."

"Hmm. That would have been Natalie. She was tall for her age, blonde, and a practical joker."

"Figures it would be a girl."

"We did everything together. We used to scale the wall of the mayor's *potager* and eat his strawberries."

"Are you still good friends?"

"Very much so. She's my sister. Are you hungry?"

The crowd at the park was thinning, and the sky was getting dusky. She still had work to do, too.

"A little," she admitted.

"I know a crêpe window near here. I'd love to have dinner with you, but I'm afraid it's not possible. A ham and cheese crêpe would be nice, though."

Minutes later, they were tearing into buckwheat crêpes with melted Gruyère cheese and thin strips of ham. Café terraces were filling with chattering groups clutching wineglasses. Luc led her to the Odéon metro station.

"You know how to make your way home from here?" he asked.

"Easily." She stepped toward the entrance, then turned. "Thank you, Luc."

"Thank you, Joanna, married lady."

Chapter 13

Joanna emerged from the metro at La Motte-Picquet Grenelle. As she crossed the street, she threw a glance over her shoulder at the intersection where Pearl had died, and her giddiness from the afternoon with Luc dissolved.

What had she been thinking? She was in Paris to get a job done, not flirt with suspiciously charming professors. Or at least serial daters of perfect French women with lipsticked moues and a knack with eyeliner. What would she think if Paul had done the same thing? She wouldn't like it.

As penance, she decided to spend the evening with Parfum d'Antan's financial records. Then she'd check in with Ruth.

Stuffed in the crack of Joanna's front door was a folded piece of stationery. Who would leave her a note? Who would be able to get past the two digital entries to the building? Martin Saunier, maybe. Or Madame Chomette.

No, the note was from Madame Dédé. "Dear neighbor, if it would please you to visit me tomorrow morning at 10 a.m. I am in the apartment above you. Amina Dédé."

Joanna stared at the note a moment. Still clutching it, she absently fed Jicky, then froze as the cat's tail wound around Joanna's ankles as she ventured forward to sniff her kibble.

Well, well. All sorts of surprises, Joanna thought. She set down the note and made a mental note to be ready the next morning.

She opened the French windows to let in the slight breeze and took the income-expense printout that Elise had given her to the armchair that had clearly been Pearl's favorite place to read. Elise had offered the whole laptop, but Joanna had smiled and said a year's worth of records on paper would be fine.

Reviewing financial records had never been Joanna's strongest skill, but thanks to running Tallulah's Closet, she knew what a competent income and expense report looked like. This one was solid. Someone—Pearl, presumably, but maybe Elise—had logged each day's total sales with monthly subtotals. Expenses were noted on a separate tab, with rolling offsets against taxes and rent noted.

According to these records, Parfum d'Antan made a modest profit, enough to keep Pearl and Elise afloat and pay the bills, but not much else. Every few months, expenses hiked as Pearl purchased more stock for the shop. In short, the business looked financially solid, if not especially lucrative. Mrs. Littlewood might make more money by selling off the shop's perfume bottle by bottle than by selling the business as a whole.

Joanna stretched. Somehow, a few hours had passed. Now it was completely dark outside, and a cool breeze rustled the curtains. Joanna set the papers aside and moved to the office. If Pearl had other investments, records would be here. Joanna stood in the center of the room, her hands on her hips. Jicky jumped into the office chair behind her and watched.

The office clearly belonged to someone who wanted to be orderly, but who wasn't at heart a bookkeeper. Cardboard banker boxes at the bottom of one shelf were crammed with tax records. Binders on the shelf behind the desk held hard copies of the ledgers Joanna had just examined, filed and tabbed by month. She flipped through them to make sure nothing else was there and stopped at the income-expense report for the past December. If she wasn't mistaken, the income number was higher than she'd seen on the ledger Elise had given her. She remembered because it was so much higher than January's income.

Joanna retrieved the printouts from the living room and compared numbers. Yes. In fact, a clean two hundred euros a month for the past nine months should have been added to the file Elise had given Joanna. This was interesting. She paper-clipped the page and pushed away from the desk, dislodging the cat.

What else would she find? Joanna continued her search of the office. She set aside a few photo albums for Pearl's mother—and, if she were honest, her own perusal later. Here was something. At the bottom of the bookshelf behind the desk was a wooden chest. She tested its lid. Locked. She fished around in the desk's top drawer and found an old key right away. Typical. Why people locked things then put the key in the closest drawer, she'd never know.

Joanna pulled the chest to the center of the room and slipped in the key. It unlocked easily. If Pearl had a separate bank account for unreported income, she might have the records here. The chest opened to a segmented wooden tray. Pearl's U.S. passport lay on top. It held stamps for Morocco and the Caribbean. Maybe vacations with Philippe?

Joanna lifted the tray to find bundles of unopened letters. Lots of them. A quick glance showed letters going back twenty years. All to Ruth Littlewood in Wilfred, Oregon. And every single one marked "return to sender."

Joanna sat in the middle of the floor, just beyond the pool of light cast by the desk lamp. All at once, she felt like crying.

*
**

That night, Joanna stood in the living room with the phone in one hand and a glass of wine in the other. "Why did you cut off your own daughter?" she said as soon as Mrs. Littlewood answered.

"Excuse me?"

"I found piles of letters that Pearl wrote you, and you didn't even bother to open them. Stacks of them." She set the glass on an end table and grasped the phone with both hands. "What could she have done that was so awful?"

Silence.

Joanna braced herself. "Mrs. Littlewood? Ruth."

"Did you read them? The letters?"

"No. Of course not. They were sealed. But she'd saved them all. Every single one. Locked them away."

Again, no response.

Joanna took a deep breath followed by a mouthful of Sancerre to cool her emotions. "I'll bring them home," she said softly. "Give you another chance to get to know her. When you're ready."

"If you're finished railing at me, maybe you'll let me know what progress you've made with the estate." Her voice might have cracked.

Fine, Joanna thought. "For the most part, her finances look solid. The shop was doing all right, making about a five percent profit over the past year. There is one thing, though…"

Joanna told her about the discrepancies between the records Elise had given her and the ledger she'd found on Pearl's desk. "It's consistent. Not much money, but every month."

"It's that manager, I bet," Ruth said. "She's skimming."

"Or it could be a way to hide from the tax man," Joanna said. "Or the accountant might be taking a cut, and Pearl is on to him. I don't know who does the books. It doesn't come to much more than fifteen hundred euros total."

"Question the manager. She has the easiest access. I've seen skimming before, and it's almost always someone on the front line."

"It's barely enough worth prosecuting for." Or killing for, Joanna thought.

As if reading her mind, Ruth changed subjects. "What about the waiter? The one who might have written the note in the guestbook. Did you talk to him?"

"He didn't come in today. I'll check again tomorrow." This time she'd have to do it herself, rotten French language skills or not. "Mrs. Littlewood?"

"Call me Ruth, honey. You make me feel old."

Tonight, Ruth sounded old, in fact. Joanna clicked off the table lamp. Only the meager pendant lamp in the hall and the nearly full moon illuminated the room.

"I'm sorry for asking about Pearl, for butting in where I'm not wanted. Something's been on my mind, that's all."

"I thought so. I thought so the moment you jumped on my offer to go to Paris. Didn't even run it by your husband."

That's right. She hadn't. She'd presented it to him as a fait accompli, in fact. That thought burned at her. Ruth Littlewood had noticed something she hadn't even wanted to notice herself.

"I had a rotten childhood. I don't wish that on any kid."

Nearly a full minute of silence passed. Joanna knew Ruth

Littlewood was still on the line by her breathing and the toll of a grandfather clock.

"I don't know what to tell you," Ruth said, finally. "Pearl is my only child, and I failed her. Mind you, she failed me, too. I'm afraid I don't have any advice for you."

"I know you don't like talking about it, but what went wrong?"

Joanna sank to the floor, her back against the couch. Jicky tucked her head under her hand, and Joanna absently petted her. The cat jerked back suddenly, seeming to realize she was letting herself be petted, and hissed. Joanna dropped her hand.

Ruth sighed. "Pearl was my only child. Then she went so far away. I needed her—didn't she know that?"

"I'm sorry," Joanna whispered.

"Never mind. You'll follow up with the finances and check in with the waiter, then call me tomorrow night," Ruth said, all business now. "I'll be waiting."

"Yes, Mrs. Littlewood."

"Ruth. And, Joanna?"

"Yes?"

"Hang on to those letters. I might want to look at them after all."

Chapter 14

At ten the next morning, Joanna knocked on Madame Dédé's door. What did she want? It couldn't be that Joanna was too loud, unless the sound of her evening phone calls to Ruth had drifted out the French windows Joanna opened to let in the evening breeze.

A woman Joanna's age opened the door. Age was about the only thing they shared. This woman was tall and thin with an assured beauty and skin the color of fawn suede gloves. She wore a suit.

"Welcome. I'm Michelle," she said in flawless English. "Come in and meet my mother, Amina Dédé."

Joanna walked into an apartment exactly like hers below, but full of light and a sectional sofa with stark lines. Full bookshelves lined the walls. The apartment looked like a man's home, maybe a professor's. Amandine had mentioned that Madame Dédé had married her employer. Perhaps she was too sentimental to change the décor.

Today, Madame Dédé wore a pink and blue print of swallows in flight. She stood and offered a hand.

"It's nice to meet you. I'm Joanna Hayworth."

"Pleased to meet you," Madame Dédé said with an accent that spoke of Africa and birds and common sense.

"My mother doesn't speak much English. She asked me to come and interpret for her. Please, have a seat. Would you like a cup of coffee?"

Joanna took the edge of the leather couch nearest Madame Dédé. "No, thank you." From this angle, more of the living room came into view. A silver lamp curved over a side chair.

Madame Dédé's gaze seemed to absorb Joanna. After a moment, she said, "Thank you."

"For what?"

"For coming to her defense," Michelle said. "Yesterday. Across the street, the gardienne's nephew insulted my mother. You took her side."

"I had no idea what he said, but it didn't sound nice."

"He hasn't been there long, apparently," Michelle said. "I talked to the gardienne, and he's supposed to leave by the end of the summer. But his insults are unconscionable."

Madame Dédé at last shifted her gaze from Joanna and spoke to her daughter in French.

Michelle translated. "My mother says he's out of work and insecure, and she understands his pain."

"That's no excuse—" Joanna started.

"No. That's no excuse for his comments. But we forgive him. After all, it's only words." Michelle reached out and held her mother's hand. "My mother wants to thank you, but also wants you to understand that she is not hurt."

"I'm glad."

"And you don't need to defend her. She says it's best just to let it go."

Maybe her response had been fueled by uncertainty in her own life, but, still. "Why? Why not tell him to lay off?"

Madame Dédé tapped her daughter's knee and spoke to her again. "Have you met any of the neighbors yet?"

Apparently, she'd decided to ignore Joanna's question. "Yes. I had dinner with Martin Saunier. And I spoke with Madame Chomette the morning after I arrived. I haven't met her husband yet, though."

Michelle looked at her mother, and her mother erupted into a deep, rumbling laugh. She must understand more English than she lets on, Joanna thought.

Joanna smiled. "You've met him, then?"

"No one's met him," Michelle said. "Mother doesn't think he exists."

"But Madame Chomette talks about him all the time."

"*Précisément*," Madame Dédé said, before launching into another ripple of French.

Michelle rolled her eyes. "My mother has a lot of theories about love. She says Amandine likes being single but is ashamed, so she doesn't admit that her husband left her long ago. Maman hasn't seen him for at least a decade."

"Why would she be ashamed of living alone?" Joanna asked.

"Because she is lonely," Michelle said. At Joanna's puzzled look, she said, "I know. It's complicated."

"You," Madame Dédé said. "In love?"

"Me?" Joanna didn't know why she hesitated. "I'm married."

"Children?"

"No." She wasn't ready to add, "Not yet."

Madame Dédé nodded and rose. She took a small box from the fireplace mantel and handed it to her. A gift.

Joanna lifted the lid to find a silver and ebony pendant of a bird. "Thank you. It's lovely. You really don't need to do this."

"Thank you again," Michelle said. "The pendant is for luck. Pearl may not have had much luck—at least, not at the end—and every bit will help." Her mother whispered in her daughter's ear. Joanna didn't know why, since she wouldn't have been able to understand, anyway. "Maman says if you want to talk about it, you come to see her."

That would be a trick, Joanna thought. "I won't be in Paris long. Just another week and a few days. But thank you."

Chapter 15

Joanna hesitated before opening Parfum d'Antan's door. She didn't relish asking Elise about the discrepancies in the ledger. Over the past few days they'd developed an appreciation for each other. Joanna appreciated Elise's skill with customers, efficiency, and even her willingness to do what needed to be done to close Parfum d'Antan, even though it meant the end of her job. Joanna thought Elise valued her respect for perfume and everything she and Pearl had created.

Even if Elise stomped out, Joanna knew she'd be all right. The shop's inventory was almost finished, and the police could follow up with Elise, if Ruth chose to press charges.

"Hello, Joanna," Elise said, opening the door just as she'd wrapped her fingers on its handle. "We just finished the inventory."

Joanna stepped in, grateful for the fan on the counter whooshing air scented with amber and sandalwood through the boutique. "I was going over the shop's financial records last night—"

Christophe appeared at her shoulder, waving a clipboard. "Just put it in the computer, and we're finished. Too bad the store will close now. It would be so easy to keep the list updated."

"Good news?" Anything to delay her message.

"We may have found the bottle of Lys Bleu."

Elise stepped back. "No!"

"You're joking," Joanna said. "Where?"

Christophe laughed at their reactions. "I told you I'd ask around. It's the baron. He actually tweeted that he had it."

Joanna set her purse on the counter. "That doesn't make sense. Why would he do that? It's a stolen bottle."

"He doesn't know it's stolen. Says he bought it from a fan. Look here." Christophe held up his phone. *Reference bottle of Lys Bleu parfum now in my possession*, the screen read. The baron's profile photo showed a man in an ascot who could have doubled for a younger Thurston Howell, III, from *Gilligan's Island*.

"That's him?" Joanna asked.

"Not like I've ever seen him," Christophe said. "All hail the magic of photo filters. But he has it. Has to be the bottle. I bet he bought it on the black market. Maybe even paid someone to break in here for it."

"*Oh, là*," Elise said. "We should call the police."

"We call the police, and he'll deny everything and hide the bottle. No. We can't do that."

"How do we get it?" Joanna asked. "And how do we find the person who stole it?"

Christophe slid his phone in his pocket. "We might never find out who stole it. The question is, do we want the bottle back?"

"Well, yes," Elise said.

"Then we visit him, and we take the bottle home with us. Joanna, you come with me, and you tell him that you're handling Pearl Littlewood's estate. He'll be forced to return the bottle to us. Then, I'll bring it to the Osmothèque, as Pearl wanted."

"Why would he show us the bottle?" Joanna said.

"It's simple. I'll appeal to him as a perfume writer. I'll praise him and tell him I must smell it. He won't be able to refuse, I promise you. Here, I'll get in touch with him now." Christophe snatched up his phone.

"So soon?" Joanna said. "You think he'll see us right away?"

"Why wait?"

Joanna had never seen such elation in Christophe. She'd seen him happy, as when he was explaining the differences between Chamade eau de toilette and parfum, but she'd never seen him joyous to the point that he could barely keep from laughing, as he was now.

"This will be a cinch," Christophe said. "Count on his ego to help us." He tapped at his phone. "Look! A response already."

Elise stepped up to his shoulder. "What does he say?"

Christophe read from his phone. "He would be pleased to show us the flacon, but no samples." He typed furiously, then raised his head and smiled. "Just wait."

"You had something to tell me about the shop's records?" Elise said. She'd backed away from Christophe and set a dust rag on the counter.

"He writes to bring a bottle of champagne, and he will unveil the real Lys Bleu. Can we leave now?" Christophe said.

"Already?" Joanna said.

"Why wait? He's feeling the flush of new ownership. Let's get to him while he's still giddy."

Joanna looked at Elise, then Christophe. "Yes, let's do it," she said to Christophe. Then, to Elise, "I wanted to talk to you about the shop's expenses, but we can settle it later."

Joanna and Christophe crossed the grassy Place du Commerce with its tables of old men playing cards under the shade trees. Toward the sunnier end of the park, a few sunbathers spread out towels.

"I'm afraid I don't have a metro ticket. Could I borrow one from you?" Joanna asked.

"Metro?" Christophe said, barely breaking stride. "Oh, we're not taking the metro. He lives in the 19th arrondissement, on the other side of Paris. We'll take my car."

They arrived at a vintage car with a forest green body but black roof and fenders. "This is yours?"

He dabbed at a speck of dust on the rearview mirror with his forefinger. "A Citroën Deux Chevaux. Used to belong to my parents."

Joanna took in the rounded fenders and utilitarian shape. "The design looks a lot older than that. Fabulous. I see why you held onto it."

He unlocked her door. The inside of the car smelled of oil and old rubber. "That's the beauty of a classic," he said. "Just like classic perfumery."

"Just like Lys Bleu," Joanna added, not because it was the first thought that came to mind, but because Christophe seemed to expect it.

"Exactly. Let's take the scenic route, what do you say?"

With a muscled arm on the rolled-down window and the other on the leather-wrapped steering wheel, Christophe piloted the car down the boulevard de Grenelle and over the Bir Hakeim Bridge strung with hanging lights that to Joanna lent a steampunk feel. The Eiffel Tower vanished in the rear view mirror.

"The stock at Parfum d'Antan. Do you have a buyer lined up yet?" Christophe asked.

Joanna wrenched her gaze from the passing buildings with their iron-worked balconies and stonework. "Nothing yet. I suppose that will happen after I'm gone. The notaire gave me a list of auction houses."

"Some of the bottles are quite valuable. A few are even important to perfume history. I'd hate to see them go to someone who doesn't care about the fragrance just because they like the looks of the flacon. Pearl would have felt the same way. I know it."

Joanna understood. "Mrs. Littlewood might be willing to sell some of the collection independently, as long as the prices were fair."

Seeming satisfied, Christophe returned his gaze to the road. "Thank you. You—well, Pearl, actually—would be doing a service to the art."

"You're so dedicated to fragrance," Joanna said. "Why aren't you a perfumer?"

His jaw tightened. "I quit perfume school. It was all so commercial. Imagine you study painting, and all you're allowed to paint are labels for detergent bottles. It was like that. Once I had the basic principles down, I knew I could do better myself. I started with a study of the great noses."

"Like Ernest Beaulieu."

"Especially Beaulieu." He downshifted and turned up a busy street, deftly avoiding a bicycle with a suitcase in its front basket. His expression relaxed again. "In reading his writing on fragrance composition and beauty, I understood every word."

"Like he was speaking directly to you," Joanna said.

"Like I'd written them. Like they were my words, my formulas."

Joanna knew this look, this tone of voice. She'd seen it a few times in seamstresses who turned a dress inside out, anticipating the seams, feeling the fabric's weave. They knew a garment they'd never seen, as if they'd designed it themselves. They had some sort of intense connection with the designer.

"Are there a lot of people like you? People who view perfume as art?"

"Not so many. Some. Pearl knew them. They came to see what she'd collected."

"And the baron's one of you."

"Oh, no." The force of Christophe's words shifted Joanna's attention from the passing buildings to his expression. "No," he repeated. "The baron knows plenty about fragrance, but he's completely beholden to CosmeCorp."

"The luxury cosmetics company? You've mentioned them."

"So-called 'luxury.'" His upper lip curled. "As if luxury were all about advertising and a fat price tag. As if art were dictated by a bunch of men in suits in a board room."

"So, they sell a lot of perfume," Joanna said.

"And the baron is their—how do you say?—patsy. As long as he's on their payroll, he'll do anything."

Who knew that feelings could run so high about perfume? Christophe's certainly did. For him, it was a fight about art—what he saw as a dying art. One he was determined to uphold.

"And you think CosmeCorp is interested in Lys Bleu."

Christophe tapped the steering wheel with his thumb. "I don't know. Lys Bleu is too complex, too old-fashioned a fragrance to sell well for them. They'd love the cachet of the name, though." He squeezed the wheel. "I'd hate to see what they'd do with the perfume if they got their hands on it."

"They'd only have the fragrance. Not the formula."

"Oh, they'd run it through the gas chromotographer and make up their own formula, then reproduce Lys Bleu with cheap materials and a fruity note to make the masses happy."

They were now in a grubby neighborhood. People set up folding tables on the sidewalk and sold fruit from cardboard boxes. Graffiti covered the walls. Christophe steered the car up a narrow street between a dingy building constructed sometime in the 1960s and a grand old building with most of its windows open and laundry hanging from some. He parked the car at the end of a street that stopped at a brick parapet above a canal.

"There's the address." He pointed at a Deco-style building that rose like a limestone cruise ship above the canal. That is, a cruise ship that had been put in dock during the last big recession and had been left to rot since. Christophe consulted his phone, then punched a code into the pad outside the door. The lobby smelled faintly of urine.

"The baron lives here?" Joanna asked.

He looked at his phone. "That's what the address says."

"You don't think—" She drew back. "You don't think this is some kind of trap, do you?"

Christophe only looked concerned for a second. "No. The email was definitely from him, and, for all his faults, he's not a tough guy." He pointed at a note taped to the elevator. "But it looks like we'll have to walk. To the seventh floor."

By the time they reached the baron's apartment, Joanna needed to stand for a moment with a hand on the stair rail and catch her breath. Christophe had taken the stairs easily, but he waited patiently, casting an eye toward the baron's door.

"Ready?" he asked.

"Okay."

Christophe turned to her and raised his arms as if to grab her by the shoulders, but dropped them. "You won't let him talk you out of it? The bottle of Lys Bleu?"

"Absolutely not. It's not his. Let's go."

Chapter 16

The baron's frame filled the doorway. In a different world—a world with less cheese and pastry, plus a gym membership—the baron might have looked like Christophe. They were both on the short, sturdy side. But the baron was bald and plump, with a fat gold signet ring on his pinkie and a twist of silk around his neck, even in the heat. It was as if he wore a Halloween costume that came in a box titled "British Dandy with Pretensions."

"Christophe," the baron said, all the while looking past him at Joanna. He stepped forward, offering a hand. "Ellsworth Barking. *Enchanté.*" Even in French, his British accent showed.

"Joanna Hayworth. Pleased to meet you."

"American? Nice."

"Ellsworth?" came a voice from within the apartment, followed by steps. A small woman in a pink and orange caftan appeared. Her Asian eyes and delicate frame gave her the air of a Japanese schoolgirl. A schoolgirl holding a cocktail shaker, that is. "For Christ's sake, don't just stand there. Invite the guests in. The martinis are getting watery."

"Allow me to introduce Mitzi. Won't you come in?"

Unlike the rundown building, the baron's apartment was bright and sparkling. They stepped through a small hall and kitchen into a room shaped like the prow of a ship, with floor-to-ceiling windows letting in full afternoon sun. Beyond the windows was a terrace with olive trees and blooming angel's trumpet. In a cage next to a bookshelf, a parrot groomed its wing.

Mitzi cracked an ice tray into the cocktail shaker. "We were just settling down to tea. I'll make a fresh batch, extra dry with olives. Won't you join us?" She held a gin bottle with one hand while she waited for their response.

Joanna looked at Christophe. It was barely noon.

"Apéros for lunch, you know," Mitzi added.

Joanna shrugged. "That would be nice, thank you. I'm Joanna, by the way. It sounds like you're American, too. From the South, maybe?"

"Texas, honey." The gin glugged over the ice. "Ellsworth and I met over a bottle of Mitsouko at Guerlain. Truth be told, I'm more of an Alien type of gal. Love my jasmine."

Oh, Mitsouko. A benchmark chypre, Christophe had said. Strawberry pink toenails peeked from under Mitzi's caftan. Maybe there was something to this fragrance-typing by personality, after all.

"So, you want to see my bottle of Lys Bleu, do you?" The baron settled back onto a white leather couch with a chrome frame. He reached forward to accept a martini from Mitzi.

Joanna tensed at the "my." "Thank you," she said as Mitzi handed her a champagne coupe with an olive rolling in its bottom.

"How could we resist?" Christophe didn't look tense at all. He was clearly playing to the baron. "Anything by the great Beaulieu, and especially his chef d'oeuvre. Lys Bleu."

"You always did worship him, didn't you?" the baron said.

"You've read my blog?"

"I might have caught an article or two. You've done quite a bit of research."

"Of course I have. I spent time at Beaulieu's home in Cabris and went through his papers—what's left of them, that is. Have you?" There was no missing the challenge in Christophe's voice.

"Why should I? It's the perfume I'm interested in, not the personality."

"The baron's blog is very popular," Mitzi said. "Although not as popular as his book."

Then Joanna realized that the bookshelf was full, but of only one book, white with metallic mauve lettering. *The Everything Guide to Perfume*. Best to nudge discussion away from Beaulieu. Christophe might get testy. "That must be your book, then."

"You haven't seen it?"

"I'm new to perfume, but Christophe has taught me a lot."

"Mitzi, give Joanna a copy," the baron said. "You might learn a few things here, too. Would you like me to sign it for you?"

"Thank you. I understand you'd come by Parfum d'Antan looking for Lys Bleu, that you're writing something on Beaulieu, too."

"A little something I'm doing with CosmeCorp. They're issuing a deluxe retrospective book on Beaulieu and asked me to write it for them. Of course, I needed to smell reference-quality samples of his work."

It struck Joanna how much the baron looked like a king on his throne. Maybe a disco king, given the cocktail and white leather, but definitely royalty. "Have you been to Parfum d'Antan lately to see if there's anything of Beaulieu's for your collection?" Pearl was killed nearly two weeks ago now. Where was the baron at that time? "We just finished an inventory."

"Perhaps I'll stop by," he said. "I only just arrived in Paris two days ago. Family issues in London have kept me away."

Christophe seemed not to have heard. "Pearl Littlewood wanted the special bottles to go to the Osmothèque. Especially Lys Bleu. She was clear about it."

"But someone stole the bottle," Joanna added, keeping her gaze on the baron.

He was nonplussed. "You're not going to accuse me of stealing it, I hope." He laughed, but it sounded forced. The parrot echoed his laugh in a raucous *ha ha ha*. "I bought mine legitimately. It cost me something, too."

"I'm sure CosmeCorp will pick up the tab," Christophe said.

Joanna shot him a warning glance.

"It wasn't easy to find. Once Pearl turned me down, I put out word."

"Ellsworth is so popular that he got a lot of help," Mitzi said. "Emails came in from everywhere."

"*Ha ha ha*," said the parrot.

"Why is CosmeCorp putting out a book? They haven't bought more of Beaulieu's work, have they?" Christophe said.

The baron averted his eyes. "I don't know. You'd have to ask their lawyers."

Christophe hadn't touched his cocktail. He was squeezing the chair's arm and releasing it, leaving deep marks in the leather.

"Now, boys," Mitzi said. "How about another drinkie-poo?"

"Better yet, let's look at the bottle of Lys Bleu. That's what you came here for, right? Come into my office." Using both hands on the armrests, the baron hoisted himself from his chair.

Joanna followed him into the hall and then to a room with the curtains drawn.

"I keep the room dark because of the perfume, of course," the baron said. He clicked on a switch, and spotlights illuminated glass-fronted bookshelves full of bottles. Perfume. Row upon row of perfume bottles. Parfum d'Antan's storage basement held more, sure, but they were mostly in boxes and stacked for utility. These bottles were arranged like Cartier jewels against a velvet backdrop.

The baron laughed. "Impressive, isn't it? I always love a newcomer's face when she sees my collection."

Either Christophe wasn't impressed, or he didn't want to show it. He stood in the room's center, his hands clasped behind his back. "That must be the Lys Bleu." He nodded toward a velvet-swagged item on the desk.

"Ah, yes." The baron waved back Mitzi, who had stepped into the room clutching her cocktail glass. "No food or beverages. Yes, that's the Lys Bleu. I don't mind telling you I paid a good sum for it. Once I finally tracked it down."

"Where did you get it?" Joanna asked.

"As I said, I put out the word. Finally, one of my readers wrote to me that she had a friend who had inherited a bottle. Not just *a* bottle, I should say, but *the* bottle. The bottle Beaulieu had made for his wife."

They stared at the velvet lump.

"That can't be," Joanna said finally. "Parfum d'Antan had that bottle. Pearl and Elise were sure. You saw it, too, right, Christophe?"

"Yes." Christophe shifted his gaze to the baron. "Yes, I saw it. It was the real thing. Now it's missing. How sure are you of this bottle's provenance?"

"Absolutely certain," the baron said. "I saw a photo taken ten years ago, when its prior owner received it at Christmas. No, I'm afraid Parfum d'Antan was snookered." He shrugged. "It happens sometimes. You shouldn't feel bad."

"Does yours have its box?" If so, it couldn't be Parfum d'Antan's bottle.

"Alas, no," the baron said. "But the box is hardly important compared to the fragrance."

In a sudden movement, Christophe stepped forward and snatched the velvet cover from the bottle. The baron frowned, then quickly regained his smile. "Eager to see it, are you? Well, there it is."

The bottle was cut crystal, with "Lys Bleu" engraved on its side. Its contents shone like topaz. Gold cord affixed the ground-glass stopper. And the bottle was huge. It might have held a full quart of perfume.

Christophe's stern expression relaxed. "That's not it."

"Of course it is. How can you be so sure?"

"It's not the bottle from Parfum d'Antan."

Joanna agreed that it couldn't be the shop's bottle. For one thing, it was too large to fit the box she'd seen. Then she had another thought. Perhaps the baron's bottle was Ernest Beaulieu's original bottle and not the one in the shop. Yet that didn't make sense, either. If so, why had the shop's bottle been stolen?

"So, you saw the wrong one," the baron said. He loosened his ascot with one hand. Beads of sweat popped at his hairline.

Christophe folded his arms. "No, this one's a factice. If it were perfume, why didn't anyone open the bottle and wear it?"

"A factice?" Mitzi asked from the door, her martini refreshed.

"A phony bottle, for display in a boutique," Christophe said. "Lalique probably made one or two, thinking Lys Bleu would be marketed soon."

The baron shifted feet. "It's real, I say. I should know."

"How exactly is it that you should know?" Christophe said, widening his stance.

"Knock it off, boys," Mitzi said.

"A factice is full of colored water, then," Joanna said.

Christophe understood right away. "We smell it. That's the only way to know for sure that it's Lys Bleu."

Light gleamed from the Lys Bleu, giving it the look of a science fiction amphora.

The baron looked from Christophe to Joanna to Mitzi, who'd seen this as important enough a moment to ditch the martini and join them. "Okay," he finally said. "I was planning to open it, anyway. Eventually."

"You mean you were planning to give it to CosmeCorp to open to analyze and make a cheap copy of," Christophe said.

Joanna gave him a dirty look. He wasn't making this easier. "I'd love to smell it," she said. "It would be a real honor to smell it here, with you."

"You don't think I stole it, then?"

"How could you?" Joanna was really pouring on the oil now. "You have proof, right?"

The baron brought a small pair of gold scissors from a desk drawer. "For Joanna, I'll open it. I'll prove to you it's the real thing." He snipped one of the cords. "The bottle will be sealed with animal skin, too. We may need to apply a warm cloth to its neck." He snipped another cord and unwound it. "What an experience this will be, Joanna," he said, pointedly ignoring Christophe and apparently taking Mitzi for granted. "They say Lys Bleu is as haunting as old Armagnac. Rich and deep, but with a lifting, almost transparent lily note. Not meaty, but like lilies played by a cello." His voice took on a lecturing quality, as if they were in an auditorium instead of a small office. "Be prepared for a real treat." He placed his hand over the stopper. It twisted easily.

"I have a cloth ready," Mitzi said.

"No cloth necessary." The baron looked up triumphantly. "It's as if it's begging to be released."

Eyes half closed, expression already dreamy, he lifted the stopper to his nose. His eyes flew open.

Joanna didn't have to be told what he smelled. He'd smelled nothing.

Ha ha ha, the parrot laughed from down the hall.

Chapter 17

"You should have seen his face when he realized he'd been taken," Christophe told Elise.

The baron hadn't wasted a minute shooing them from the apartment, and Christophe had laughed all the way back to Parfum d'Antan.

Joanna was more circumspect. They hadn't found the stolen bottle of Lys Bleu, and neither had the baron, despite his connections and, if Christophe was right, the lure of a fat payout by CosmeCorp. As the car drew closer to the Place du Commerce, Joanna's anxiety had grown. She still had to confront Elise about the difference between the income and expense logs.

After Christophe left, Elise handed her the shop's laptop. "The inventory is finished. Every last bottle is logged in."

"Thank you." She set it on the counter. The sun's slanted rays fell in a diamond pattern through the night gate. "Elise, I want to talk with you about the shop's accounts."

Elise's smile dimmed a few watts. "What about? The file I gave you was okay, no?"

"The file was fine. At Pearl's apartment, I found another set of books, this one written by hand and backed with receipts. They don't match up with the records you printed out for me."

Elise averted her gaze. "They are less, perhaps, a few hundred euros a month?"

"That's right. What do you know about that?"

She sighed. "I noticed it, too. That was Pearl. I questioned her about it."

"And?"

"She didn't want to tell me at first. She'd started seeing a psychiatrist. She'd been estranged from her family in the United States for so long, and I think it was beginning to weigh on her."

Joanna's jaw relaxed. She turned to face Elise. "What does that have to do with taking money and not marking it as an expense?"

"She was self-conscious. Perhaps she didn't even want to admit it to herself. So she paid the doctor in cash. She took it from the till. No checks with the doctor's name, no record to remind her." Elise picked up her purse. "I think she was feeling better, too. Until..."

"Yes." Until she was killed, Elise had been about to add. "I guess that makes sense. From looking at her papers, Pearl wasn't the most organized person around."

Elise laughed. "So true. We're organizing for her. Do you mind if I go now? I want to visit my father before it gets too late, and the home is a long metro ride from here. The back is already locked. All you have to do is lock the front door, then pull the night gate down the rest of the way and lock that, too. You have the keys and the alarm code, right?"

She did.

"I wish I could have been there to see the baron uncap the Lys Bleu factice." Elise shook her head. "At least the bottle's probably worth something, even without the perfume. Well, good night." She stopped and turned around. "Oh, I left something for you next to the cash register. Jean Patou's Que Sais-Je, a fruity chypre. I thought it would suit you."

"You can't sell it?"

"The label's damaged, and it's not especially rare—this is the 1980s remake. It will have a better home with you. Something to remember us by in Portland. See you tomorrow."

A squat bottle with sloping shoulders and black stopper sat between the register and the telephone. Joanna opened it and sniffed its sharp, mossy elegance. Fred Astaire in a bottle.

For the first time, Joanna was alone in the shop. In a few days, she'd turn Parfum d'Antan over to someone to sell, and she'd probably never see it again. It was a shame, really. Over the years, Pearl had created something beautiful, a destination for people who appreciated perfume as something more than a bottle of pink juice to spray on for date night. People like Christophe, who really saw perfume as an art. And the baron, who, according to Christophe, exploited that art.

She turned toward the shop's office. Elise had worked with Pearl for years. Her story about Pearl's appointments with a psychiatrist was plausible. Plus, if Elise had been stealing from the shop, why had she started so recently? Pearl clearly knew the ledgers didn't match, but she hadn't fired Elise. There was no one else to pilfer from the shop. Joanna would be more comfortable if she had receipts from the doctor's office to offset the expense, but if Elise were right, on some level Pearl hadn't wanted to own up to the appointments. Yet, she'd kept a private record at home.

Joanna should have a solid report for Ruth that evening. Except for the failed mission to find the bottle of Lys Bleu.

Everyone seemed to want that bottle. Why?

Christophe thought CosmeCorp wanted to remake the perfume.

She couldn't imagine a major corporation bumping off a perfume shop owner to get a bottle. Hire the baron to find them the bottle, sure.

Christophe himself wanted the bottle saved at the Osmothèque for posterity. He was passionate about it. She remembered his fury as he talked about the baron. But Pearl had promised him that the bottle would be preserved. He had no reason to steal it.

Then there were Luc's hints that the bottle might somehow link to the Beaulieu family's treasure. That seemed far-fetched, at best. But it would provide the motive both to steal the bottle and to prevent Pearl from giving it away—even if it meant killing her. Could there be some sort of secret code on it?

Joanna had thought the world of vintage clothing was rich with quirky characters, but in Pearl's world of perfume, passions ran unusually deep. In fact, she'd met a number of interesting people in Paris, including her neighbors. Like Monsieur Saunier, for example.

She had a free evening ahead of her, and a plan began to come together. This plan might not be worth sapphires, but she hoped its benefits would last a long time.

Night was falling. A floor below, Monsieur Saunier would be awake by now, perhaps having coffee. Joanna glanced at Philippe's hamper, which she'd filled with sandwiches and a bottle of wine, plus Pearl's best linen napkins. She'd wait just a bit. Another half hour to give her target time to wake up fully.

Plus, she needed to dress. The occasion required something a step up from her cotton dresses—something that would make the evening feel plucked from an old movie. Joanna remembered the full-skirted cocktail dress she'd seen in the wardrobe. She and Pearl were close in size. Just maybe…

With a swish of tulle on skin, Joanna pulled up the dress and zipped it up the side. Not a bad fit at all. The spider's web of rhinestones glittered against the black tulle like a constellation on a winter's night. Perfect. She pulled back her hair and dabbed Que Sais-Je behind her ears.

Jicky watched her from the armchair by the window. Over the past few days, they'd struck a truce. Joanna would care for her but leave her alone, and Jicky would lay off the growling and hissing. Joanna couldn't help but feel if she had more time, they could be real friends.

As for tonight, it would feel good to do something positive, something that could have a happy ending, no matter what happened at Parfum d'Antan, or with finding Pearl's killer, or—her heart seemed to shrink into itself—with Paul.

Might she strike out? Sure. But trying felt right. No one was here to tell her "no" tonight.

Chapter 18

Joanna set the picnic hamper in the hall, readjusted her borrowed dress, and pressed Monsieur Saunier's doorbell.

The brass cover over the peephole flicked back, and the door opened. "Joanna?"

"Will you take me out this evening?" Joanna replied.

Monsieur Saunier looked behind him, as if an answer would come from his empty apartment, then returned to her. "Take you out?"

"It's a lovely evening—warm with a bit of a breeze. And dark. Sun won't be a problem now." She lifted the hamper. "I brought dinner."

Monsieur Saunier's gaze dropped to the hamper, searched the wall behind her, then settled on Joanna's face. "Come in, won't you? Have a seat. I'll return in a moment."

He disappeared down the hall, and Joanna took a hardback chair at the dining table. A crockery plate with a piece of torn bread sat at Monsieur Saunier's place, but he hadn't yet dished up his meal. On his easel was a landscape of summer-blown trees framing a pale meadow.

"There." Monsieur Saunier reappeared in the living room in a brown suit complete with a vest. He'd smoothed back his frizzled hair, and a blue paisley bow tie showed beneath his beard. "Now I'm fit to be seen with a lady. Shall we go?"

Joanna couldn't help but laugh. They crammed into the building's tiny elevator, Joanna's skirt billowing to fill the corners, and emerged into the street. The florist's shop on the avenue de La Motte-Picquet had packed up its gardenias and geraniums for the night, but the café terraces hummed with conversation and laughter as white-aproned waiters dashed between tables.

"What is our plan, madame?" Monsieur Saunier asked.

"I thought we'd sit on the Champ de Mars and have a picnic. Then maybe you'd show me a little bit of Paris at night."

"You should be doing this with a handsome young man."

"I should be doing this, full stop," Joanna said. "And so should you."

"You are a forceful thing, aren't you?" He didn't look like he minded.

They laid a linen tablecloth on the lawn that stretched from the École Militaire's yellow stone bulk to the Eiffel Tower. They weren't the only couple with this idea. The lawn was dotted with people on the grass, sipping wine and eating sandwiches, and all facing the same direction—toward the gently lit tower and the river. A spotlight revolved at the tower's tip.

"Do you believe in the grand gesture?" Joanna asked.

"Ah. The grand gesture." Monsieur Saunier slipped off his oxfords, revealing a quarter-sized hole in one of his socks. "Why, yes, I do, in fact."

"So do I." Satisfied, Joanna unpacked their dinner. She set Pearl's porcelain plates on the cloth and folded napkins next to them. "You might have to walk a bit further to climb marble stairs, but it's important to take a building's prettiest entrance."

"I agree. A few tuberoses in a vase are very nice, too."

"And silverware that feels good in your hands, even when you eat alone."

"Good sheets are key," Monsieur Saunier said. "I have someone hunt down the old cotton ones at the flea market for me."

"I completely agree." Joanna dished out slices of poached salmon and sugar snap peas with ribbons of basil. "I hope you like fish."

Monsieur Saunier didn't answer. Lost in thought, he stared toward the Eiffel Tower's pulsing spotlight. "You remind me of my wife."

Joanna set down the serving spoon and leaned back. "Tell me about her."

"I met her in art school. We used to set up our easels next to each other when we copied paintings at the Louvre. We married young, and she died—young."

"Oh."

"Cancer." His chest rose. He stripped off his jacket and folded it next to him. "She believed in the grand gesture, too. She would have liked this." He pointed toward her ring finger. "You're married."

"Yes."

"But you're here alone."

"Yes," she repeated.

Monsieur Saunier raised an eyebrow but didn't press the subject further.

"Maybe we can see the Louvre tonight," Joanna said. "I'd love to hear your stories."

"Perhaps. And I'd like to hear your stories about Paris, too. Did you ever find the bottle of Lys Bleu that had gone missing?"

As they ate, Joanna told him about the day's visit to the baron. "The bottle might have been stolen so its formula could be reproduced," she concluded. "Although a big company like CosmeCorp wouldn't have to steal it. They could buy it and presumably pay as much as was demanded."

"So they hired the baron to find the bottle, even if it was on the black market."

"That's what Christophe thinks. The baron didn't deny it."

"And someone else might have stolen it with the idea of selling it to CosmeCorp via the baron."

"Maybe. There's one other theory, too, although it's kind of outlandish."

Monsieur Saunier ripped from the baguette. "I'm listening."

"I met someone else at the store, a history professor at the Sorbonne. He says the perfumer's family was well to do and had a sapphire-studded reliquary they'd hidden during the French revolution. He thinks the bottle of Lys Bleu might hold the clue as to where the reliquary is."

"You mean, an etched map or something like that?"

"Luc says the perfumer was part of the Resistance during World War II, and he knew there was a good chance he'd be killed. He didn't want the Nazis to seize the reliquary."

"Surely, his family would know where it was."

"That's just it. He was an only child and married a Jewish woman who died at Auschwitz. They didn't have children. Then the Nazis killed him. The bottle of Lys Bleu that disappeared was a one-off, and he had the flacon specially made."

"Hmm. I suppose it's possible to etch crystal with a map. Or maybe write something on the reverse of the label." Monsieur Saunier squinted as he thought. "No. Beaulieu must have had an old map. It would be an heirloom at that point. Why would he destroy it?"

A map. A piece of paper. "You think he might have kept the original map."

"Sure. The map would have been part of his family's legend. He would have found some way to preserve it. You say this perfume was special to him. If the map were small enough, he might have affixed it to the underside of the label."

" Or even lined the box with it," Joanna said all at once. The bottle of Lys Bleu was gone, but the box remained on the shelf at Parfum d'Antan. Could it be?

"Look." Monsieur Saunier pointed a cobalt blue-spattered finger toward the Eiffel Tower.

Joanna inhaled sharply, then laughed. The tower had erupted into a fizz of sparkling lights.

"Now that's a grand gesture," Monsieur Saunier said.

The Place du Commerce was deserted. Joanna unlocked Parfum d'Antan's night gate as quietly as she could, feeling she was doing something illegal, despite her right to enter the shop anytime she wished.

The gate creaked as she lifted it. She bolted the door behind her and keyed in the alarm code but kept the lights off. She shook her head. No use thinking about bogeymen. She had a job to do. The Lys Bleu box was still downstairs. She'd never be able to sleep until she'd checked it for a map.

Joanna pushed aside the heavy velvet portière and made her way to the basement stairs. She clicked on the bank of fluorescent lights and went to the back of the room, where the really valuable inventory was locked up. It was so quiet down here. The hum of the dehumidifier was the only noise.

She flipped through the key ring. There it was, the key to the vault. After a bit of fidgeting, the door opened. Joanna half expected the Lys Bleu box to be gone, but it was just as she and Elise had left it. Her back prickled, as if someone were watching her. But that was impossible.

She took a deep breath and examined the box. It was white with gold lettering and made of a stiff rag cardboard. She lifted the lid and peered inside. Tipping it in the light, she saw nothing but black linen paper lining. There could be a message under the lining, though. Before taking it apart, she picked up the box's base and shook it. It was heavy—not like today's cheaper boxes—and presumably hollow.

Would the Lys Bleu be worth less if its box were destroyed? Probably. The box wasn't hers, either. What would Ruth Littlewood say?

Ruth would want her to go for it. Slicing a key along the base's seams, Joanna pried it open. The key ring fell to the floor with a clatter. Folded inside the box's base was a piece of yellowed paper.

Hands shaking, Joanna smoothed it against the shelf. It appeared to be some sort of map. On instinct, she looked over her shoulder. The basement was quiet—she was alone. She breathed deeply to calm her racing pulse.

The map was handwritten in black ink that was now faded at its center. It showed an address and a rough floor plan of a house with an arrow pointing to a staircase, then to another door. Where the arrows ended was a drawing of a lily in a paler ink. Ink that might once have been blue.

This map was old—far older than World War II when Ernest Beaulieu created Lys Bleu. Luc had been on to something. The map showed where the reliquary was hidden. Had to. She refolded it and slipped it into her purse.

She took a moment to catch her breath. The shop around her was quiet and gently scented with the ghosts of a hundred perfume bottles. Her skirt rustled against the shelf as she patted her purse again to make sure the map truly was there.

She folded the box back together and, taking a fortifying breath, returned it to the shelf. She hurried up the stairs, pulled down the heavy night gate, and plunged into the night.

Chapter 19

It was well past midnight now. With the map in her bag, Joanna rushed down the deserted square toward the café at the corner of rue du Commerce where a few couples still sat on the sidewalk sipping coffee and brandy. The comfort of the presence of strangers wouldn't last long, though.

She rounded the corner and moved purposefully by the darkened shop windows, her skirt swishing against her calves.

The map. She'd found a map in the Lys Bleu box. Luc had been right. Whoever had stolen the bottle wasn't after the perfume at all. He wanted the map, and, ultimately, the reliquary. The thief's error had been in assuming the bottle held the answers.

It would soon become obvious that he didn't have the information he wanted. Would he return for the perfume box? Her feet rap-rap-rapped on the sidewalk as she hurried. Two young women, laughing tipsily, stumbled from a hotel. Across the street, a group of people emerged from the Café du Commerce and paused, as if unsure what to do next.

In a few blocks she'd be at the Boulevard de Grenelle and among the people in the surrounding cafés. She clutched her bag closer. At one point, she heard someone behind her, gaining on her, but the steps turned up the boulevard.

At last, she was at the apartment building. Looking over her shoulder, she punched in the building's code to get to the lobby, then the lobby's inner code. Now she was at her door. She fumbled with the key, turned the bolt, and stepped inside.

The apartment was quiet. Undisturbed. As always. She sighed in relief and locked the bolt behind her. She set her bag with the map on the dining room table and closed the curtains. Now what?

She drummed her fingers on the counter, then nodded. She would hide the map, but she had one thing to do first.

She changed into the closest cotton dress, leaving the cocktail dress draped across a chair in a billow of sparkle. Then she went downstairs and rapped once again on Monsieur Saunier's door.

Monsieur Saunier was still dressed in his eveningwear, although his bow tie lay limp around his neck. His vague look of dreaminess turned wary when he saw her. "Joanna?"

She spoke quickly. "Remember our talk about Lys Bleu? I have a question for you." Then, quickly, "I'm not disturbing you, am I?"

Monsieur Saunier chuckled, then stepped aside to let her enter. "I'm an old man. I don't know what I was thinking."

"That I'd come to seduce you? Don't think I'm not tempted." She tugged the end of his bow tie. "It's about this." She held up the map.

"I see you brought a friend."

Jicky ran between her legs and darted into the apartment.

"I'm sorry. She must have escaped when I opened the door. I didn't see—"

"Oh, it's no worry. Madame Littlewood used to let her down the back steps sometimes to say hi. We're old friends, aren't we, Jicky?" The cat raised herself to nestle her head in his palm. He expertly scratched her ears. She jumped onto the chair at his easel and began to groom herself. "Now, how can I help you?"

Joanna told him about finding the map in the Lys Bleu box at Parfum d'Antan. She unfolded it on the table. "It looks old. I wondered if, with your art history background, you could tell me anything about it?"

He touched the paper between his fingers. "Just a moment." He brought the map to his easel and clicked on the light. Jicky jumped down from the chair, and in a silent leap landed on the table and curled up next to Monsieur Saunier's napkin. He swung a magnifying glass the size of a sheet of paper over the map.

Joanna stood with her hands at her sides, afraid even a breath would disturb his analysis.

Finally, he pushed the magnifying lens away. "You guessed correctly; it's old. From the yellowing in the vellum and the fading in the ink, I'd estimate late 18th century."

"Luc was right, then. It's a map to the family's reliquary."

"Definitely a map. In those days, amateur maps were drawn much as they are today. People used landmarks like these" —he pointed to the tree and the well— "with lines and arrows."

"There's an address, too," Joanna said.

"Not a street I recognize." He withdrew a small book from his bookshelf next to the fireplace and flipped to the index. "Not listed here, either. Perhaps it's not in Paris. But it does seem to indicate houses on both sides. Maybe…"

"Maybe, what?" Joanna said, barely breathing.

"Streets were renamed over time. This one might have been, too. It wouldn't be unusual. I have a friend who specializes in old maps. I could ask her, if you'd like."

"Yes, please."

"Once we've found the address, the map is quite straightforward. There's only one bit I don't understand." He placed a finger on the map's corner. "This."

Joanna moved forward. "S. S." was carefully lettered in the lower right corner. "Could it be the initials of the person who drew the map?"

"You said it belonged to the Beaulieu family, *non*?"

"That's my best guess."

"It would be more normal to sign an initial and a surname. But you could be right." He clicked off the lamp next to the easel and took off his glasses. "In the meantime, you have to decide what to do with it."

"Yes." She pulled at a curl and wound it around a finger. Who did the map belong to? She didn't know the law. Pearl had owned it, but maybe it should go to the Beaulieu family, if relatives, however distant, could be found.

And, it might be evidence for murder.

She double-checked the bolt on the door to the back stairway. Locked. She'd put the map somewhere safe while she decided what to do next.

Where to hide it? She scanned the apartment. If she were looking for a map, where would she start? She'd look with other papers, in a desk or dresser drawer, or in books. Those places were out. She'd heard of people storing jewels in the freezer, but that would destroy the old paper.

Under the cushions on the dining room chairs was too obvious, as were the cushions on the couch or armchair in the living room.

She could hide it behind a picture frame, but she thought she'd seen that in a movie. No, a burglar would definitely check there, just as he'd check under the mattress.

Jicky yowled from the kitchen in hope of an early breakfast.

"Not yet, baby cat. Here. Why don't you play with this?" Joanna reached for a toy mouse in a bowl on the fireplace mantel.

Yes. That was it. The chimney. She fumbled through a kitchen drawer for a plastic bag and slipped the map inside. She pushed away the fireplace screen and reached up the flue. There should be some sort of damper where she could rest the bag. Just until she could figure out what to do with it.

Cheek pressed to the fireplace's marble front, feeling gingerly up the chimney, her fingers reached a ledge. Here it was. She stretched just a few inches further, hoping she wasn't getting soot on her dress, and she felt something else. Something with a rounded edge.

Soot be damned, she thrust her arm and shoulder into the fireplace and grasped the object and pulled it out. She coughed and turned the object in her hand. It was a bottle, wrapped in paper.

Catching her breath, she unrolled the bottle from the paper. Its gold lettering glinted in the light of the table lamp. No way. She dropped to the armchair and stared. It was the missing bottle of Lys Bleu.

"You've got to be joking," she said aloud. They'd been shaking down social media networks across the globe to find the bottle of Lys Bleu, and, all the while, it had been here. Pearl must have hidden it.

Joanna took the bottle to the kitchen and wiped it down. It was a heavy crystal flacon full of amber liquid. Gold cord affixed the stopper to the bottle. Attached to the stopper was a thick ornament—bronze, maybe—with strangely rustic edges and twists that might have been

Brancusi's approximation of a lily. A vellum label crossed the bottle diagonally with Lys Bleu printed in gold.

She turned the bottle in the light and examined its bottom and what she could see of the back of the label. No marks at all.

Well. Tonight was a double whammy. First the map, now this. Where was a martini when you needed one?

Joanna set the bottle on the counter. For the meantime, she'd hide it in one of Pearl's boots. The Lys Bleu was still valuable, but it was the map that was the real treasure. Once the reliquary was found, she'd give the bottle to Christophe to pass along to the Osmothèque.

And that would be that.

Chapter 20

Joanna rubbed her eyes and swung her legs to the floor. She shouldn't have slept well last night. She should have tossed and turned and fretted about the mystery unfolding with Lys Bleu. Instead, she'd passed out as soon as her head touched the pillow.

She slipped on Pearl's kimono—really, this was getting to be a habit—and picked up her phone. A message from Ruth Littlewood.

Joanna tensed as she listened. "Joanna," Ruth's unmistakably irritated voice said, "do we have daily appointments, or do we not? Call me."

Damn. In the excitement, she'd forgotten. She couldn't call now. Ruth would be in bed. Tonight. She'd have plenty to report then. Before discussing the map with anyone else, she'd run it by Ruth. And one other person. Once she'd put water on to boil for coffee, she picked up the phone again.

"Philippe?" She imagined him reading the orange-tinted pages of *The Financial Times* or maybe *Le Monde Diplomatique* over a croissant and a porcelain cup of coffee with milk in his bachelor apartment. He'd mentioned having a roommate. Maybe there were two gentlemen bachelors. "I have something important to talk with you about. About Lys Bleu."

Philippe was out of breath. "Sorry, I just stepped off the treadmill.

I'm at the gym."

"Oh." She recalculated her visual. "Do you have time this morning, maybe? I'm going to Parfum d'Antan to work, but those are my only set plans for the day."

"I'm booked solid, I'm afraid." He'd regained his breath, and the background was quieter, too. He must have stepped into the locker room. "But I would like to see you and hear this news. How about dinner? You can come to my home, if you'd like. That way, we can talk in private. Eight o'clock?"

An hour later, she was at the perfume boutique. Today, she'd inventory the shop's fixtures. In the warm light of the summer morning, the boutique had shed the prior night's sinister feel. A group of older men played pétanque in the Place du Commerce while a woman in a colorful head wrap pushed a baby stroller.

Elise was already at work. A half-eaten fast food breakfast sandwich sat at her elbow. "*Bonjour, ma belle.* Did you have a good evening? Maybe you found Pearl's receipts for the difference in the ledgers?"

Joanna looked at her blankly for a split second. The ledgers had been the furthest thing from her mind. "Not yet, but I'm sure you're right."

Elise shrugged. "A small thing. I didn't want to bring it up, but I suppose it doesn't matter now. Oh, our first customer of the day."

Joanna turned to see a middle-aged brunette clutching her handbag to her chest. She hesitated at the door. "*Bonjour, madame,*" the woman said.

American. Joanna was sure. She leaned on a case to watch Elise at work.

Elise's face lit up as she discreetly pushed her breakfast sandwich out of sight. "Welcome. May I help you?"

The woman's face relaxed. She dropped her arms to her sides and stepped in, her head swiveling to take in the rows of bottles, the velvet draperies. "Is it okay if I speak English?"

"Yes, of course. It will give me the chance to practice."

Nice ploy, Joanna thought. Elise's English was already perfect.

Elise added, "Is there a particular fragrance I can help you find?"

"I'm looking for a signature scent," the woman said. "I know I probably should have one by now. I mean, I'm no kid." She stole a sideways glance at Joanna, who responded by tidying papers.

"Nonsense," Elise said. "I must have a dozen signature scents." She laughed. "At least, that's what I call them. I add one every year, it seems. After all, I wouldn't wear the same dress every day, would I?"

Yet she did wear the same uniform, Joanna thought. Crisp white blouse and man-tailored trousers with delicate jewelry and her ever-present chignon. But Joanna got her point. No wonder Pearl had made sure to hold on to her.

The customer set her purse on the glass-topped counter and scanned the shelves. "I've been to every department store in Sacramento—that's where I'm from—but nothing feels right on me. I read about your shop in a magazine."

Elise came from around the counter and clasped her hands in front of her. "Most of our business comes from people who already know which fragrance they want to take home. Since we sell perfume that isn't made any more, we don't have many testers. But we do have some. And, frankly, it's customers like you I really enjoy. What's more fun than helping someone discover a fragrance they'll love?"

The woman faced Elise, a smile on her face, shoulders relaxed. "I'm so glad I came in."

"Would you like a cup of tea, maybe?" Elise raised an eyebrow toward Joanna, who dipped beyond the velvet portière to fill the electric kettle. She glanced over her shoulder. Elise stepped closer to the customer and gestured toward a bottle. Joanna slipped through the door to the basement, keys in hand, and passed the darkened rows of perfume to the locked room at the rear. She opened the door and let herself draw a full breath. The Lys Bleu box was still there.

When Joanna re-emerged, Elise was in full interview mode with the woman. "It sounds like you want something subtle. Shalimar is beautiful, but certainly not quiet."

"I don't know why the saleslady kept insisting I try it. 'Shalimar is for brunettes,' she kept telling me. It just wasn't me."

"Let's talk about what it is you are, then," Elise said. "When you are relaxing at home, in the garden, say, what do you like to drink?"

"Chardonnay," the woman promptly responded.

Elise nodded. "Where is your favorite place to visit on vacation?"

"I teach, so we can only travel during school breaks. Mostly we go to Fresno to visit my daughter. This trip is special, for our fortieth anniversary." The woman's face lit up. "But if I could go anywhere, I'd go to the lavender fields in Provence. Wouldn't that be wonderful? I'd love to walk through rows and rows of lavender bushes, with the bees buzzing all around me."

"Joanna, the kettle."

Joanna had been so fascinated that she hadn't heard it boil. She quickly filled a teapot with a smattering of leaves from a black Mariage Frères tin, poured water over it, and brought it to the front where she could continue to listen in.

"Crisp white sheets," the woman was saying. "But I'm not into that minimalist thing. I like Sallie—she's my dachshund—to nap on the bed, and I can't have too many photos of my grandkids around."

Elise was on a rolling ladder behind the counter, reaching for a bottle. One bottle was already on the counter. Now Joanna knew why Elise stuck to trousers and elegant loafers. Better for climbing ladders.

Elise set a cube-shaped bottle on the counter. "It sounds like current perfume trends aren't right for you. You like lavender, but you don't want anything too terse. Here are a few options we have testers for. Lavender is an unusual note in women's perfumery, but wonderful. Too seldom used, I think." She took a tester strip from a crystal tumbler, sprayed it, and handed it to the customer. "Voilà. This one was created in 1889, but is still in production. We keep older bottles with real civet."

The woman sniffed the tester strip, and her face relaxed, then tightened. She handed the strip back to Elise. "There's something, well, poopy about this one."

"You have a sensitive nose. That's Jicky eau de toilette. Its civet is assertive."

"Jicky?" Joanna said, stepping from behind the portière.

"Yes. Pearl named her cat for the fragrance. Is the tea ready?"

"Oh." Joanna poured tea through a strainer into a violet-sprigged teacup.

"Try this one. It's by Dior and more modern. Dune."

"I remember ads for Dune." The woman closed her eyes and moved the strip under her nose. "It's nice. Lots of lavender. I like it."

"But you don't love it." Elise watched as Joanna carried the tea to the customer. "Would you like sugar or milk?"

"No. This is wonderful. Thank you."

"We have one more lavender-centered fragrance to try. I've saved the best for last." The tester didn't have an atomizer, so Elise dipped the scent strip into the bottle and pulled it out stained with amber. "It's Moment Suprême by Jean Patou. It's lavender, but with a warm, woody amber base. Like a California Chardonnay," she added.

Again the woman, eyes closed, smelled the strip. This time her eyes popped open. She sniffed the strip again, taking long huffs. "I love it. How can it be fresh but warm at the same time?"

"Henri Alméras composed this one. He's the nose behind Joy. Give me your wrist." Elise dabbed the stopper on the customer's wrist, then wiped the stopper with a cotton ball before replacing it. "It's getting nearly impossible to find, but it's so lovely and unusual."

"I love it," the woman repeated.

"Enjoy your tea for a moment, and let's see how it wears."

Joanna was fascinated. So, this was how the boutique worked. She looked at the rows of bottles and had the urge to pull down every tester for a sniff.

The bell at the front door jangled. "Moment Suprême. A masterpiece." The baron stood at the door. "Madame Noiret." He nodded. "Joanna, I'd hoped you'd be here." He set a fat book wrapped in an orange ribbon on the counter. "I'm sorry for yesterday's tantrum. I was out of line. Here's the copy of my guide you left behind, and I hope you'll accept my apologies. I'm afraid I'm apt to get passionate about fragrance."

The customer looked from Joanna to Elise.

"Madame…"

"Debbie. You can call me Debbie."

"I'd like you to meet Baron Ellsworth Barking," Elise said.

"Baron!" Debbie set down her teacup. "Oh, my goodness. I have a copy of your book at home. I can't believe I'm meeting you."

The baron bowed from the waist. "Madame. I hope you've enjoyed it."

"Oh, yes. I know I'll never smell half of the fragrances, but it's so fun to read the descriptions."

The door opened again, and Christophe stood behind the baron, dangling his car key on a finger. "*Bonjour, mesdames. Monsieur.*" He didn't stick around to weigh in on Moment Suprême, but went straight behind the velvet portière.

Joanna and Elise exchanged puzzled glances. Elise wrapped the customer's bottle.

"Joanna," the baron continued, "If you're free, I'd like to take you to lunch today to make up for yesterday. I hope you'll say yes."

"Now? Oh, thank you, but I can't. We're working."

"I don't think you can afford to pass up this chance. It's a special lunch."

"You didn't mention it yesterday."

"An opportunity that only just came up." The baron was intent on Joanna.

Just then, a small, dark man in a business suit entered the shop and slipped his sunglasses into his breast pocket. The silken green wool of his suit looked like it might have been milled from hundred dollar bills. He stepped aside to let the customer from Sacramento, fragrant and holding her prized bottle, exit the shop.

"Ellsworth. I came in to see what was taking so long." The man's gaze roamed the shop with focus.

"Joanna insists she has too much work, but everyone needs to eat. Monsieur Valmy, I'd like you to meet Joanna Hayworth, Pearl Littlewood's legal representative."

"I'd suggest dinner, but I already have plans," Joanna said. Who was the suit, anyway?

Christophe emerged from behind the curtain and stopped short at seeing Monsieur Valmy. "You."

"You've met?" Joanna asked. "Monsieur Valmy is a friend of the baron's."

Christophe's expression iced over, and he turned to Elise. "I'm here to pick up my check for helping with inventory, if that's all right."

Elise shrugged and handed him an envelope.

Christophe folded it into his wallet and spoke to Joanna, steadfastly ignoring the baron and Monsieur Valmy. "I'd like to come visit before Parfum d'Antan shuts down for good, if you don't mind. It's a one-of-a-kind place. I'll be sad when it closes." He shot a glance at the men. "Perfume today simply can't compare. No offense, Monsieur Valmy."

Monsieur Valmy extracted a business card from a platinum holder and handed it to Joanna. "Vice President of Business Development, CosmeCorp," it read.

"We'd really enjoy lunch with you, madame. Ellsworth has had such interesting things to say."

"Go," Elise mouthed behind them and mimicked telephoning.

Joanna quirked an eyebrow, as if to say, "Are you sure?"

Elise nodded.

"Well, then. Let's go."

Chapter 21

"Over here, madame," Monsieur Valmy said, pointing to a black sedan purring at the curb. Its interior smelled of chilled leather.

Joanna slid onto the bench seat.

"Where to?" the baron asked.

Monsieur Valmy took the seat next to her. "Would you mind terribly if we ate at the executive dining room at CosmeCorp? It's the August holiday, and many of the better restaurants are closed."

"That's fine," Joanna said. What bizarre twists her trip to Paris was taking. She'd have stories to tell when she returned home.

"I promise you, it's not cafeteria food. Our chef trained with Ducasse."

This should be good. Joanna's budget didn't allow her a meal at one of Ducasse's restaurants, but she'd dreamed of Michelin-starred cuisine.

The limo edged through side streets and slipped onto the busy Boulevard de Grenelle. Both the baron and Monsieur Valmy busied themselves with their phones, Monsieur Valmy begging Joanna's pardon and the baron simply following suit without apology.

Less than ten minutes later, the limo had left old world Paris and pulled into a parking garage under a glass and steel skyscraper somewhere west of the Arc de Triomphe. Monsieur Valmy led the way to a small lobby with an elevator flanked by potted palms. He pressed his hand to a scanner, and the elevator opened. They rode it up nine floors.

The elevator opened into a vast room sparkling with sunlight from a solarium, yet still cool. A Grace Kelly look-alike greeted Monsieur Valmy, and, after a brief conversation in French, led them to a side room paneled in elaborately carved oak, but with a wall that was floor-to-ceiling plate glass.

Joanna was drawn instantly to the window. "That's the Champs Elysées down there, isn't it?" She caught her breath. "And the Louvre. Amazing."

Monsieur Valmy barely smiled. "I'd hoped you'd enjoy the view. The menu with today's lunch is on the table. If you don't like what the chef has planned, I'm sure he'd be happy to prepare a substitute."

The baron had the menu in his hand and was studying it with relish. "Seafood salad. Wonderful. I don't suppose you'd have a nice Puligny Montrachet to go with it?"

"Please, have a seat," Monsieur Valmy said to Joanna. "As for wine, I thought we'd do well with sparkling water, Baron Barking. I'm sure you don't mind."

The baron tossed the menu on the table and took a chair. It was clear he did mind. "Of course not."

A waiter brought two icy bowls brimming with greens and marinated seafood. A second waiter followed with a white platter of nearly raw meat, which he positioned in front of Monsieur Valmy. He set a bone-handled steak knife next to the executive's plate.

"Now, Madame Hayworth," Monsieur Valmy said.

"Joanna, please."

"Joanna. You must call me Antoine." He stabbed a slice of meat with his fork. "You don't mind if we talk business, do you? I don't normally like to mix business with food, but my schedule is tight."

"No. Please." There could only be one reason he'd asked her to lunch. Joanna could have given him his answer at Parfum d'Antan.

"You know we're interested in acquiring Parfum d'Antan's bottle of Lys Bleu. Baron Barking has informed us that it's gone missing."

"Yes, sadly." Joanna busied herself with a forkful of octopus and pictured the bottle in its current spot in one of Pearl's winter boots.

"How unfortunate for you, especially since you're responsible for Madame Littlewood's estate."

She set down her fork. "It truly is unfortunate, but it's not my fault."

"No, no. Of course not. I didn't mean to imply that. I suppose you've searched the shop and Madame Littlewood's home?"

As for how much searching she'd done, she didn't think it was any of his business. "The Lys Bleu is gone. We've reported it to the police," Joanna said.

The baron kept picking up his glass and replacing it on the table, as if disappointed in its contents. "Lys Bleu. A brilliant fragrance."

Monsieur Valmy made a noncommittal noise.

"Named after a sapphire-encrusted reliquary lost during the French Revolution, they say."

Joanna discreetly raised her eyes. The baron was ready to regale them with further stories, but Monsieur Valmy seemed unimpressed. Was it a show?

"I'm quite taken with the boutique. CosmeCorp would like to purchase it and its inventory."

Joanna stopped chewing and, with effort, swallowed her food. "Excuse me?"

"The shop has many examples of lovely old fragrances that would make valuable additions to our archives. Maybe we could adapt some of them for today's market."

"You want to buy the whole shop?"

"Yes. Is that a problem?" Monsieur Valmy's plate was now nearly empty, except for the sheen of blood on porcelain. "I thought this would simplify things for you. Instead of having to sell the shop's contents piecemeal, you can sell it all at once."

The baron watched both of them as if it were a championship game and he had money on the outcome. Come to think of it, maybe he'd see a commission.

"We are ready to offer a substantial sum, of course," Monsieur Valmy said. "You have power of attorney for the estate, *non*?"

As if on cue, a suited man, this one gray-haired but clearly Monsieur Valmy's inferior, entered through a door set into the paneling and placed a leather-bound folder on the table before slipping out.

Joanna had no doubt CosmeCorp was capable of a stupendous offer. Everything she'd seen so far—the limo, the marble-floored elevator, the antique paneling—smelled of pure money.

"Yes, I have power of attorney, but I'd need to talk this over with Pearl Littlewood's heir, first."

"Her mother, am I right?"

How did he know all this? Joanna's appetite vanished. "Yes. Ruth Littlewood. She'll want time to think it over."

Her heart dropped. She knew what Ruth's response would be. Sell the shop, and sell it now. The more money, the better. Ruth would be over the moon to think Joanna had pulled off this kind of a deal. Christophe, on the other hand…Joanna now understood more deeply how perfume could be art. As with vintage clothing, a beautifully constructed perfume required sophistication to appreciate thoroughly. CosmeCorp didn't manufacture that type of perfume.

"Our offer is good for a week. That's all." His tone had chilled. He slid the leather portfolio across the table. "I'll expect to hear from you." A waiter soundlessly appeared and removed his plate. "Oh, and if the bottle of Lys Bleu reappears, it will be included, of course."

Chapter 22

Joanna was five minutes early. She paced to the end of Philippe's block and circled back. The day had been excruciating, waiting to meet up with Philippe and enlist his help in figuring out what to do about the map. She'd stopped by the café to look for the waiter and had received shaking heads when she mentioned Olivier's name. Someone else had written out the day's specials.

Finally, she'd left the apartment early and walked the forty-five minutes past the École Militaire, behind the Hôtel des Invalides, and deep into the seventh arrondissement. Here, the sidewalks ran narrow next to tall limestone walls, leaving her only to imagine the buildings and gardens beyond.

Now she stood on a quiet side street with an expanse of buttermilk-hued wall rising next to her with a monumental double door painted peacock blue. A brass doorknob as big as her head studded the center of each door. This was not what she'd been expecting. She'd envisioned a traditional Parisian apartment, probably a bit smaller than Pearl's, with a stodgy gardien at its entrance. Or, she was willing to concede, he might live in a new high-rise toward the edge of town. If so, his apartment would be decorated in minimalist furniture, and he'd have nice stereo equipment.

Of course, she didn't know what lay behind the double doors. As instructed, she pushed the buzzer.

"Madame Hayworth?" a man's voice—not Philippe's—said.

"Yes—*oui*."

"*Attendez, s'il vous plaît.*"

A moment later, one of the blue doors opened, and a muscular man in a navy blue suit beckoned to her. "Follow me, madame."

The gates opened to a cobblestoned courtyard edged in huge pots of olive trees and flowers. White climbing roses, pale pink begonias, and even gardenias basked in the August heat radiating off the stone walls. To the side was parked the black sedan Philippe had taken with her to Pearl's funeral.

"Joanna." Philippe met her in a tiled entrance hall with a spiral staircase rising in the rear. He greeted her with a kiss in the air in the approximate vicinity of each cheek. "Did you have trouble finding the address?"

"Not at all. This is quite some home."

"The Le Galls have lived here for more than two hundred years. We've been fortunate."

A tapestry covered one wall, fronted by a table flanked by two gilded chairs. Through the doorway was a more welcoming looking room with upholstered furniture, and, she was startled to see, an older woman in a wheelchair. Joanna recognized her from Pearl's funeral.

"My mother. Come into the salon."

"Mother, I'd like you to meet Joanna Hayworth. Joanna, this is my mother, Marie-Chantal Le Gall."

"You're young," Philippe's mother said. Her accent carried more French than Philippe's, but it was distinctively upper class. And accusatory.

Joanna forced a smile. "It's taken me all my life to get this old."

So, Philippe lived with his mom. In palatial splendor, maybe, but Joanna was beginning to understand why Pearl didn't take their relationship to the altar.

To Joanna's surprise, Madame Le Gall laughed. "Well said." She gestured toward Philippe, and a Boston terrier galloped toward her, jumping into her lap. "*Viens, chéri.* This is Filou."

"It's nice to meet you, Madame Le Gall. And Filou."

"I'll let you have dinner privately. Filou and I will take a turn in the garden, then watch some television before bed."

The muscular man materialized at a French door on the other side of the salon leading into a grassy yard lush with black-eyed Susans, zinnias, and more begonias. It was a crazy mix of colors, and not what Joanna would have anticipated for a fancy house in Paris, but it worked.

"We'll have dinner on the back terrace, if that suits you. Nothing elaborate, I'm afraid. Just a tart and salad. Once we've eaten, I'm looking forward to hearing your news."

Joanna's hand dropped to her purse, where the map was carefully folded. "Sounds wonderful."

The simple tart and salad turned out to be a mouth-watering smoked salmon quiche with lightly dressed arugula sprinkled with calendula and pansy petals. The wine was also faintly floral, smelling of violets.

When the dinner plates had been cleared and a tender wedge of cheese served and eaten, Joanna and Philippe sat back with demitasses of coffee. The garden was now dark except for gentle lights illuminating the terrace and, deeper in the garden, a gazebo. Crickets chirped from the shrubs.

"Now, tell me what's on your mind," Philippe said.

At last. "First, have you heard anything from the police about who might have pushed Pearl into the street?"

His cup steamed at his elbow, but he showed no sign of lifting it. "Nothing. The nearest shop was closed, and the metro's surveillance tapes had been erased. The driver was adamant, though, that it wasn't an ordinary accident."

They'd waited too long. "Too bad."

"Indeed."

"There's one other thing. It's flimsy, but it's worth passing along to the police. I was at the café across the intersection from" —Joanna looked up— "you know…"

He nodded. "Café de l'Espérance, I think it is?"

"The daily specials were written on a chalkboard with the same handwriting in the guestbook. I've been trying to catch up with the waiter who wrote it, but we seem to keep missing each other."

"I'll let them know. Is this why you wanted to see me?"

"No. Something else." Joanna pushed aside her coffee and told Philippe about finding the map and about Monsieur Saunier's assessment of its age. As she talked, Philippe moved to the edge of his chair.

"You have this map with you?"

"Right here." Joanna lifted her purse to her lap.

"Let's take it to the library where there's better light."

They left the table—this wasn't the sort of place where you cleared your own dishes, Joanna thought as she glanced back—and entered the house through the salon's French doors. They passed through the salon into another, smaller room lined in bookshelves and decorated in watery Venetian blues and greens.

Philippe clicked on a lamp on the mahogany desk perpendicular to the wall. "Let's have a look at that map, Joanna."

Half fearing it wouldn't be there, she took it from her purse and handed it to him. He smoothed it on the desk's green leather top.

"Definitely a map. An old one, too. And you think it leads to the Beaulieu reliquary?"

"I can't think of what else it could be." She pointed to the stylized lily on the map's corner. "Apparently, the family may have hidden it during the Revolution and never moved it." Joanna took the chair across from him. "Someone knew it was there. And, if the note in the funeral guestbook is right—"

"Does anyone else know about the map?"

"Monsieur Saunier, the downstairs neighbor, like I mentioned. He also helped with the address."

"I haven't heard of this street name. Did you look it up?"

Monsieur Saunier had slipped a note under her door with a brief explanation and the map's new address. "The street was renamed. Here's the new address." She laid Monsieur Saunier's note on the desk. "I wasn't sure what to do next. Should I give the map to the police? I wanted to consult with you about it."

He tapped a finger on the desk. "It's quite near. The address, that is. The Beaulieus almost certainly had a town home. In the late eighteenth century, many families moved from the Marais to the Saint Germain neighborhood."

Joanna nodded. Monsieur Saunier had explained all that.

"Before we decide next steps, what do you say we check it out?"

"It's within walking distance," Philippe said. "I know people in the arts and culture ministry, and I may be able to get us into the building as early as this week, although the holidays might slow things."

Joanna was already on her feet. "Let's go."

In the entry hall, Philippe exchanged a few words with a man watching television in a small office off of the entry hall. He wasn't the man who had met Joanna when she'd come in. It was nearly ten at night now, and they must have changed shifts.

"Do you have staff on duty all day and night?" she asked.

Philippe didn't look at her. "It's a big house. Plus, my mother," he said, as if this explained it.

On the street, they turned left and walked in the direction of the Seine. The sound of a baritone's moody aria drifted from an open window. A small café was closing for the night, and a stocky man with a cigarette dangling from his mouth stacked chairs.

"Down here," Philippe said, and they turned again. This street was wider, more commercial. Philippe halted and consulted the address Joanna had given him. "This is it."

They stood outside of a small grocery store. "Bio Nature," the sign said. It was closed, and shopping carts were chained inside the entrance. A poster in the window featured ready-made salads with the cartoon of a laughing apple in the corner.

In her mind, Joanna heard trombones playing "wah-wah-wah." She and Philippe stared at the storefront.

"What now?" she said.

"The map is useless. The house's courtyard is filled in, and the layout has completely changed. Probably has been for years. If anything valuable was hidden in a cupboard or in the walls, it's long gone." He handed her the map.

"Construction workers might have found it."

"And sold it, either as is or in pieces." He shook his head. "I'll make a few calls tomorrow to see when the building was reconfigured, but it doesn't look promising."

Joanna looked at the storefront again. At one point, a wealthy family had lived there. They'd stabled horses in the courtyard and drunk from a well in the garden. Now it sold gluten-free crackers. And they called this progress?

Chapter 23

Philippe had offered to drive her home, but Joanna wanted to walk. She needed to think.

She may have been at a stalemate as far as finding the Beaulieu reliquary went, but Pearl's death was still an open question. The waiter had seen something. Someone may have tried to break into Pearl's apartment the first night Joanna was there. And Pearl had hidden the bottle of Lys Bleu at the apartment, even though it had been locked up at Parfum d'Antan. She had known it was valuable. Was it because of the Beaulieu family's treasure, or because of CosmeCorp? Or something else? Maybe instead of focusing on the "why" of Pearl's death, she should be considering the "who."

The lit dome of Les Invalides rose in the distance like a golden mountain, but the streets were dark and nearly deserted. She was in a residential neighborhood, and it was August, she reminded herself, when the whole of Paris—at least the residents of chi-chi neighborhoods like this—went on vacation.

Her phone chirped from her purse. A text. Maybe Paul was wishing her goodnight, even though it was the middle of the afternoon in Oregon, and he'd be deep at work. She smiled as she pulled out her phone. No, the text was from Luc.

In your neighborhood, he wrote. *Should I drop by the Café de l'Espérance to check on waiter?*

Joanna began to type a response, then on impulse hit the button to call.

"Joanna," he said. "I'd wanted to call, but I was afraid it was too late. How are you?"

"I'm…good. A lot has happened over the past twenty-four hours."

"I know it's last minute, but I happen to be nearby. You wouldn't want to meet up for a drink and talk about it, would you?"

She passed the moat surrounding Les Invalides and turned up the avenue de La Motte-Picquet. Restaurants and boutiques posted signs announcing they were *congé* until the end of the month.

"I'm not home, but I'm close."

"Why don't we meet at the café? We can check in again on the waiter who might have seen Pearl's accident."

"I'll be there in ten minutes," Joanna said.

Luc was at the café when she arrived. Unlike the café she'd passed earlier on their hunt for the reliquary, the Café de l'Espérance was bright and still busy with customers. Luc had staked out a table inside, in the warmth of the wood-fronted bar and burgundy wainscoting.

He rose to give her the traditional kiss on each cheek. Although Parisians were experts at avoiding actual skin contact, she got a bit of Luc's whiskery jaw.

"He's not here," Luc said as he sat.

"Has he come in at all?"

"The manager says not. When he does come in, no job will be waiting for him. Apparently he was a bit shifty, anyway. The night manager—that's who I talked with—said they suspected he'd been dipping in the till."

"*Désirez?*" A busty brunette with streaks of gray appeared at their table. Although she was there to take their order, she looked directly at Luc.

"Joanna, this is Madame Véronique, the cafe's night manager." He flashed one of his wide smiles.

Figured. Everyone else had the attention of a waiter, but Luc reeled in the management. "It's nice to meet you."

The manager smiled blandly at her.

"*Un petit calva pour moi.* Joanna, what would you like?" Luc asked.

"Same for me."

"You said you had news," Luc prompted. "About Lys Bleu?"

"Oh, yes." She tucked her purse under the table. "A lot has happened over the past couple of days. We thought we'd found the bottle, but it was a fake. Then I discovered an old map in the Lys Bleu box—"

"What?"

"*Voilà.*" The manager placed two small snifters of golden liquid and a carafe of water on their table.

"*Merci, madame.*"

"*Je vous en prie,*" the manager said, adding a note of huskiness to her voice.

She'd barely left when Luc said, "You found a map?"

Joanna nodded. "And the real bottle of Lys Bleu. You should see it. It's gigantic."

"But the map. What does it show? Tell me."

"I can do better than that. Here." There was no longer a reason to hide it. She hoisted her purse to her lap and handed the map to Luc. "Don't get too excited. I went to the address tonight. It's an organic food mart now."

Any trace of seductive charm had been replaced by steel-trap attention. "Start at the beginning. Tell me everything." He glanced at the map, then back at Joanna. His expression softened. "I mean, please."

She told him first about visiting the baron and about his link to CosmeCorp. She described finding the map and showing it to Monsieur Saunier.

"You've already made friends in the building?" Luc asked.

"He's such a nice man and so interested in the world. But he hadn't been getting out much, so we walked around the city last night. He was the one who found the modern street address for this." She pointed at the map.

"You say it's a grocery store now?"

"I just came from visiting it with Philippe. Pearl's boyfriend," she added.

Luc squinted for a split second. "Philippe Le Gall."

"You know him?"

He smiled. "I know of him. I know everyone, remember?"

"What's his story, anyway? He lives in a gigantic *hotel particulier* in Saint Germain. He seems awfully well connected, too."

"I get the impression his background has to do with intelligence, or maybe Interpol. Not sure."

Joanna lifted her chin. "How do you know so many people? You can't tell me they've all taken your history classes."

He laughed a bit louder than usual. "I get around, and maybe I'm a bit nosy. That's all."

She gave him a moment, but he didn't add to his explanation. She folded the map and returned it to her purse. "Well, if there's treasure there, it's long gone now."

Luc turned the snifter in his hands. "The S.S. on the map. Did Monsieur Saunier know what it meant?"

She hadn't even seen that Luc had noted the initials. "He didn't, in fact. He thought it might have been the initials of the person who drew the map."

"Presumably, that would have been a Beaulieu."

"With a 'B.' True." It was nice to sit here and ponder old mysteries with Luc. Everything seemed cloaked in amber light tonight. Bad 1970s music played low from behind the bar, complemented by the murmur of conversation and spoons clinking on saucers. The apple brandy was going to her head. Luc leaned back, and his foot touched Joanna's. He pulled it back.

"So, I guess that's it, then," she said.

"I hate to let it go. We have a valuable old bottle of perfume, an antique reliquary hidden during the French Revolution, an unexplained death—it's all such a great story."

"It really is," Joanna admitted. "But the bottle is found and will be donated to the perfume archive. The map leads nowhere. Which leaves Pearl's death."

"How much longer will you be in Paris?"

"Eight days." Her time was slipping away. If she were home, she'd be watching a Cary Grant movie and finishing a mug of herbal tea. And arguing with Paul about children, she feared, or, worse, living in unresolved tension. She'd never forget this trip. Or tonight. "I suppose I should get home. It must be near midnight."

Luc left a bill on the table and pulled out Joanna's chair. The terrace was now empty except for a young couple with a bottle of champagne at their elbows.

"Oh, look," Joanna said. "It's Cassoulet." The dog lay against the café wall, soaking up the heat. "Come here, darling. Poor little guy." She scratched his ears. "Ugh. I think he has fleas."

Luc knelt next to her. "He looks pretty healthy, otherwise."

"Do you need a dog?"

"I wish. My cat wouldn't be happy about it."

"Somebody needs to take him home. Winter's coming. I hate to think of him sleeping in the cold. What if he gets sick? Who's going to take care of him?"

Luc smiled. "You can't take care of every stray animal."

Joanna stood. "I have an idea. Madame Chomette. She's lonely."

"Who's she?"

"The neighbor across the hall. She spends a lot of time talking about her husband, but my upstairs neighbor thinks she's bluffing and that he left years ago. She'd love a dog. I know it. She might not admit it, though." She cast a last look at Cassoulet.

When she turned to Luc, he was watching her.

"You have a beautiful spirit," he said.

She wouldn't meet his eyes. The streetlights through the trees cast mottled light on the sidewalk. "Well, I guess this is goodbye," she said. "We probably won't see each other again."

He bent to give her the double kiss goodbye, and this time his lips did touch skin.

Never had a night felt so alive. The air was charged. Conversation from a late-night dinner party drifted from open windows above her. A baby cried somewhere. The two-toned wail of a siren passed in the distance.

Emotion fizzled and took flame within her, bringing a smile and the sudden desire to skip and laugh.

She punched in the code to the building's lobby. And froze. *Shoot.* She was supposed to call Ruth.

Well, she'd do it as soon as she got in and fed Jicky. It was still mid-afternoon in Oregon. When Ruth heard what she'd been up to, she'd forgive the delay.

Joanna bypassed the elevator and worked off some of her jubilant energy by walking up the curving stairway to the fourth floor—fifth floor, American style. As she crossed each landing, the crystal-encased ceiling lamp snapped on its timer.

And now she was home. Catching her breath, she stood in front of her door—Pearl's door, she reminded herself—and inserted her key in the heavy tumbler. It didn't turn. Had she forgotten to bolt it behind her? Singing "La Vie en Rose" under her breath, she pushed open the door.

She dropped her purse and gasped. The apartment had been ransacked.

Chapter 24

"Jicky!" Heart pounding, Joanna burst into the apartment and ran room to room, barely taking in the thrown pillows and pulled-out drawers, until she found the cat cowering under the armchair in the bedroom.

"Come out, honey. Are you okay?"

Stretching a paw forward, Jicky inched from under the chair and looked around. She let Joanna pet her as she decided whether it was safe to relax.

At a creak, Jicky shot back under the chair. The creak sounded again, and Joanna realized it had come from downstairs. Monsieur Saunier. It would be the middle of his day. Then another thought occurred. Could the intruder still be in the house?

Joanna scanned the bedroom. No one was there, and there was nowhere to hide. She drew a breath, then threw open the closet connecting the bedroom to the office. This was empty, too, except for its row of garment bags. The office had received an especially thorough tossing. Papers covered the floor ankle-deep, and every drawer was open. No one was in the living room or kitchen.

Joanna let out her breath. Now she was sure. This wasn't the first time someone had broken in.

Who could it have been? Both Philippe and Luc knew she was

out tonight. At Parfum d'Antan, she'd mentioned she had plans. Of course, anyone could have seen her leave.

Lys Bleu. Whoever he was, he wanted the Lys Bleu. She back-tracked to the bedroom, where Jicky had decided the coast was clear and sat on the armchair grooming herself. Joanna pushed open the wardrobe door and reached for Pearl's toppled boot. The Lys Bleu was gone.

She closed the door. The bottle was unimportant now. She knew that. It was the map that mattered. The map! She rushed to the hall, where she'd dropped her purse, and rifled through its pockets. She closed her eyes in relief. The map was still there.

Clutching her purse, she took a moment. What to do next? She'd have to call the police. She surveyed the upturned chair, the books thrown from their shelves, the pictures hanging askew. Her gaze returned to the map. There was no telling what someone would do to get their hands on it. The reliquary could too easily fall into the wrong hands.

She bit her lower lip and released it. She needed Monsieur Saunier to do something for her. He had the expertise, and he knew the story. Yes, this would be the safest solution. She stepped into the hall and double-bolted the door, taking the map with her.

The next morning—was it still morning? The bedroom was full of sunlight—Joanna awoke to the chime of her doorbell. She pulled on Pearl's kimono, and pressed her face to the peephole. Amandine Chomette's face showed through the fish-eyed lens.

At a crack in the door, Amandine pushed her way in. She was

carrying a lidded casserole dish.

"You were still in bed? It's past noon," she said, making herself at home in the kitchen.

Joanna sleepily reached for the foil packet of coffee. "I was up late. Really late." That's why Amandine had come across the landing, of course. Not for a neighborly French lesson or an update on the gardienne's love life.

"I know. The police woke Monsieur Chomette."

Joanna raised an eyebrow. Madame Dédé would have snorted a laugh at that remark. "I suppose you'd like to know what happened?"

"I brought a *potage de legumes*," she said in reply. "It's lunch time, you know."

Joanna filled the electric kettle. "What, Monsieur Chomette doesn't like vegetable soup?"

Amandine faced her head-on. "He prefers a nice chop. Now tell me what happened."

The possibility that Amandine pushed Pearl into traffic or raided the apartment was nil. Still, Joanna didn't need to stoke the neighbor's imagination with stories of Lys Bleu. So, she started her recitation with the night before.

"When I came home, the door was unlocked. Someone had broken in."

"You were out late," Amandine said.

"Dinner with Philippe and a drink later with someone else." Joanna hurried on with the story. "Whoever broke in searched the place pretty thoroughly. He dumped out drawers and cupboards and pulled the cushions off the furniture. He even yanked the books from the shelves."

Amandine wandered across the hall and put her hands on her

hips. "You've tidied up."

That was part of the reason she'd gone to bed so late. The break-in had unnerved her enough that even after considering that the thief had what he wanted, she couldn't sleep. She'd put the living and dining rooms in order, but she hadn't had time to take care of the office yet.

"A little bit."

"Then the police came," Amandine prompted.

"I went downstairs to see Monsieur Saunier. He called the police for me. The police arrived right away and took a report." He'd also done her another, significant favor that neither Amandine nor anyone else could know about.

"*Oh, là là.* How do you feel? You must be horrified. *C'est affreux.* How did he get in?"

"As far as the police could tell, he came right in the front door."

"A master thief, then. Or he had the key."

"The locks were changed first thing this morning." Ruth wasn't going to like the bill for it, either.

Amandine scanned the room. "Was anything missing?"

Joanna drew a breath. "One thing."

"What?"

Joanna returned to the kitchen to pour hot water over the coffee grounds. "A bottle of perfume."

"That's not possible," Amandine said. "The drawing in the gold frame. A Pissarro, *non*?"

Keen eye, that one. Philippe had pointed it out as a gift to Pearl for their tenth anniversary. "It was a valuable bottle."

"So the thief knew what he was looking for." Amandine faced Joanna. "And he got it. And probably won't be back."

"So I hope. The police said hundreds of apartments in Paris are broken into during August when people are on vacation. They took a report so I have something to give the insurance company, but they didn't even bother to dust for fingerprints."

Her story to the police about the map and Pearl hadn't invited more than a curt note taking. Joanna was torn between a frenzy of wanting to find the thief and relief that he wouldn't be back.

Jicky appeared at the kitchen doorway staring at her food bowl beyond Amandine's feet.

"That cat," Amandine said. "She does you no good. What you need is a dog to bark if someone tries to break in again."

Hmm. Joanna poured coffee into a mug and dumped in a healthy portion of milk. She worked to keep her voice indifferent. "Do you like dogs?"

"Of course. The important question now is, do you have bread to go with this vegetable soup?"

When Joanna heard Amandine's door close across the landing, she turned toward the apartment. Pearl's office still needed to be put back together, and it was a good excuse for diving more deeply into her papers.

Joanna caught sight of her phone and groaned. Damn. Another evening had passed without a report to Mrs. Littlewood, and she had no doubt she'd received a peeved text—or two. After braving the phone and finishing the office's cleanup, she'd stop by Parfum d'Antan to fill Elise in on the bottle of Lys Bleu and the break-in. She deserved to know.

Joanna picked up her phone, and, sure enough, found two voice-mails from Ruth. She hesitated before listening.

"You've missed our nightly call. I'm expecting one tonight." The next: "Joanna, this is not professional. I did not send you to Paris to waste my money gallivanting around on evenings. Call me."

Joanna jotted back a text that she'd definitely, one hundred percent, absolutely be in touch today. She set down the phone and leaned back, closing her eyes. She snapped them open again. She was actually petting Jicky! The cat had come to her and was purring.

"At least you appreciate me, kitten."

As if suddenly realizing what she was doing, the cat leapt off of Joanna's lap and sat under a chair grooming herself.

Joanna pushed the phone aside and made her way to the office. The sooner she started, the sooner she'd be finished. She stood in the doorway and reflected there was a reason she'd kept this room for last to tidy. Each of the desk's drawers was pulled out and dumped upside down, and the filing cabinet was half open and half closed, with file folders dumped helter-skelter. Only the glass-fronted cabinet with its dozen or so bottles of perfume was undisturbed. Joanna approached it. Strange, since the intruder had wanted a bottle of perfume all along. Of course, simply looking through the glass door was all he'd have to do.

She pushed papers aside to clear an area in front of the French window. On one side she'd stack papers that didn't bear on the estate. On the other, she'd gather the papers that Ruth might be interested in—anything having to do with property, investments, or insurance, for instance. She'd also keep a lookout for the bills Elise had mentioned that would offset the regular debit in the shop's accounts.

Over the next few hours, Joanna worked steadily, stopping only to change the CD on Pearl's stereo. Fortunately, she and Pearl shared a love for Cole Porter and Blossom Dearie.

Joanna was reaching into a filing cabinet when she saw, again, the chest containing the packets of letters from Pearl to her mother. Joanna touched the address. So strange to see "Oregon" written on each. Thirty years of letters, and not one opened. But Pearl had kept them.

Joanna wondered what news the letters contained. Maybe in the early letters Pearl had written about discovering Paris and her plans of opening a perfume boutique. Maybe she'd wanted to reestablish some kind of bond with her mother. In later years, fewer letters were written. Five years ago or so, they'd stopped.

The office was filled with sunlight now, and the warm breeze through the French window ruffled the lace curtain. Jicky lay on the tiny balcony, absorbing the sun. Across the narrow street, a woman washed dishes at her kitchen window. At the florist's at the corner down the block, a woman in a straw sunhat carried a pot of gardenias inside.

Joanna reached for two of the large padded envelopes she'd seen in the desk and stuffed the letters inside. She sealed them. She wouldn't need to look up the address. It was carefully written across dozens of envelopes.

Chapter 25

Joanna's vision swam as she stepped onto the street. Too many hours of stacking papers and staring at spreadsheets. It was nice to breathe the afternoon air and take in the buildings around her—many still shuttered for the holidays, but some with pots of herbs and geraniums, and at least one with a puffy duvet airing over the balcony railing.

She had nearly all the information on finances and assets Ruth would need to sell Parfum d'Antan. Today's visit to the shop was to fill Elise in on the stolen Lys Bleu. And the offer from CosmeCorp. She likely wouldn't take either piece of news well.

Elise was dusting the display bottles when Joanna arrived at the shop. On seeing Joanna, she set down the feather duster. "What's wrong?"

"You can tell?"

"It doesn't look like you had much sleep."

Joanna pushed open the velvet portière so she could sit in the armchair while Elise had a clear view of the door for customers. "Someone broke into the apartment last night while I was out."

"No!" She paused, then shook her head. "So many break-ins during the August holidays."

"That's what the police said, too, but it was more than that." Joanna swallowed. "You see, they stole the bottle of Lys Bleu."

Elise's whole body seemed to rattle. "What? You mean the shop's bottle? You had it all along?"

Joanna put a hand up, palm out. "It's not like that. I only found it the day before yesterday. Really, I haven't had the chance to tell you. I found it when I was looking for somewhere to hide the map. The map I found in its box."

Elise grew deadly still. Her gaze shut down in the way Joanna was discovering Parisian women must have mastered since kindergarten. Joanna waited until Elise was ready to speak.

At last, Elise returned to life. "Start from the beginning. You found a map in the Lys Bleu box."

Joanna nodded. "Remember how we talked about the Beaulieu family's reliquary? The one Lys Blue was named after?"

"Yes," she said uncertainly.

"It came to me that maybe the bottle was stolen because someone thought it held the answer to where the reliquary was. Apparently—Luc, the history professor told me this—it's been missing for centuries. Then, I wondered if the box might hold the clue."

"The map was in the base of the box, wasn't it?"

"Exactly. I knew it was valuable, so I decided to hide it up the chimney. But the Lys Bleu was already there."

Elise leaned back. "*C'est impossible.*"

"I know. I was flabbergasted. Well, to make a long story short, last night someone broke into the apartment and turned it upside down. The bottle of Lys Bleu is missing again."

Elise slowly leaned forward again. "Do you think—I mean, if it's true—that Lys Bleu is why Pearl was murdered?"

Joanna shrugged. "I don't know what to think anymore."

According to Philippe, other than the driver's story, they didn't have evidence to prove Pearl's death was anything but an accident. After all, the driver would fervently want to believe he hadn't been responsible. He'd imagine Pearl had been pushed, whether it was true or not. Joanna wondered if the police had had any luck getting in touch with the waiter.

"And the map? Was that stolen, too?"

"No." She glanced up. "It's safely hidden now. Not that it matters. The map is twohundred-plus years old. Philippe and I followed it, and there's nothing there now but a health food store."

Elise stared toward the front door. Joanna stood to see if someone was coming, but the sidewalk was empty.

"Are you okay?" Joanna asked.

Elise drew a deep breath. "Yes. It's just—well, it's all so strange. I don't know how to make sense of it." She tilted her head. "Is the box still downstairs?"

Joanna nodded.

"Probably smart, if the thief had the same thought and decides to come back for it. Better for him to find an empty box." Elise nodded, first faintly, then with purpose. She strode to the front door and locked it, hanging the "back in five minutes" sign in its window. It was clear she wasn't planning to go out for a coffee, though. "Show me the box."

They descended to the basement, to the familiar scent of cold stone and a mélange of perfume notes. The dehumidifier hummed in the corner.

"In the vault?" Elise asked.

"Yes. Exactly where the bottle was."

She extracted a bundle of keys from her pocket and fit one into the padlock securing the door. The light was dim, and it took two tries, but at last the door opened. The closet's light was brighter than that in the basement, and Joanna blinked.

"It's still there." She let out a long breath. She didn't know what she'd been expecting, but with the craziness of the past few days, it could have been anything. She turned to Elise, but Elise wasn't looking at the box.

She was looking on the ground, and her eyes were frozen wide, her mouth taut with horror.

Propped in the corner was a dead man.

Elise erupted into a laugh, then stopped as suddenly as she'd started. She fell against the doorjamb.

"Elise?" Joanna said. "Are you okay?"

Elise's chignon fell out, and the silver pin holding it clattered to the floor. She stared at the body but didn't respond. Her breath came in rasps. Joanna had seen more than one dead body, and while it was always a shock, the first one was definitely the worst.

"Elise," Joanna repeated. "I'm calling an ambulance."

Elise steadied herself, and her breaths, while still erratic, quieted. "No. No, I'm okay. What are we going to do?"

They both looked at the body. It was a man perhaps in his forties, with a shaved head that dropped chin to chest. He was tall, and, curiously, wore cowboy boots. His hands and face were the color of paraffin tapers.

"He's really dead?" Elise nearly whispered.

Joanna toed the sole of his boot. It wiggled, but the man didn't move. Not that she'd expected it to. He looked like he'd been dragged in from Madame Tussaud's.

"Do you know him?" Joanna asked.

"No."

Elise took a sudden step forward and flipped the man's head back. She and Joanna flattened themselves against the vault's opposite wall. The man's glassy eyes stared straight ahead, with deep bags under them. That's not what froze Joanna's breath and sent blood beating a timpani in her ears. It was the purple sash of broken blood vessels ringing his throat. He'd been strangled.

Elise gasped.

"Come on." Joanna pulled her away. They left the vault door open, its light shining on the body behind them.

"I do know him," Elise said when she'd caught her breath. "But I don't understand."

"Who is he?"

She shook her head. "A waiter. At a café where Pearl and I used to lunch."

Joanna knew Elise's next words before she spoke them.

"The Café de l'Espérance."

Chapter 26

That night, Joanna didn't forget to call Ruth Littlewood. This time, Joanna was waiting, hand on phone, until the clock struck eight in the morning, Oregon time. Five p.m. in Paris. The bells at Saint Léon chimed the hour, and Joanna punched in Ruth's number. As the phone rang, she squeezed her eyes shut in dread.

"Hello?" Ruth answered, a decidedly frosty tone to her voice. She had caller ID, of course.

"It's Joanna. I wanted to give you a report."

"It's about time. While I've been sitting here, waiting to hear how you're spending my money, you've no doubt been passing the time seeing the sights and lounging in air-conditioned museums. I—"

"No, Ruth, that's not true. You see—"

"I have to register your unsatisfactory service. Two nights now you've missed your reports. Two mornings I might have been bird watching. I missed the pipeline protest, thanks to you. I—"

"Wait!" Joanna said. "Just wait a minute." The silence over the line might have dripped icicles. Joanna decided to hit with her biggest news first. "Listen. The police are at the perfume shop right now. We found a dead body in the basement."

When Joanna had left, a team of technicians had taken over the shop. They spoke in lightning speed French, pushing her and Elise behind a corner display of old Chanel No. 5 bottles for a cursory interview with a detective. After taking each woman's step-by-step description of the afternoon, he'd let them go, with a promise to follow up within the day. Joanna expected a detective to show up at her door any time. She sighed. Amandine would sure like that.

"What?" Ruth's response rang like a cannon's boom. "Who was it?"

"A waiter. Probably the one who wrote the note about Pearl in the guestbook." Joanna dropped to the couch. "And that's not all, either."

She filled Ruth in on finding the map, then the bottle of Lys Bleu, then the break-in when the bottle was stolen. "That's why I didn't call."

Instead of the rush of words Joanna had expected, Ruth was silent. Joanna rose and pushed open a French window to ease the room's stuffiness.

Finally, Ruth said, "The police are investigating?"

"Yes. Definitely."

"I want you to come home."

That statement should have been comforting. Joanna should have jumped on the chance to escape from the drama and, as Ruth suggested, let the police get on with it. But all she could choke out was, "Why?"

"You've done the shop's inventory, right? How's your assessment of my daughter's assets?"

"Nearly finished," Joanna said. "I want to take photos of some of her art and furniture, but that's all."

"Then your job is complete. It's too dangerous for you to stay. If I'd had any idea what Pearl was mixed up in, I never would have asked you to go. Besides, you're not a professional. I should have hired someone from my attorney's office."

"It's only another week, Ruth. The apartment has new locks now.

I'm perfectly safe."

"I'm not buying it. Besides, you don't have to worry about putting the shop up for sale. A gentleman contacted me with a huge offer. I had no idea old perfume was worth so much."

"A gentleman? Monsieur Valmy, by chance?" Shoot.

"Antoine Valmy from CosmeCorp. He's sending over a contract for me to look at sometime this week. So, there's really no point in your staying."

"But…but I can't leave." She nodded as the thought dawned. "The police still want to talk with me. They'd never let me go. Not yet. Besides, imagine the fees to change my ticket."

The silence on the other end of the phone told Joanna that Ruth was considering her decision. "Then I insist you stay out of trouble. I mean it, Joanna."

She might have protested with a "what do you mean?" but they both knew how that conversation would go, and Joanna would not come out on the winning side of it. A parade of managers at Ruth's cannery could probably share her pain.

"And you will report back to me every single evening. Every one. If you miss a day, I guarantee you'll come home immediately. Understand?"

"Yes. Definitely."

"And I want to know everything. Don't keep any of it from me. Everything. For instance, what's going on with that English teacher across the hall?"

Now they were on safer ground. Ruth might be tough, but she was gratifyingly nosy. "Rumor has it that Amandine isn't actually married anymore," Joanna said.

By the time Joanna hung up, she knew she was on thin ice, but thought she might escape an early exit from Paris—narrowly—if she cleaved to the rules.

⃰

A few hours later, while Joanna was eating her way down a buttered baguette with ham, the doorbell rang.

A new detective, not the one she'd talked with earlier, stood at the door. He pushed the hair out of his tired-looking eyes. "Superintendent Batignolle. May I come in?"

"Please. Any news?" Joanna said and pointed toward the sofa. Across the landing, Amandine's door cracked open, then shut.

"One thing." He turned to face Joanna head-on. "Just the name of the victim. As you said, he's a waiter at the Café de l'Espérance."

The detective folded his tall frame into an armchair like a spider would, and he smoothed his hair again.

"Your English is excellent." Thank goodness for that. Her interview with the police at Parfum d'Antan, brief as it was, had been cut even shorter when hand gestures and grammar school language skills failed to deliver the message.

"Thank you. That's why I'm on the case." His hand absently picked at a milky stain near his collar. He saw Joanna watching him and dropped his hand. The police detective leaned forward. "Do you know this waiter?"

"No. I mean, yes, sort of." When the detective didn't respond, she continued. "I'm in Paris for only a few weeks because Pearl Littlewood—the owner of this apartment and the perfume shop—died. Her mother hired me to tie up loose ends."

If any of this was news to Detective Batignolle, he didn't show it.

Joanna crossed the room for the funeral guestbook and set it, open, on the coffee table. "The first morning I was here, I saw this." She tapped the page with the message.

Reading, the detective raised an eyebrow. "Lys Bleu?"

"It's a perfume. A valuable perfume."

"The perfume stolen last night."

She nodded. So, he had read the report on the break-in. "The driver who hit Pearl came forward on Sunday and said Pearl was pushed into his path."

The detective picked at the milky stain on his sleeve.

"You'll want to dab that with cold water, then an enzyme-based spot remover, if you have one," Joanna said.

"What?"

"That's baby formula, right?" She had to be on target. Only a new baby could generate the depth of exhaustion she saw in his eyes.

"Two weeks old." For a moment, his exhaustion flashed into a radiant smile before the bags under his eyes and sour expression reappeared. She wondered if she'd ever feel that way herself. "Let's stick to the case at hand."

"Fine. I suspect the thief was actually after a map."

Once again, she recounted the story of the perfumer, reliquary, and map. Each time, from Philippe to Luc to Elise to Ruth, and now to the detective, she had a bit more to add. She went to the chimney and reluctantly withdrew the map. She'd already memorized it, but letting go of the original felt like letting a talisman slip away.

The detective barely glanced at the map before slipping it into a folder. "You say you visited the café with a friend to ask about the waiter?"

"Yes. Luc. My French is awful, and he helped."

The detective posed a pen over his pad. "His surname?"

"Luc Cazaubon. A history professor."

The detective's pen froze. "A professor, eh?"

"At the Sorbonne. Do you know him?" She wouldn't be surprised. As they'd joked, Luc seemed to know everyone.

"It's a common enough name. Do you know how to get in touch with him?"

Joanna gave him Luc's phone number. "I was with him when someone broke in. Not all evening, but long enough that I don't suspect him. Plus, he was the person who told me about the reliquary. Why would he bring it up if he were out to steal it? I don't suspect him."

Detective Batignolle's tired eyes sharpened. "Who, then, do you suspect?"

"Well, no one person stands out." Joanna settled into the chair. "But the murderer knew Lys Bleu was at Parfum d'Antan, knew where Pearl lived, and knows about the reliquary. He also knew I'd be out yesterday evening."

"Anyone could have seen you leave," he said. "A few questions might have pinpointed where the perfume was and where Madame Littlewood lived. As for the reliquary, we still haven't established that's what the murderer was after. However, you've clearly thought about this. Who wanted Lys Bleu, and why?"

He was systematic. This was good. "First, you might consider the store's manager, Elise Noiret. She's mentioned having extra expenses, and someone has been skimming from Parfum d'Antan's income. Not a lot, but every month. She has the easiest access. She could use the money from selling Lys Bleu."

"And yet—"

"And yet she has the key to the perfume vault. That's what you were going to say, right?" Joanna said. "She could have taken it anytime. Anytime before Pearl took it home, that is."

The detective nodded. "Yes. Who else?"

"Christophe—he helps out at the shop a few times a year—says Baron Ellsworth Barking wants Lys Bleu. The baron is writing something about it and its perfumer, but he says the baron would sell the perfume to CosmeCorp to reformulate and sell."

The detective jotted this down. "And this Christophe? Could he be a suspect?"

"He definitely wants to keep the perfume out of CosmeCorp's hands. He worships Ernest Beaulieu, the perfumer, and believes Lys Bleu should be in the national perfume archive." Joanna remembered the waiter's purple-ringed neck. "He's strong enough to strangle someone, that's for sure. But why the waiter? I suppose you could see if he was in the neighborhood when Pearl was killed."

"May have been killed," the detective said. "We don't know for sure, remember. Now, who else?"

"I suppose we can't rule out Philippe Le Gall, Pearl's boyfriend. I had dinner with him last night. He knew I'd be gone."

Detective Batignolle didn't even lift his pen. "Who else? Neighbors?"

"Amandine keeps an eye on the building's comings and goings, but she and Pearl weren't close. Monsieur Saunier, downstairs, has seen the map and didn't need to steal it. He wouldn't be interested in perfume. Madame Dédé, upstairs, seems completely uninterested in it." Joanna shook her head. "No, I don't see it."

The detective rose. He was alert, but judging from his stifled yawn Joanna would have guessed he hadn't had much more sleep than she last night.

"Will you let me know what you find?" Joanna asked.

"I'll certainly keep you informed of anything that concerns you or Madame Littlewood's property."

"You mean the bottle of Lys Bleu. Like I said, I think it's the map that's important."

"Someone clearly doesn't agree with you."

Chapter 27

Joanna couldn't focus, and she didn't see the point of trying. She had neither the patience to sort through the papers in the office, nor the heart to tell Elise about CosmeCorp's offer—not after the questioning the detective had alluded to having in store for her very soon. Although Joanna couldn't buckle down to work, neither could she relax enough even for a walk, despite the miles of Paris awaiting her exploration.

She was locking the apartment's door behind her and on the street before she was even fully aware of what she was doing. Five minutes later, she stood on the sidewalk in front of the Café de l'Espérance.

Two middle-aged women sipped tea on the terrace, while next to them a man with a beer adjusted the top of a baby buggy to keep sun from a child's face. A girl ate a pain au chocolat while her mother examined something on her phone. A waiter darted in and out, his tray empty then full then empty again.

It was all so normal. As if nothing had happened. No one would have guessed a man who'd worked here had been strangled and left dead only blocks away.

Joanna turned toward the intersection. She had an almost clear view of the corner where Pearl had been struck by the delivery van. The waiter would have been standing. He would have seen everything, down to the identity of the person who pushed Pearl.

And it had all been for nothing. The map led nowhere. The reliquary—assuming it had ever been where the map indicated—certainly wasn't there now.

At a nudge at her foot, Joanna looked down. Cassoulet wagged his tail low and whined. Joanna crouched beside him and scratched his gnarled fur. Someone would have a heck of a time getting a comb through that. There was a good chance the mutt had fleas, too. Her fear and shock from the past week stacked like kindling and caught fire. She had to do something to relieve it. She clenched her fists and released them.

This dog needed a home with someone who had time on her hands. Now was the time to make it happen.

"Cassoulet," she whispered.

The dog wagged his tail, this time with more vigor. He knew his name.

"How would you like to come with me?" The waiters at the café didn't seem invested in Cassoulet's future, except to feed him scraps from the back door.

The dog didn't have a collar, and, even if he did, Joanna didn't have a leash. She scanned the café, then the block.

"Wait here," she instructed him and hurried to the newsstand just across the boulevard. She plucked at the string bundling a stack of the day's *Le Monde*. "*Un peu de,* um—" she pulled at the string and made a snipping motion with her fingers.

The newsagent didn't even pause. He pulled a ball of string from beside him and cut her a length. She handed him a euro and ran back to the café.

Damn it. Cassoulet was gone. Her shoulders dropped. She'd only been gone less than a minute—

A whimper caught her attention. The dog was crammed under a table, trying to look as unnoticeable as possible while the waiter distributed a tray of Aperol spritzes nearby. She doubled the string and prepared to loop it around his neck when Cassoulet leapt into her arms in a whoosh of rough fur and the stench of unwashed pooch.

The short walk to Pearl's was a cinch. The dog only started to wiggle when she tried to get him into the elevator. At last, the door was closed, and the elevator started its ascent.

Cassoulet didn't like it one bit. He started to pant, then bark, then howl. Joanna dropped him to the floor and put her hands over her ears. When they reached the fourth floor, she didn't know if she should open the brass cage that shut them in. Would the dog bolt down the stairs, barking the whole way?

Amandine's door flew open. She didn't even look at Joanna. "*Le pauvre!*"

Cassoulet's howl hit a higher pitch.

"What should I do?" Joanna shouted.

"Open the door." Amandine crouched and spread her arms as if she were waiting for the quarterback to deliver the ball.

"Are you ready?" Joanna put a hand on the latch.

"*Vas-y,*" she said.

Joanna snapped open the door, and the dog plastered himself to the back of the elevator. "Come on," she said from the hall, one hand holding the door open.

Cassoulet refused to move. But at least he'd stopped howling. He whimpered once.

"Do you have any beans? They say he likes cassoulet."

Amandine disappeared into her apartment and reappeared seconds later with a sausage. "Cassoulet is about more than just beans," she said.

The dog appeared interested in this development. Amandine waved the sausage, and his nose followed it from side to side. He took a step. She lunged forward and grabbed him, just as he snatched at the meat. Amandine stood now, holding Cassoulet, whose tongue wrapped up to clean every last morsel of pork from his jaw.

"You brought home a dog?" she said. "Jicky isn't going to like that."

"He's a stray," Joanna said. "He really seems to like you."

Truth was, Joanna didn't know if Cassoulet liked Amandine or not, but he didn't seem *not* to like her. The sausage had made sure of that.

"What are you going to do with him?"

"I don't know. He was eating scraps at the café." Joanna leaned forward. "I think they were going to send him somewhere, well…"

"Come in," Amandine said and pushed open the door of her apartment.

"What about Monsieur Chomette?" Joanna couldn't help asking.

Amandine dropped the dog in the hall. He ran toward the living room, wagging his tail the whole way, but Amandine froze.

"Isn't he sleeping?" Joanna said.

The neighbor's gaze slipped to the side, then back to Joanna. "No. He's out."

"Will he be out long?" Behind Amandine, a woman's slipper lay under a chair. Women's magazines were stacked on the hall table next to a small bowl with keys and a lipstick. The coat tree held a woman's cardigan and a pink umbrella. No sign of a man at all.

"I'm not sure," she said.

"Amandine…"

"Yes?"

"Do you have anything to tell me?"

Her nostrils flared and her chin rose. "What do you mean?"

"About your husband," Joanna said patiently.

She folded her arms. "All right. You guessed, there is no Monsieur Chomette." The words came all at once. She stared at Joanna as if challenging her to deny it.

Joanna's brow raised. Madame Dédé had been right. "Okay."

"Okay? Is that all you're going to say?"

To her surprise, Amandine's eyes filled with tears. Joanna led her into a sparsely furnished living room, all in white. It might have been featured in a magazine of minimalist décor. The only touch of color was a single ginger flower leaning from a glass vase.

Joanna took in Amandine's burgundy hair and streaming tears, then the décor, then returned to the neighbor. Looking as out of place as burnt toast at the Tour d'Argent, Cassoulet wagged from a white shag rug.

"It's okay," Joanna repeated. "No one cares."

"I'm a fraud," she whispered. "No husband. And a decorator did the apartment ten years ago. Just before he left. I haven't had the heart to change it."

Joanna swallowed the lump in her throat. Today had been too full of emotion. If she didn't watch out, she'd be grabbing at the tissues along with Amandine.

"Should we get the dog some water?" she asked.

Amandine mopped her eyes and nodded. She set a full bowl—also white, Joanna noted—of water on the kitchen floor, and Cassoulet trotted over and lapped happily. Then he returned to the rug and plopped over.

Hiccuping a sob, Amandine asked, "Did the police come by to

ask more questions about the break-in?"

Joanna sighed. "We'd better sit down for this. We have a lot to talk about. But before I get started, what are we going to do about the dog?"

Cassoulet, aware they were talking about him, rose to sitting. He wagged his tail and looked from woman to woman.

Amandine drew a long breath. "I suppose he can stay here." She blew her nose. "But I'm going to have to get a new rug."

Chapter 28

Joanna was halfway through her morning coffee, Jicky in her lap, when her phone rang. It was Luc. Early, too. Jicky jumped to the floor as Joanna rose.

"Hello?" Why would he call? She'd been sure she'd never see him again. Even so, her heart skipped a beat.

"A police detective called."

"Oh."

"He said you found a body in Parfum d'Antan. Are you okay?"

Now, there was a good question. "I guess so. Remember when we had a drink the night before last? When I got home, the place was turned upside down. Someone had searched the apartment. Elise and I found the body the next day."

The pause on the line told her he was thinking this through. "I don't know what to say. I don't suppose you know—"

"It was the waiter. The one who saw Pearl die." Suddenly, in her underwear and Pearl's kimono, Joanna felt a bit exposed. She drew the kimono firmly closed.

"And the apartment. Was anything stolen?"

"Yes. The bottle of Lys Bleu. That's all. The map is safe, though."

"And you're safe."

"I'm fine."

"It's Saturday."

"Yes. Why?"

"The Porte de Vanves flea market is open. That's where Pearl got the bottle, right?"

He'd remembered that detail. "That's what Elise told me."

"Will you meet me at the metro station? I can be there in an hour. Let's see what we can find out about it."

The train swayed as it rounded the tracks. "Gaïté," a woman's recorded voice announced a stop. "Plaisance." The metro station names were so much more romantic than simple names like "Forty-second Street." Joanna read some more from the map on the train car's wall: Bonne Nouvelle, Chateau Bleu, and Filles du Calvaire. Who were the "girls of the calvary," anyway? "Picpus" was less alluring.

The train took her further from the center of Paris, and Joanna's fellow travelers were an African woman dressed in bright orange and green, reminding her of Madame Dédé, and a young man with wire-rimmed glasses bent over a book.

At last, she arrived at the Porte de Vanves station. She took the stairs to the street, unsure of where to wait for Luc. She needn't have worried. He stood against an apartment building and pulled a hand from his pocket to wave at her. A stray bit of hair blew into his eyes, and he brushed it away.

She felt unusually awkward. "How do you know who to talk to?" she said. No "hello," no "nice to see you." She'd get straight to business.

"Hello to you, too," he said.

She laughed. "Sorry. Hi."

"To answer your question, we don't." He turned and started around the corner, where a couple of old men sat at a corner café next to a grocer fronted with an artful pyramid of melons. "We'll have to do some asking. The flea market isn't huge, though. The vendors tend to know each other. If we don't find the right person, we may be able to get a name."

They turned the corner to a wide sidewalk lined with tables on both sides, with a walkway down its middle. Joanna breathed in pure joy. She was right at home. The tables were heavy with goods: Footed crystal glasses covered one table, and next to it, a U-shaped table held stacks of linens. Lace-trimmed chemises hung from the chain-link fence behind it. Other tables held a mishmash of goods, from books to chipped plates to picture frames to statues of the Virgin Mary. A warm breeze jostled the leaves on the plane trees.

A woman so old her face might have been carved from a shrunken apple pushed a cart with a coffee kettle down the walkway. "Café!" she shouted in a voice outsized for her frame. The plinking of an off-tune piano came from up the block.

"It's amazing," Joanna said, her embarrassment at seeing Luc forgotten. "This happens every weekend?"

"Hmm," Luc replied absently as he scanned the vendors.

Joanna stopped in front of a table lined with velvet. Rows of hand-painted ceramic cameos lay on it. She picked up one with a woman's head. The woman had billows of white hair with a spray of pink flowers spilling from them. Joanna flipped over the cameo. "Limoges," it read.

"Do you like that?" Luc was right at her elbow.

"It's lovely. I've had one or two in my shop over the years, but we don't get many in the States."

Luc said a few words to the dealer and handed Joanna the brooch. "It will look nice on your dress."

"For me?"

"Why not? How have you been?"

"Good," Joanna said, forgetting all about dead bodies, break-ins, and corporate takeovers. What was she saying? She pulled herself together. They were here for a reason. "How are we going to find the perfume vendor? There must be a hundred dealers here."

He pulled her by the hand. "Let's ask them."

She followed him to two men smoking pipes and playing chess behind a table covered with lamps. A terrier snoozed on a blanket under a chair, making Joanna wonder how Amandine and Cassoulet were getting along.

"Bonjour, messieurs," Luc said with one of his patented, easy smiles.

After a moment of conversation, one man advanced a rook while the other man pointed the bowl of his pipe further up the row of vendors.

Luc took Joanna by the elbow. "They said a woman named Clothilde sells a lot of perfume. They don't know if she's here—apparently, she's a bit odd—but if she is, she'll be near the bend in the market."

Ahead, Joanna saw what Luc meant by the "bend." The market took a ninety-degree turn to follow the street to the right. At its crook, a man banged out what might have been a child's tune on a weatherbeaten piano.

Luc stopped to talk to another vendor, this one with crates of prints and magazines in front of her.

This had to be it. They'd found the source of the bottle of Lys

Bleu. Bottles covered the table, some in boxes. A rectangular bottle of Chanel No. 5 sat next to a green- and white-striped boxed Ma Griffe amid a sea of full and partially used bottles. A shoebox of mini-bottles had an "À choix 1 euro" sign taped to it. Christophe would have expertly examined them, but all Joanna could do was gawk. How many dressing tables had been raided for this display?

"She's gone," Luc said. "Where's the vendor? No one's here."

"*Attendez*," a cracking voice came from behind them. "*Je suis là.*" A woman limped to a folding chair behind the table and plunked down a thick tumbler half-full of dark red wine. She held a sandwich wrapped in paper in the other hand. "*Américaine?*" She waved the sandwich at Joanna and advanced a bottle of Evening in Paris. "*Voilà.*"

Joanna had seen enough of these bottles at estate sales to know the violet-rose fragrance wasn't for her.

"Madame Clothilde," Luc said. Joanna couldn't understand the words that followed, but his tone was all butter and honey.

Clothilde appeared unimpressed. As he talked, she balled up bits of the bread from her sandwich and tossed them to the growing number of pigeons at her feet.

The table next door held boxes with old prints in cellophane envelopes stacked in boxes for easy perusing. As Luc and the perfume vendor talked, Joanna flipped through a few. The aquatints of flowers would be nice hanging near the cash register at Tallulah's Closet. She especially liked a print of a beehive and a man swathed in beekeeping garments.

The next print was of a cutaway of a chateau. Above, eighteenth century dandies danced in a hall. Below, a servant filled a bottle from a barrel of wine. The basement was marked "sous sol." Sous sol. S.S. Slowly, she returned the print to its box.

Could the Lys Bleu map be of an underground room? Maybe that's what the map was trying to say. In that case, the reliquary might still be somewhere under the grocery store she and Philippe had found.

Joanna pushed the prints upright and returned to Luc. Madame Clothilde examined Joanna, then Luc, and responded in a gravelly voice.

Luc was able to get in another question before Clothilde waved him away and pushed the bottle of Evening in Paris toward an Asian woman with a white cotton sunhat and a camera.

"What did she say?" Joanna asked as they left the table.

"She used to work with Pearl regularly, and she definitely remembered the bottle of Lys Bleu. Said she bought it from Beaulieu's housekeeper after he died. The housekeeper figured the Nazis would take everything, anyway, so she squirreled a few things away from Beaulieu's apartment. She'd kept the bottle in a closet for years. When the housekeeper died, her son got ride of some of her things, including this bottle. Clothilde sold it to Pearl for a nice profit."

"Oh."

"Also, she passes along her condolences to Pearl's mother."

Joanna imagined the housekeeper. In her mind's eye, she saw women with wide-shouldered dresses riding bicycles down the street and soldiers posted at street corners.

"There was one more thing she mentioned." Luc's easy charm grew serious, and his eyebrows drew together. "Someone was asking about the bottle of Lys Bleu only a few weeks ago."

"Did she say who?"

He sighed. "She couldn't remember, just that it was about Lys Bleu and the person didn't buy anything. She couldn't even tell me if it was a man or a woman."

Joanna glanced back at the table. With her French, questioning the vendor further would get her nowhere. They were weeks behind the murderer. Would they ever catch up? However...

"While you were talking, I had an idea. My downstairs neighbor told me about the Paris catacombs."

"Sure." He steered her past a man carrying a rolled-up rug over his shoulder.

"The map has the initials 'S. S.' in the corner."

She didn't need to finish her thought. Luc grasped it immediately. "Of course. The underground. Why didn't I think of that?" He picked up the pace. "Come on. I need to get home and make some calls."

Chapter 29

As Joanna unlocked the apartment door, she wondered if they'd ever catch up with the person who'd stolen the bottle of Lys Bleu. Before she'd even heard of the perfume, someone had sought it, confronted Pearl, and searched the apartment. He questioned the flea market vendor and silenced the waiter. He was ahead on all counts, except one: she had the map.

She braced herself and pushed open the door. The apartment was calm, as usual, with Jicky flopped on her side in the hall. Joanna knew she'd never open that door with flinching, not in the week she had left in Paris.

She crossed the room and unlatched the French windows. On the street, around the corner came Amandine, walking Cassoulet on a brand new leash. Joanna leaned forward. At least, the dog was Cassoulet's size and shape. This dog was creamy tan instead of gray, and he was luxuriant with curls. He trotted with a spring to his step and his head up high. Joanna laughed. Amandine must have been up all night combing him out.

"Amandine!" Joanna waved to the street.

Her neighbor waved back. Her grocery bag was slung over her shoulder. Joanna bet it was full of dog treats.

Joanna congratulated herself on a success. If it weren't for her,

Cassoulet would be looking at a long, cold winter he might not survive, and Amandine would be sitting in her antiseptic apartment pretending to have a husband.

Amandine and the dog disappeared into the building just as Madame Dédé came out. Madame Dédé turned in surprise at the dog, then smoothed her dress—this one adorned with giant orange watches—and moved, chin held high, at a serene pace up the street.

A man shouted from across the street. It was the man who'd yelled at her before. This time he left his post leaning against the doorway and approached her.

Madame Dédé turned her head only a millimeter and continued purposefully on her path.

The man stepped up close. Too close. Joanna gripped the iron balcony and leaned forward. The man's shirt was unbuttoned nearly to Vegas performer standards, and his pants were so tight it was no surprise he'd been leaning on the wall instead of sitting.

Then he growled something at Madame Dédé and pushed her. She didn't fall but stood frozen on the sidewalk. The man pushed her again. This time Madame Dédé tumbled to the street.

Joanna flew down the stairs, not trusting the elevator to be fast enough. She came at the front door with both hands and stopped, gasping, at Madame Dédé sitting on the street, wiping gravel from her forearm and elbow.

The man was nowhere to be seen. Joanna thought she glimpsed a bit of his dark head through the gardienne's sheers covering the ground floor window, but he drew back.

"Are you okay?" Joanna helped Madame Dédé to her feet. That disgusting man. What an entitled jerk.

The woman looked into the distance for a moment, then at Joanna.

"*Merci. C'est bien.*"

"Your arm." Joanna pointed to Madame Dédé's scraped skin and wished she could speak better French. "You ought to clean that."

Madame Dédé readjusted her head wrap. "*Merci, madame.*" She continued on, chin high as before. Her first few steps were tentative, as if she were testing her knee, then her pace picked up.

Bastard. Joanna turned to the gardienne's apartment. The man emerged from the front door, examined Joanna with a lascivious stare, and sauntered down the street in the opposite direction. Joanna stared at his back and too-tightly wrapped derrière. He was probably going somewhere to leer at more women and insult others.

Her anger sprouted like Jack's beanstalk in the fear and confusion that already composted in her mind. *Watch out*, a small voice said, but she was livid. Pearl's death, the strangled waiter—maybe she couldn't do anything about them. But, by God, she was going to do something about this.

Joanna lay on her belly, her elbows on the balcony and opera glasses pressed to her face. Jicky rubbed her nose on Joanna's elbow. Conveniently, Pearl had kept a set of mother-of-pearl opera glasses in a leather case on the bookshelf in her office. Joanna adjusted them until their focus tightened on the door across the street.

A mother pulled a shopping cart and a toddler up to the door. *Action.* Joanna grabbed the pad and pen next to her and jotted down the code punched into the building's outside keypad. The gardienne's apartment was still dark.

Joanna slipped the bag of tools she'd prepared into a shopping bag. To anyone else, it would look like she was on her way to run errands. Her errand this time was a lot more important than fetching a baguette and a demi-kilo of coffee. This was about justice.

Paul's voice intruded into her thoughts. "When we have kids, you won't be able to do this sort of thing. Are you sure, Jo?"

The emotion running through her system responded with an emphatic "yes." Yes, she was sure. No one should treat another person the way that loathsome man had treated Madame Dédé.

"Positive there's not another way to do this? Something less risky?" Joanna heard in a whisper.

She had no time to stand around and argue with imaginary voices. The gardienne could be back any minute. Joanna hurried down the stairs, paused only a moment in the lobby to make sure the street was clear, and crossed the street to tap in the code. Success.

Now she was in a lobby much like her own, but with a different pattern of tiny black and white tiles on the floor. The gardienne's apartment was on the left. Showing the confidence of a resident, Joanna passed a bank of mailboxes and found the maid's staircase through a door at the building's rear. Beyond that, as she'd anticipated, was a courtyard with garbage cans and the apartments' rear windows. Including that of the gardienne. Right on the ground floor.

Not only were the gardienne's windows easy to find, one of them was open. She wouldn't even have to use the screwdriver. This was almost too easy. The ease of years of playing in the woods with Apple and her brothers came back as Joanna hoisted herself onto the ledge and pulled herself into the bathroom. She untangled herself from a rack of drying underwear and T-shirts and stood still, listening.

Someone was watching television, but the canned laughter she heard came from behind her, through the courtyard. The apartment was still empty.

The gardienne had apparently been enjoying an onion-laden stew. It smelled heavy for the day's heat, but Joanna didn't have to eat it. The sole bedroom was hung with flowered housedresses, and lipsticks and half-used bottles of perfume covered the dresser. Drugstore bottles, Joanna couldn't help noting, including lily of the valley she would have been tempted to smell, had she time.

Judging from the mess of blankets on the couch and the stack of clothing, the nephew slept in the living room. He might be a slob, but he was vain about his clothing. After a quick glance at the front door, Joanna settled on the couch and took out her stitch ripper.

Twenty minutes later, she was finishing up the last of the nephew's pants when she heard the front door's bolt snick.

Leaping up so quickly she nearly cut herself, she ran to the bathroom window and pushed aside the clothes rack. A flurry of surprised French erupted from the living room—and it wasn't just the gardienne. The nephew had come home with her, and one of them had caught a glimpse of her. Joanna didn't need to be fluent in the language to get the drift. One word in particular stood out: police.

Lightheaded, she heaved herself out the window and was again in the courtyard. She could dash through the lobby and into the street and hope they were too distracted to look out the window—or, worse, anticipate her escape and wait for her. The thought of running into the nephew was too awful to consider.

What else? She could sneak up the maid's staircase and huddle, waiting, until the coast was clear. Wouldn't that be the first place the police would check? By now, they were surely on their way.

Shoot. She'd blown it this time. Goodbye Paris, goodbye job. Hello, jail cell. Another thought, worse, came to her. She swore under her breath. She'd left the bag behind.

A lace curtain flicked across the courtyard. Lots of windows were open this afternoon in a vain attempt to catch a cross breeze. Joanna didn't think twice but ran for the window and pulled herself in.

She found herself in a dining room crowded with furniture stacked high with old newspapers and canned goods. The television blared from the room next door. She ran through to the front door, fumbled with the bolts, and let herself into the front hall and burst onto the side street, gasping, next to an Indian restaurant.

Sirens slowed around the corner.

She took a moment to calm her breath. What had been in that bag? Anything to identify her? Two screwdrivers and a knife to pop a window latch. She still clutched the stitch ripper. She dropped it and kicked it into the gutter. At least her keys were in her pocket.

Her heart beat madly, but with what she hoped was a relaxed smile on her perspiring face, she rounded the corner and approached her building. A police van idled across the street.

Madame Dédé's head popped into the window above Pearl's. They locked gazes.

Joanna was soon in the safety of the apartment, closing her eyes and leaning inside the door. She had gone too far this time, taken too much of a risk. Never again.

That night during her check-in with Ruth, Joanna didn't mention her excursion across the street. She'd spent the rest of the afternoon inside, only venturing to the window from time to time to see if the police car was still parked at the curb. Once, she saw the gardienne and a police officer on the sidewalk, and she could have sworn the gardienne's nephew had looked up at her apartment. After that, Joanna had stuck to the back of the apartment and scavenged leftovers for dinner.

She did, however, fill Ruth in on the trip to the flea market. "Someone had been asking about the bottle earlier," she said.

"Did the vendor describe the person?"

"Someone in a hat and sunglasses. That was all she could tell us."

"Not even a gender?"

"No," Joanna said. "The vendor was an odd woman. It was hard to tell how much she really knew."

Ruth sighed. "Have you found out any more about the discrepancy in Pearl's books?"

"No. Not yet. The detective brought up the possibility that Elise might be involved with the murder, too. If you could have seen her when we found the body, though…I don't think she did it. No one is that good an actress."

"Oh, her fear might have been real, all right. Fear that she'd get locked in the pokey for a good long stretch. You're being safe, right? Careful?"

"Absolutely," she lied. "The bottle is gone, and the map is a dud. The only witness to Pearl's death, as far as we know, is dead. The police are sorting it all out."

As she talked, her phone beeped to tell her a text had come in. Probably Paul.

"How's the rest of the job going?" Ruth said. "Time's running out, you know. You have less than a week left."

"Good. The notaire is on top of things, and I have a solid accounting of Pearl's estate. Philippe referred me to a good real estate agent.

The last thing will be to find a home for Pearl's cat." The phone was silent for a moment. "Hello?"

"What kind of cat is it?" Ruth asked. This was the most interest she'd shown so far in how Pearl had lived her life.

"Siamese. Her name is Jicky." Jicky chose that moment to stroll into the living room and stretch out on her back, revealing a plush tan tummy with a white spot. "She's adorable. It took us a few days to make friends."

"We used to have a Siamese when Pearl was a girl. Molly, we called her."

"Pearl must have adored her."

Ruth cleared her throat. "Quite. Well, I'll expect to hear from you tomorrow. Don't forget."

"Definitely."

She ended the call and checked the text, ready to give Paul the Cliff Notes version of the day. However, the text wasn't from Paul, but from Luc. *I can get us into the underground. Can you be ready tomorrow morning at 9?*

Chapter 30

Joanna hadn't packed anything appropriate for poking around in catacombs, so the next morning when she emerged from the apartment—glancing across the street to make sure the gardienne wasn't watching—she wore her loosest 1950s sundress, the one with the print of poker players—and flat sandals.

A plump, bearded man stood next to Luc. He looked like he might have strolled out of one of Portland's hipster bars, complete with a neck tattoo of a rose twined around a pickaxe. "Don't tell me she's going to wear that," he said.

"It's all I have," Joanna replied. "Unless you want to stop by an outdoor store on the way."

"Joanna," Luc said, "I'd like you to meet Dominique."

Dominique looked her over with a mixture of intrigue and disgust. "We'll make do."

He led them to a small van and opened the passenger side for Joanna. Luc took a seat in the back among plastic ponchos, bungee cords, and a bucket of rope.

"You'll need boots," Dominique said as he turned the key in the ignition. "Luc, look behind my seat and find a pair to fit Joanna. There should be some socks down there, too."

Luc handed her a pair of thick socks—clean, surprisingly—and boots to try.

"Where are we going?" Joanna pulled on one boot. Too small. She reached for another.

"There aren't as many tunnels in the seventh, so we're going to have to park a few blocks away from the address Luc gave me. We'll make our way as close as we can, using GPS, until it gives out. You aren't claustrophobic, are you?"

"Nope." She'd certainly squeezed into enough darkened closets.

"Dominique had a stern talk with me about you," Luc said. "He wanted to be sure you were up to climbing on rocks and getting dirty."

Joanna turned toward the street, now feeling more comfortable than ever. "I'm fine. I do everything in dresses and have never had a problem." She'd jumped out of windows, broken into boats, and leapt from a burning house in a dress. This should be a cinch.

"And breaking the law. The fine isn't steep, but the catacombs are strictly illegal. Are you okay with that?"

"Whatever it takes to see if my hunch is right about the map."

"Luc said you were all right. But there are a few ground rules."

"Yes?" They weren't far from Philippe's now, or from the Luxembourg Gardens, where she and Luc had strolled only a few days earlier.

"First, you must do exactly as I tell you. No wandering on your own. Stay close. Don't touch anything unless I say so. And, if we run into anyone else, let me do the talking." He parked in a narrow side street and cut the engine, but didn't make a move to leave the car. "*Compris*? Understood?"

"Yes," Luc said. Joanna said "*Oui*" at the same time.

"Hand me that bag, Luc."

Luc passed up a canvas backpack. "This one?"

"Yes. I've spent years exploring the *souterrain*, but this is a new cave for me. It's a branch of the underground of the old Chartreuse monastery."

"Why would monks have underground tunnels?" Joanna asked.

"They were carved out in the thirteenth century for the limestone they needed to build the monastery. The monks used the tunnels later as a distillery." Dominique opened the van's door. "When the monastery was destroyed during the Revolution, the tunnels were closed."

"For a while," Luc said.

"True. Most of it's been mapped out. Not where your address is. I'm not even sure the tunnels go that far, but there's only one way to find out. Come on."

They walked up the rue Auguste Comte, past the Closerie des Lilas and onto a side street.

"Follow me." Dominique led them to the Raspail metro station and through the turnstiles. "Don't question what I do, just follow."

Luc looked at Joanna with a raised eyebrow, and she nodded. So far, so good. They went to the platform as if waiting for a train.

"*Le prochain train arrive en trois minutes,*" a pleasant female voice announced over the loudspeakers.

Dominique edged toward the end of the platform, looked both ways, and dropped to the gravel tracks. He darted into the tunnel. Luc jumped to the ground and held out his hand for Joanna, but she easily slipped next to him.

In the distance, a train rumbled. On instinct, Joanna flattened herself against the wall.

"*Un moment,*" Dominique said, fumbling with a key ring.

At last, Dominique turned the tumbler and pushed open a heavy door. They were inside a dark tunnel, just as the train rolled to a stop outside. The dank air smelled of urine, oil, and damp rock. Joanna gasped as something—a rat?—ran over her boot.

"There are a few other ways down here, but this one was the easiest," Dominque said. "Believe it or not."

"Where are we?" Luc asked. Joanna couldn't see him in the dark, but she felt him near enough that she could have touched him by leaning toward his voice. Luc sounded wary, maybe a bit afraid. Paul would have handled the dark and the unknown with confidence.

"A side track the metro doesn't use anymore." He fumbled in the backpack, and the tunnel was suddenly illuminated. He wore a headlamp and passed them out to Luc and Joanna, too.

"I saw cameras on the platform. How come the police aren't after us?" Joanna asked.

"The guard on duty this morning is one of us," Dominique said. "A cataphile. He knows me. Remember the rules."

"Follow you, stay close, don't talk to strangers," Joanna said.

Dominique turned toward her. "I like you."

"We're on a mission here, remember?" Luc said.

Dominique's phone lit up as he punched coordinates into it. "The GPS will be good for a few blocks until we lose the signal. All right. Let's go."

They walked along the abandoned track for what felt like a few blocks. Empty bottles and dirty blankets showed they weren't the first people along these tracks. The rumble of trains grew fainter. Thick wires roped the tunnel, and gravel crunched under their feet. Way, way above them, people lounged on café terraces, took naps, and labored in offices.

"Now for the best part." Dominique turned into a dead-end hall and opened a creaking metal door. "I'll go first. Then you, Joanna, then Luc. Got it?"

Joanna nodded. Dominique dropped into a hole. Only his head showed, and that not for long. She followed him, gripping rusted iron protruding like staples from the chute. Down they went, hand over hand, one foot then the other. The tunnel couldn't have been wider than four feet. Dominique had been wise to ask her if she was claustrophobic.

"*Et voilà*," he said at last. He held out a hand to help her jump the ladder's last few rungs.

"Whoa." It was the only word that suited what Joanna saw. They stood in a huge cavern of yellow-tinted walls, some of them scrawled with graffiti. Pillars of rocks supported the tunnel's ceiling here and there. The air smelled moist, and was blessedly cool. She turned the balls of her feet in the sandy soil.

"Rue d'Assas couchant," Luc read from a street sign carved into the wall.

"So beautiful," Joanna whispered.

Dominique smiled and turned his head, and his lamp illuminated a stretch of tunnel ahead. "This is the carrière de la Grande Chartreuse. It's well explored, although that didn't stop the concierge at the Val de Grâce from losing his way here, back in the day."

"What happened?" Luc said with the air of someone expecting a good story. They were making their way through the catacombs easily now. This was clearly well trod ground.

"They found him eleven years later with four empty Chartreuse bottles. Apparently he'd planned to dig into the monks' stash but his candles ran out before he got home. There's a nice marble monument to him down here."

"My downstairs neighbor said there's a popular dance club down here," Joanna said.

"À la Folie," Dominique said. "The other side of the boulevard Saint Michel. I bet Luc's been there."

"He does seem to get around."

"You're right. Been there once or twice. I know one of the owners."

"Figures," Joanna said. "How long do the batteries on these headlamps last, anyway?"

"*Pas de souci*. I have spares plus regular flashlights in my pack." He laughed. "The concierge died two hundred and fifty years ago, at the other end of this stretch of catacombs. Don't worry."

They walked companionably, passing a quiet stream at one point, then a wide pit of glistening blue water.

"People swim there," Dominique said. "You have to be careful, though. These tunnels are riddled with wells."

He checked his map now and then, leading them into side tunnels. After a while, he stopped and turned toward Luc and her, his headlamp throwing fractured light across the rough stone walls. "According to this map, we are within a block—probably two or three buildings—from the address you gave me, Luc."

Despite the short distance, the next half hour was slow going. The tunnel was narrow now, and chunks of limestone littered their path. Graffiti had ceased a while ago. Trickles of water streaked the walls.

"The tunnel is deliberate," Dominique said. "See the marks on the ceiling? It's been mined. But I don't know if anyone has been here for decades. Maybe longer."

Ahead, due to fallen rocks, the tunnel tightened to an opening they'd have to squeeze through on their bellies. Joanna glanced at Dominique. He was a big guy.

"Should I give it a try?" Joanna said. "I can poke my head through, see if the tunnel widens on the other side."

"I don't know if it's worth the risk," Dominique said.

"If you get stuck on the other side, you could be there for a long time," Luc said.

"Remember the concierge and his bottles of Chartreuse," Dominique added. "We don't even have Chartreuse."

She'd be damned if they'd come all this way to be stopped by a little pile of rocks. "I'll just look. That's all. If the tunnel is clear on the other side, we'll widen the entrance." She looked from Luc's face, queerly serious in the dark, to Dominique's bearded one.

"Just a look," Dominique said. "I'll hold your feet."

"I knew you were a true explorer," Joanna said as she hurried toward the bottleneck before they could change their minds.

She scrambled up the rock pile and easily slid on her stomach through the hole. She would have slipped through to the other side, but hands on her ankles held her back.

"What do you see?" Dominique asked.

By the distance of his voice, Joanna realized it was Luc who steadied her. His hands were warm on her calves. "It's wider through here. I can see as far as my headlamp shines. I think we'd make it."

The hands slid to her ankles and released, and she slid through the opening with only the barest scrape on her knees. She stood, crouching a bit, on the other side and peered through the hole.

"You guys coming?"

After a few minutes of clearing fallen limestone, Luc and then Dominique scrambled through the opening. Joanna might have to duck her head, but Luc was definitely hunched over, and Dominique's headlamp pointed ahead only with an effort.

"How close are we?" Luc said.

Dominique consulted the map. "Can't be sure—it's not detailed enough—but I'd guess less than ten meters."

Picking their way over the rocks, they made slow progress.

"Here." Dominique pointed to a small outlet to the left.

"That's it?" Joanna said.

The tunnel was shut off by debris. She imagined the health food store above her, grocery carts trawling the aisles, health-conscious shoppers tossing heirloom tomatoes and bags of kale into their baskets. Once it had been a home with children playing in the yard, among them Ernest Beaulieu.

"That's it," Dominique said. "Got to be."

They stared at the rocks. Joanna stepped forward and began tossing rocks into the tunnel behind her. "I don't know about you two, but I didn't come here to be disappointed."

Dominique chipped in first, laughing. Luc, serious, finally joined them. After half an hour of digging, they hit something hard. Metal.

"It looks like iron," Dominique said. "Yes, it is. A door. A locked door."

Only the door's midsection was exposed, but it was, indeed, locked. And the lock, built into the door, was unlike any Joanna had seen. Its keyhole bore a strange outline, not the usual pear shape. It was familiar. All at once she understood.

"There's no way we can clear this all out without tools. And there's no way we can pick this lock." Luc tapped Dominique's headlamp. "Unless you brought something special in your backpack."

"Bread, Port Salut cheese, and a few beers. It always pays to carry the essentials."

"I've never seen a keyhole like that," Luc said.

Tearing her mind away from lunch, Joanna said, "It looks like… it looks like a lily, doesn't it? A stem, a crude triangular flower, and three stamen."

Luc laid a hand on her arm. His face was smeared with limestone, and the low ceiling forced him to lean over her. "The bottle."

"Exactly. Just like its stopper."

Chapter 31

"We've got to get in. We could blast the door open," Luc said.

"Bad idea. You'd bring the whole street down on top of you," Dominique said.

"It's the lid, the flacon's stopper. The whole time, the bottle actually was important," Joanna said as they turned back. At the opening to the larger tunnel, Joanna squeezed through first, relieved to be able to lift her head fully as she stood on the other side. "Now we don't have it."

"And the person who stole the bottle doesn't have the map," Luc said.

Dominique marched ahead. "I'd ask what this is all about, but as with all Luc's plans, I don't want to know. It's better that way."

The trip out was much faster than the walk in. Dominique took them past their original entrance to a manhole in a narrow street near the Luxembourg Gardens before heading back to the van.

"What do you say to a picnic?" he asked, swinging his backpack full of snacks. "It's lunch time, you know."

Joanna unclipped her headlamp and handed it to him. She pulled a handkerchief from a pocket and wiped her face. She had the sudden urge to talk to Paul. "I should get home and get cleaned up."

"I think you look great." Dominique took a step forward. "Perhaps later on?"

Luc looped an arm around her shoulder. "Joanna says she needs to be getting home. Will you drive us, or should we take the metro?"

"I don't mind walking," Joanna said. "It's nice to be in the sun again."

"Fine. I'll come with you," Luc said. "Thank you," he said to Dominique. "I'll be in touch." He marshaled Joanna down the street.

She waved at Dominique, rapidly shrinking as they marched forward. "Bye!"

Luc's arm on her shoulder, they turned yet again, and he dropped his arms to his sides. "So, now what do we do?"

"Could we tell the police? Get them to blast through the door?"

"Maybe. It's risky, though, and we'd have to explain that we were down there. On top of that, with the way French bureaucracy works, it could take weeks."

"I see." She had five days left in Paris. She had to follow this through. Not only to know what was behind the locked door, but to find whoever killed Pearl and the waiter. "The person with the bottle has the key to get in the door. But we have something he needs. The door's location. Without that, the key is useless."

"Remember, he'll do just about anything to get in that door."

Joanna remembered all right.

"Yes. The trick is, how do we bring both pieces together? And how do we do it without ending up in the morgue?" Luc asked. A chic woman in nearly chopstick-high heels clicked past. Luc's gaze followed her a second before returning to Joanna.

Why did he care so much about Pearl and Lys Bleu, anyway? She'd suspect him of having stolen the bottle, except that he was with her when the apartment was ransacked. Or had he been? Someone could have broken in earlier, when she was at dinner with Philippe.

"Well, let's be logical," Joanna said. "The thief is either a member of the perfume community or has been pretending to be to get information about the bottle. He's been in Parfum d'Antan, and he knows enough about Ernest Beaulieu to have heard of the reliquary."

"That sounds like me," Luc said.

She didn't reply.

Luc stopped and pulled her next to a shop window hung with Moroccan lamps. "You can't be serious. You think I'm a murderer?"

She looked him over. Luc was smart and too charming for his own good, but he was right. She couldn't see him as a murderer. "No. I guess not."

"All right, then." They continued down the boulevard.

Joanna gratefully inhaled the warm air. She felt like she should say something. "We don't have much to go on right now."

"True." After a few steps, he added, "You really thought I could have done it? Broken into your apartment, even?"

"Luc, hush. What about this? How about we put out the message that we have important information about Lys Bleu? We can ask the Baron and Christophe" —Joanna turned to Luc— "he's a perfume historian and blogger. We can ask them to spread it. We could even put a note in the window of Parfum d'Antan. We'll ask them to get in contact with us."

Luc nodded. "It could work. We'd have to give my phone number as a contact, though, since the message will be in French."

Damn it, he was right. "You could buy a throwaway phone. Anyway, we'll make sure he's the one with the bottle, then we'll say we have the map and say we'll split the loot." Joanna's voice picked up excitement. "We'll arrange for a meeting and invite the police to be hanging out nearby. What do you think?"

"I think we'd better talk it over with the police first."

"But?"

"But it could work."

Joanna was finishing her bath when the doorbell rang. The afternoon light warmed the living room, and Pearl's kimono swished on Joanna's calves as she passed up the hall and pressed an eye to the peephole. It was Madame Dédé and her daughter Michelle.

"Can I help you?"

"My mother would like to talk to you about the incident across the street yesterday," Michelle said.

Madame Dédé stood gravely in the hall, her hands clasped in front of her. Michelle's hair was tied in a headscarf, too, but she'd paired it with hoop earrings and a modern dress showing her miles of legs.

"Come in," Joanna said. "Have a seat in the living room. I'll put on some clothes and be out in a minute."

When Joanna returned to the women, she'd changed into a fresh dress, the Swirl housedress with patch pockets and scenes of Paris. She'd glossed her lips with red.

"Thank you," Madame Dédé said in heavily accented English. Jicky was curled in her lap, purring.

"Whatever I did, you're welcome," Joanna said. "How did you make friends with the cat so fast?"

Michelle smiled. "She loves animals."

One hand on Jicky's back, Madame Dédé told her daughter something in French.

"Maman says she saw you go to the building across the street yesterday and saw the police arrive later."

"I had an errand." Joanna bit the inside of her lip. "That's all."

"Then, this morning—"

Here, Madame Dédé erupted into laughter. Jicky jumped off her lap.

Joanna smiled. "What happened?"

"The gardienne's nephew should wash his underwear more carefully. It was not quite as white as it used to be."

Joanna's smile widened until she remembered the police the day before. She'd gone too far. It wasn't like her to be so impulsive.

"This morning he came out of the apartment, as if he were waiting for my mother to pass, and he shouted at her. He put one foot on the bumper of the car on the curb, and, zip!" Michelle made a motion of fabric rending.

"*C'était magnifique,*" Madame Dédé said.

"Same thing again later," Michelle said. "Maman said she could hear the shouting, even from her apartment." Her expression grew more serious. "You don't know anything about that, do you?"

Joanna clasped her hands in her lap. "Me? Why should I?"

Michelle looked at her mother, and her mother nodded back. "Maman also says that you are doing difficult work. She wants to know if you have friends to help you. She saw a man walk you home earlier."

"Oh, he's someone I met here."

Madame Dédé's gaze tightened.

"Maybe a husband at home?" Michelle asked.

"Yes." They seemed to be waiting for more, but she didn't have anything to add. All at once, she missed Paul. They needed to talk. The depth of this yearning must have shown on her face.

"He has been comforting you, *non*? It's difficult to be alone in a foreign country, living in a dead woman's apartment."

Joanna's hands sought the armrests. "I don't want to bother him."

Madame Dédé seemed to understand her without her daughter's translation. She said something decisive to Michelle, stood, and fastened her eyes on Joanna. Joanna looked to Michelle.

"Do you have a few hours this afternoon? There's someone Maman wants you to meet."

 Chapter 32

Joanna sat next to Madame Dédé as the metro car gently rocked them along its course to northern Paris. Michelle had gone off to work. Without an interpreter, Madame Dédé and Joanna communicated by gestures or, as now, sat in silence.

When they emerged from the metro, Joanna might have been in a different country. African men sold mangos and nuts from boxes on small portable stands almost like TV trays under the trees. They shouted friendly words. Madame Dédé lifted her chin and continued up the street.

They passed dingy storefronts with off-brand rolling suitcases and signs advertising cheap cell phones. Deli counters served up buns with vegetables and sauces she didn't recognize. African music blared from shops. A bridge took them over a bundle of railroad tracks, and they descended into a quieter neighborhood of apartment buildings interspersed with shops with stacks of brightly printed fabric of the same waxed cotton as Madame Dédé's clothes.

At last, they came to a shop with "Palais de Beauté" painted on a board above the door. Through the plate glass window a woman sat feeding sky-blue fabric through an old-fashioned black sewing machine while half a dozen women sat in a semi-circle around her. The woman at the machine wore a queenly ensemble of lime green fabric festooned with abstract butterflies, and her head wrap was even higher than Madame Dédé's. She was clearly holding court. Why were they here?

"*Voilà*," Madame Dédé said.

They entered to the smell of coffee, fabric, and the faint oily scent of the running sewing machine.

"*Bonjour*, Amina," the woman at the machine said, but her gaze was on Joanna. Her fingers continued her work, even without looking. "*Américaine?*"

"Yes. *Bonjour, madame. Je m'appelle Joanna Hayworth. Enchantée.*"

"Very well," the seamstress said. "We will speak English. I am Madame Gadio. Welcome to the Palais de Beauté. We were just discussing the matter of Madame La's dog. He has become quite a pest to her grandchild."

Joanna glanced at Madame Dédé, but she stared straight ahead. She'd brought Joanna here for some reason. It would be revealed eventually. The women stared at her, as if it were a sort of test, and she was the pupil chosen to provide the correct answer.

"He nips the child, and he was never that sort of dog," one of the women said.

"Always very loving until the grandson came to live with Madame La," another woman said.

"To harass a child, this is not acceptable," Madame Gadio pronounced.

All eyes turned to Joanna.

"If I might make a suggestion," she said. A girl of about ten years old handed her a demitasse of coffee and a lump of sugar.

"Yes?" Madame Gadio's foot let up on the machine's pedal. The quiet was startling.

"I grew up in the country, and we always had dogs." Not to mention Gemma, she thought, imagining Gemma trotting after Paul in the wood shop even now.

"Yes?" Madame Gadio repeated.

"Dogs are hierarchical. They think in terms of packs. Maybe Madame La's dog sees the grandson as the bottom of the pack. The dog wants to assert his authority."

The sewing machine started up again. Madame Gadio nodded. "This is what I said. Madame La must punish the dog."

"Or," Joanna said, "the grandson might be given the responsibility of feeding the dog. He has control of the food. Therefore, he has power. The dog will look up to him."

The fabric fed through the sewing machine and came to the end of the seam. In a practiced motion, Madame Gadio pulled it out and snipped the threads before feeding it in another direction.

"Perhaps Madame Hayworth has an idea that might be tried. It could not hurt. What do you think, Madame La?"

An elderly, slender woman Joanna hadn't noticed spoke up. "I'm not sure."

The sewing machine's hum ceased. "Why not? Do you doubt Madame Dédé's guest?"

The women looked at Joanna. She felt her position as a stranger, here only by the grace of Amina Dédé. Not everyone would accept an outsider—a foreigner—as gracefully as her upstairs neighbor.

The slender woman cleared her throat. "This is a wise suggestion. I will try it. Thank you."

"Madame Gadio," Madame Dédé said. "I brought Madame Hayworth here because I wanted you to talk with her about essential being." So, Madame Dédé did speak English. Quietly, but well.

But what was this about "essential being"? Joanna looked from woman to woman.

"Madame Gadio has a philosophy," Madame Dédé said. Heads around her nodded. "Essential being. Very interesting."

"Hmm." Madame Gadio shifted in her seat. "Essential being. This is a subject you are familiar with?" She didn't wait for Joanna's reply before continuing. "To live well, it is vital that we are in harmony with our essential being."

A murmur of "yeses" went around the room.

"First, one must recognize one's essential being. Then, one must calibrate one's life to be in tune with it." Madame Gadio had found her pace. "And how do you do that?"

A rhetorical question one of the women was happy to chime in on. "You ask yourself, who am I? What makes me happy?"

"Yes. You pay attention to that flutter inside. When it says, 'Self, I want to do this,' you must listen. And how does it talk to you?"

"Feeling," another woman responded. "It is a feeling of happiness and excitement."

Madame Gadio nodded. "It might frighten you a bit at first. That is okay. That is to be expected."

Madame Dédé relaxed in her chair, a faint smile on her lips. This was for Joanna. Madame Dédé had brought her here for this.

"But what if you want to do something that isn't good for you?" Joanna asked.

"Ah!" Madame Gadio had clearly been expecting this question. "You say, 'Self, why is this not good for me?' If the voice you hear is not your own voice—if the reply is someone else telling you what is good and what is not, you must ignore it. Listen only to yourself."

The coffee, instead of revving her up, seemed to relax Joanna. One of the women hummed, and the sewing machine droned hypnotically. This was Madame Dédé's gift to her, she realized. In less than a week, she'd be going home. She'd never see these women again. She could say anything to them.

"What if your self tells you to, say" —Joanna looked around the room, hesitating to monopolize their time, yet aware that problem-solving was why the women gathered— "do something damaging?"

"For example," Madame Gadio prompted.

"For example, well…"

Madame Gadio raised an eyebrow. "Yes?"

"Not to have children when your husband wants them."

"When it might break up your marriage, you mean." Madame Gadio let the statement hang in the air.

"Yes," Joanna said.

Madame Gadio resumed sewing, with only a split second glance at Madame Dédé, then to Joanna. "I see."

"Having children is to grow your family," one woman said, drawing the girl against her hip. "It's natural. You grow your family first with a husband, then with children."

"It's not without a cost," another woman, this one a generation older with white hair wound into a crown, said. "For you, having a large family was an easy choice and the life you were raised to accept. It suited you. This is not so for everyone."

"I feel like he wants me to be someone I'm not," Joanna said, surprised she'd been able to speak the words. "He wants to tie me down."

"Tie?" one woman said.

"To rein me in, to keep me from being myself," Joanna said.

It wasn't so much a question of children, she realized. It was the question of who she was. They'd talked about this before, and she'd thought he'd understood that she needed to solve problems, take risks. It was, she now saw, her essential nature.

"You can't do anything that represses your essential nature, or you repress yourself and your ability to love," Madame Dédé said. "What did self say when you went into the gardienne's apartment?"

Madame Gadio's foot lifted from the pedal, and she spoke to Madame Dédé in a flurry of French. All of the other women swiveled their heads from one woman to the other, interjecting comments here and there. Joanna drained her coffee.

At last, Madame Gadio nodded and resumed sewing. "Yes," she said. "You must be careful or your essential being will explode like a pressure cooker. You think the incident across the street was bad? You will get into real trouble then."

Nods of assent rippled through the women. The girl pressed a cookie into Joanna's hand.

"One more thing," Madame Gadio said. "Your husband. Does he respect your essential being?"

Although Joanna feared children would limit her choices, she realized that being married had actually made her freer, in a way. Paul's support emboldened her to be herself, even as his concern about her risk taking frustrated her. Being with him, she'd become stronger. Now she wondered if she'd outgrown him.

When Joanna didn't respond right away, Madame Gadio said, "You must find that out."

Chapter 33

You pay attention to that flutter inside, Madame Gadio had said.

Joanna felt that flutter now as she dialed Luc's number. She'd already made two calls, but neither of them had elicited this kind of confusion. Maybe it was indigestion from the meal of bread and Brillat Savarin cheese she'd just eaten standing up in the kitchen. Not like her "self" at all.

Did she dare compare Luc to Paul? She loved Paul. They were committed—she knew this. Yet, Paul asked a lot from her. Was it good? Maybe he challenged her to think about what she wanted and who she was. Or, maybe it was proof they weren't right for each other. If he couldn't accept her "essential nature," as Madame Gadio and her friends termed it, she would never feel truly at home with him.

Luc wouldn't pressure her at all. Judging from his interactions with women, he'd expect very little from her—and would probably give little in return. It could be fun, though. For a while.

Luc answered on the first ring. "Is it set up?"

"Yes. I asked both Christophe and the baron to send out messages on their networks with the phone number you gave me."

"Did they give you any trouble?"

"The baron wanted to know if we'd found the original bottle of Lys Bleu. I fudged a bit and told him we didn't have it. Poor man.

If we ever do get the bottle back, the decent thing would be to give him a sample."

"That's Madame Littlewood's decision, I suppose," Luc said.

"Yes. Christophe was no problem. Curious, but willing to go along with the plan."

"Good. The phone is charged up and ready to go. I recorded a greeting asking for the caller to describe what he wanted and propose a meeting place, somewhere public."

"We could hear something any minute." Joanna found that she had two hands on the phone.

"Excellent. I'll let you know the second I get the call."

That was it, then. There was no more reason to stay on the phone. "Good night," she said.

"Joanna?"

"Yes?" She might have responded a bit too quickly.

"Take care of yourself."

When she hung up, the room felt emptier, despite Jicky winding herself around Joanna's ankles. She had one more call to make. Paul. It was ridiculously late in Portland—nearly three in the morning—but she didn't care. Even listening to his voicemail greeting would be a comfort.

Maybe she didn't feel a flutter when she talked to Paul because they'd been together so long. Even caviar wouldn't draw flutters if you ate heaps of it every day, Joanna supposed. She and Paul knew each other so well. They'd been taking each other for granted. Instead of a flutter, she felt warmth.

She dialed. She was just about to leave a message when he picked up. "Joanna? Is everything okay?"

"It's fine. I just…wanted to hear your voice."

"It's nice to hear you, too. It's been so long since we talked. I was afraid—"

"I know." She didn't want to say more now.

Paul seemed to understand. "What have you been up to? Everything going all right with Pearl's estate?"

Joanna settled into the armchair and drew up her legs. No flutters, just the comfort of home, and it nourished her. She knew just what Paul would look like now. He'd be in jeans and maybe his old Twin Peaks T-shirt, his hair, so carefully combed in the morning, now mussed by the fingers he'd have raked through it while he was talking.

"It's been busy here," Joanna said. "I found a stray dog for the neighbor across the hall."

He laughed. "Really? How did you manage that?"

"He was a stray at the café I go to. They'd named him Cassoulet—that's a bean casserole—because he liked the scraps."

"That's just like you to do something like that. The neighbor was okay with it? They weren't put out? I mean, you don't think they'll just dump the dog now?"

Joanna sat up straight. "No! Of course not. You should see him now. Amandine gave him a bath and tied a pink ribbon onto his brand new collar. It's true love." She drew a breath. Time to plunge in. "I did go a bit far yesterday, though."

Somewhere outside, a stereo kicked in playing funk. The Ohio Players, Joanna guessed. Paul was silent, but she knew he was listening. Maybe it wasn't so bad that he was on the other side of the globe.

"A guy across the street has been yelling at Madame Dédé."

"The Senegalese neighbor, right?"

"Yesterday he did more than yell. He actually pushed her down." Her blood simmered just thinking of it. "Can you imagine? Just like that. He shouted something at her, then when she wouldn't look at him, he shoved her."

"Uh oh," he said. Joanna knew his response wasn't because of Madame Dédé. "What did you do?"

"I was so shocked, I couldn't even yell back. Besides, I'm on the fourth floor. Fifth floor, American style," she added.

"You said you might have gone too far."

She leaned back again and let her head flop on the chair's back. "I couldn't help it. I was so angry."

"What did you do?"

She didn't want to say it. She didn't want to admit it to herself, even. "I, well—"

"Tell me, Joanna."

"The guy is the nephew of the gardienne across the street. She has an apartment on the ground floor. Their window was open, so—"

"Oh, no."

She forced herself to continue. "I broke in and loosened the seams up the seats of his pants. I think I got them all, too."

"You were breaking and entering? In a foreign country?"

"I told you I went too far." Not exactly the behavior of the future mother of his children. She knew he was thinking something along those lines.

"You weren't caught, were you?"

"No. Not exactly. I think he saw me, though."

"Jesus, Joanna. It's, let's see, five days until you get home. We can get the ticket changed. Whatever the fee is, it'll be worth it."

"No. I'm staying. I have a job to do, and I'm staying until it's finished."

"I can't have you taking all these risks—"

"Why is everybody always trying to shut me down?" Joanna was now on her feet. She thought of Monsieur Saunier downstairs and quieted her tone. "I know I went too far yesterday. I told you. I know it."

"Then, why? Why did you do it?"

"I like helping people. I don't mind taking risks and breaking social norms to do it. I like—I like the grand gesture. It's who I am. It's why I get involved in these cases." To her horror, tears seeped into her eyes. In anger, she wiped one away. The room felt too hot, despite the night outside. She moved to the window. "Maybe I need to do things my way and not always have to be worrying about someone else."

"You mean, like me?"

Joanna felt the thousands of miles, millions of molecules between them as their words shot through the glass filaments under the ocean. She could tell him about the map and the bottle, but it didn't feel right just now. "I need to think. Goodnight, Paul."

Chapter 34

Later, at Parfum d'Antan, Joanna checked the time once again. The little crystal clock on Pearl's desk registered almost three, yet no word yet from Luc. Her sleepless night pondering her marriage and the situation in which she found herself now both exhausted and supercharged her.

Heidi, one of Tallulah's Closet's best customers, was an espresso machine repairperson, and she used to talk about a cocktail combo called the "disrupter." It was espresso next to a shot of whiskey, and it simultaneously hopped up and exhausted a person. Joanna might have downed ten servings of something like that.

As she photographed the last of the office's furniture for the inventory, her phone rang. Finally, Luc.

"Did you hear from him?" she asked. Joanna peeked out of the office into the front room. Elise was waving a bottle of Je Reviens and presenting it like a diamond ring to what looked like two Italian women, one of whom held a Pomeranian.

"I just got a text. He wants to meet tonight at the Champ de Mars."

"How do you know it's the right person?" Joanna asked.

"Let me read it to you. I'll translate. *I have the key. Bring the map to the Monument to Peace at 11 pm. No police.*"

It was him. "Did you get the phone number?"

"Definitely. It's probably a throwaway phone like the one we're using, though. I'm going to call the police straight away, but I wanted you to know first."

It was working. Their plan was actually working. She felt light-headed and sat. "Do you think they'll go for it?"

"I don't know why not. But, Joanna?"

"Yes?" The ring of the cash register outside the office door told her Elise had scored a sale.

"We don't know who this person is, but we can be pretty sure he knows where you live. I don't think it's safe for you to go home until this is all over. The last thing we need is for you to be held hostage."

"Fine. I'll meet you, and we can go to the Champ de Mars together."

"No. Absolutely not."

"What do you mean? I can't believe it. You can't cut me out of this, Luc. I found the map and the bottle. Besides" —Yes, this was the way to go— "as Ruth Littlewood's representative, I should be there. The bottle is her property."

"I completely understand. Normally, I'd welcome you. But think about it. You won't be able to understand the police. If they see a weapon, you wouldn't understand to get out of the way." His voice softened. "I admire your attitude, though."

He had a point. Joanna felt her resolve melting. "I can't just hang out at the shop all night."

"You're right. The shop's not safe, either. Where can you go? Maybe to a neighbor's?"

Elise stood in the doorway looking at her with her head tilted in an unasked question. Maybe Joanna could go to her house. Elise had been with her all morning. She couldn't have sent the text to Luc. Joanna would have known it. Elise was safe.

"Just a minute," Joanna said to Luc. "Elise, can I spend the evening with you? I can't go home tonight—at least, not right away."

"Yes. Of course. You can spend all night, if you'd like. My father's room is empty. Why?"

"I'll explain later. Luc, it's fine. I'll be at Elise's."

"Good."

"You'll call after you talk to the police, right?"

"Definitely."

"Don't forget. I'll be waiting by the phone."

"Joanna, I won't forget. Trust me."

Luc did call back, as promised, saying the police had agreed to stake out the meeting that night. Although they were still investigating the waiter's death, the Lys Bleu had definitely been stolen, and that alone was enough to apprehend whoever showed up seeking the map.

Meanwhile, Joanna had given up on labeling digital photos for Ruth. She couldn't concentrate. Instead, she killed time examining the boxes and bottles in the shop.

"Joy perfume is the one advertised 'the most expensive perfume in the world,' wasn't it? I've seen the ads in old magazines. Was it truly the most expensive?" she said.

"It came out during the Great Depression. That line had a lot of appeal," Elise said.

The door behind her jingled as Christophe entered. "Joy, huh? That 'most expensive' tag again. It still sells perfume. A certain" —he sniffed— "kitchen designer stole it for his own perfume line."

"Yet it can't simply be advertising that sells perfume," Joanna said.

"In the case of Joy, it was much more than the ads. Joy is a simple fragrance, really—rose, sandalwood, and lots and lots of jasmine." Elise took the bottle from Joanna's hands and placed it back on the shelf.

"Enough jasmine that most people think it contains civet. That's how indolic it is," Christophe added. His dreamy expression faded quickly. "But, yes, advertising definitely sells fragrance. That's how just about everything CosmeCorp puts out sells. Slap an actress or model on an ad, weave some kind of pap about seduction and the modern woman, then give the fragrance a fruity top note that will lure in the consumer before the perfume has had a few minutes to collapse into cheap woody musk."

"I know marketing sells, but is it really that bad?"

"Worse," Christophe said. "You don't know how lucky you are to be here." He waved a hand over the shelves as if presenting the grand prize on a game show.

"Christophe is right," Elise said. "I might be more willing than he to call CosmeCorp's offerings harmless—"

"Harmless? Only if you don't care about art." Christophe folded his arms in front of his chest, then dropped them all at once. "Joanna? Come to my apartment, and I'll show you some fragrance materials. Once you've smelled real Mysore sandalwood, there's no going back."

It was time to tell them, but she dreaded it. She'd already waited too long. "CosmeCorp has offered to buy the shop's entire inventory."

"No," Elise gasped.

Christophe looked too stricken to speak.

"It's true. I tried to put them off, but one of their executives got in touch with Pearl's mother directly. She hasn't said yes, though."

Joanna mustered her most hopeful expression. "Yet."

"I'm sure they offered a real packet of cash," Christophe said.

"Probably," Joanna said.

Elise let a groan escape. "Should we take the best bottles now? Leave them nothing they couldn't find elsewhere?"

"They know we've done the inventory," Joanna said. "I'm so sorry."

Christophe was silent. In shock, Joanna thought.

"I'd love to smell the materials you mentioned, Christophe," she said. "I have plans tonight, but maybe another day? Elise and I are having dinner."

"Plus, she wants to be by the phone in case a certain Luc calls."

"I am expecting information from him," Joanna said. She raised her chin. "No big deal."

"Luc who?" Christophe asked.

"What does that matter?" Elise asked.

Joanna looked at her gratefully. "He's a professor at the Sorbonne. I might be seeing him later tonight."

"I went to the Sorbonne. What's his name?"

"Luc Cazaubon. He teaches history."

"Really? At the Sorbonne?" A curious expression passed over his face.

"Sure. Why not?" Had she been wrong to trust Luc? No. Couldn't be. The police had interviewed him. They were working together at that very moment. She'd even had a phone call from Detective Batignolle about it. Besides, how could Christophe know every single professor at the university?

"Maybe I know the one. Short and kind of plump? Old?" Christophe said slowly.

"Not at all," Joanna said with relief. "Tall, thin, and in his thirties."

Christophe nodded, distracted. "I've never heard of him."

Elise shrugged and turned the shop's sign to "Fermé." "I bet he's never heard of you, either."

Chapter 35

The maitre d' at the Café du Commerce led Joanna and Elise to a table on the restaurant's balcony overlooking the ground floor's checkered tile foyer.

"I hope you don't mind eating out," Elise said. "I don't have anything at home fit to serve a guest."

Joanna looked at the potted palm and the snowy linen tablecloth. "Are you sure you wouldn't rather stop at McDonald's? I don't mind, if it will give you some comfort." Even as the words came out of her mouth, she was relieved Elise had chosen a bistro, instead.

"No. This place is a classic. You've got to try it before you go back to the States. I'll have steak-frites," Elise said and set the menu aside. "And a glass of Paulliac."

"I'll have exactly what you're having." Joanna set her menu on top of Elise's.

After the waiter had come and gone, Elise raised her glass of wine and clinked her glass against Joanna's. "*Santé.*"

"Cheers." Joanna let a sip of the Bordeaux wash over her tongue. She swirled her glass to wake it up. "If this were a perfume, what would it be?"

"Vintage Schiaparelli Shocking. In extrait," she said promptly. "Now, tell me why you can't go home tonight and what this has to do with the professor." She followed her rapid-fire question with a gulp of wine that caused her to cough once.

"Elise, you're so tense."

"You're right." She rubbed her forehead. "It's been a difficult few weeks." She pushed a strand of hair behind her ears that had escaped her chignon. "Tell me about tonight."

"Well, it has to do with Pearl. And the waiter and Lys Bleu."

"Yes?" Elise barely whispered.

Joanna told her about the map and her and Luc's journey through the catacombs. "We figured out that the bottle's cap—remember how strange it was?"

Elise nodded, her eyes wide. "Shaped like a crude lily, but thick."

"It was the key to the iron door we saw." Joanna shook her head. "The lock might not work after all these years. But it's worth a try."

"So you're planning a meeting with the person who stole the bottle— and maybe killed the waiter and" —she cleared her throat— "Pearl."

"Yes. The police will be there, though. And Luc." She answered Elise's questions about finding the underground vault and how they'd set up the meeting with the person who'd stolen the Lys Bleu flacon.

"What does Luc have to do with all this, anyway?"

The waiter appeared with two hot platters of steak and fries.

"Another, please." Elise pointed to her empty glass. "Luc," she prompted.

Joanna set down her fork. "To tell the truth, I don't know." She didn't. All this time, he'd shared her interest, but she didn't know why. She'd simply assumed he was as absorbed in the puzzle as she was. "He's a professor. He's curious."

Elise's hand shook as she cut her steak. "How much do you know about him, anyway?"

"Are you all right?" Joanna asked.

"I'm fine. It's just…"

Joanna waited, but the answer never came. The rest of the meal passed in silence. When the bill came, she set her credit card over it. Ruth Littlewood could pay for this one.

Elise lived within walking distance of Parfum d'Antan, but that was all Joanna knew. They set off toward the church at the end of the rue du Commerce and turned down a street off the square, their footsteps in time on the sidewalk. The night smelled of the glorybower trees in the Place du Commerce. Joanna glanced over her shoulder toward the shop's darkened window.

"It's not far. We'll make a pot of tea when we get in."

After a few blocks, they arrived at an apartment building fronted with old plane trees but clearly built in the 1970s. They rode the elevator to the third floor, and Elise unlocked the door and ushered Joanna inside. Through a main room with a chintz sofa and two blue armchairs, moonlight cast a pattern of leaves over a balcony with a small table and two chairs.

"Just a moment. I'll get the light," Elise said, just as the hall and living room came to life. "I can lend you a nightgown. It will only take a few minutes to make up father's bed."

"Elise." Joanna stood firm in the hall.

"What?" Elise turned to her. A messy, almost youthful, disorder had replaced her usual crisp elegance.

"What's wrong? I asked you once before, and you didn't answer. Are you worried about the shop closing? You're such an excellent saleswoman."

Elise threw her purse on a chair. "No. I have a friend who works at a perfume boutique on the rue Castiglione, and she's promised me a job." She turned off the overhead light. She clicked on a lamp near the sofa, then opened the door to the balcony. "Shall we have a seat?"

"Thank you." The night was still warm. Back home, in late summer the afternoons might be scorching, but nights were usually cool enough to require a quilt on the bed. At home, there would be crickets in the yard. She took one of the chairs. The sounds of a TV drama seeped from one apartment. An orchestral suite sounded somewhere in the distance, and the tip of the Eiffel Tower showed above the building across the street.

Elise sat across from her, her face in shadow. "I need to tell you something. For Pearl. I need to tell you for Pearl."

"Okay," Joanna said.

"I wanted to earlier, but I couldn't." Elise's eyes pled across the few feet separating her from Joanna. "I hope you'll understand."

"Elise, tell me. What could be this bad?" Joanna tilted her head and softened her voice. "It's about the two hundred euros a month, isn't it? Tell me. We can make it right."

Tears filled Elise's eyes. One spilled over and traveled to her jaw. She wiped it off.

"Can I get you anything?"

Elise didn't respond. "My father hasn't been well."

Joanna nodded and waited for more.

"He needed a night nurse, and the extra care, I couldn't afford it."

"I see." Elise had stolen from Pearl. Joanna understood. "We'll figure out a payment plan. You can make it right. We—"

Elise jerked her head back. "I killed her. I killed Pearl."

Time froze. In the space of what must have been only a second, Joanna noted Elise's worn lipstick and mascara flicked beneath her eyes. She felt a full story of emotion: concern, shame, and desperation.

"What?" Joanna whispered finally.

"I don't care anymore. I did it."

The orchestral music nearby had now switched to a rowdy march. Joanna wished whoever it was would turn off the stereo. "What do you mean?"

Now's when Elise would say she troubled Pearl or worried her, and Pearl, distracted, walked into traffic.

"I pushed her," Elise said.

"You what?"

"I pushed her. You know how the driver who hit Pearl said she'd been pushed? She was." This time her voice came more loudly. "I did it. She'd found out about me."

Joanna's mind raced. Luc and the police were planning a sting operation on the other side of the neighborhood, and she was sitting on a murderer's balcony.

"Tell me about it." As emotional as Elise was, she didn't appear ready to hurt her—or herself.

"I've told you about my father. About how he needs special care. Expensive care." Between words, she hiccuped deep, emotional draughts. "The state pays for a lot, but not everything."

"Yes. You've been a good daughter."

"I couldn't afford it. Not while working in a perfume shop." Elise paused and examined Joanna, waiting for her response.

"Of course not. How could you?"

A long exhalation. "I took a little bit of money. Not much. Just enough to make up the difference. Really," she looked at Joanna earnestly, "not much at all."

"I'm sure." Joanna nodded. As she suspected, it explained the differences in the books. Elise had been stealing from Pearl. It clearly tore her up, but she'd stolen for her father. "I love my father, too. I understand."

"Pearl would have understood, too. I should have told her. I should have. And then…"

The faraway music stopped. Someone went to bed at last. The nearby TV continued with the sound of gunshots. "And then what?"

"And then I started getting the notes."

Joanna swallowed. "What notes?"

Elise's face was still hidden in shadows, but her soft, aching voice made her meaning clear. "I got notes telling me he'd tell Pearl I was stealing, unless—"

"Unless what?"

"Unless I gave him the bottle of Lys Bleu."

Joanna leaned back. Oh, boy.

"But I wouldn't do that. The money I took, well, I'd pay it back. I knew I could. Eventually. But I could never replace that bottle."

"What did you do?"

"I asked Pearl if I could buy it from her."

That made sense. Buy the bottle, then give it to the blackmailer. Everyone's square. "But she wouldn't do it?"

"She'd already promised it to the Osmothèque. That's what she said. She refused."

Now it was becoming clear. "And you argued with her."

Elise fell silent once again.

"And you pushed her," Joanna said.

"I didn't mean to."

"But you did."

"Yes. I pushed her."

The TV had shut off. Now just the sound of distant traffic intruded onto their darkened balcony. Pearl. Poor Pearl. The funeral guestbook had been right all along. And the waiter had seen it all.

"The waiter—"

"No," Elise said sharply. "I had nothing to do with that."

Joanna remembered Elise's reaction to finding the body and believed her. "Do you know who was blackmailing you?"

"No. No idea. I found notes in the shop's night gate, and I left responses there, too. I don't know who it was."

"What did the notes look like?"

"They came in an envelope, on nice paper. Not monogrammed or anything—of course—but not the kind of paper you find at the drugstore."

"Written by hand?"

"No, from a printer."

"The waiter," Joanna said. "He must have killed the waiter, too."

Elise didn't reply.

Joanna stood. "Elise, I understand. I really do. But you know what I have to do."

Elise leaned back into shadow. Her face, crumpled in shame, darkened from view.

Chapter 36

Joanna stood on the street below Elise's apartment building, on the phone with Luc. "The police are here. I called Detective Inspector Batignolle, and he sent someone right over. The thing is, I'm not sure what to do next. As you pointed out, I can't go home—"

"No. It's nine o'clock. We only have an hour until the meeting."

"I could go to a café."

"We don't know how long this will take." From Luc's end, she heard a car honk in the background. "You can stay at my place. I'd feel better about that."

A curious racing beat in Joanna's pulse. "Where?"

"Meet me at the Villa Castel in the Belleville neighborhood. Do you think you can tell the taxi driver that? Castel. Like 'castle,' but with the last letters reversed."

"Of course," she said.

"Hurry," Luc said. "We don't have a lot of time. And, Joanna? Be careful."

Now she had to flag down a cab. She moved in a walk-run back to the rue du Commerce and found a taxi with its engine running in front of a hotel.

"*Vite, s'il vous plait,*" she urged the driver.

The driver didn't respond, and Joanna only caught a glance of his charcoal-black eyes, but the car picked up speed. They crossed the wide river, with the hanging pendant lights of the Bir Hakeim Bridge glowing above them, then took an abrupt right up an avenue lined in fancy apartment buildings.

Joanna leaned back. What a night. And it was only beginning.

They crossed town, and the driver slowed as the taxi crawled up a narrow street busy with residents and Asian restaurants before turning into a dark side street.

Luc was resting against a low building and stood and waved when he saw them. As Joanna emerged onto the sidewalk, he leaned in and said a few words to the driver.

"Come inside. I told the driver to wait."

They entered through a metal gate into a courtyard with a bicycle leaning against the wall and large pots of begonias. Luc unlocked an apartment door and motioned her inside. Table lamps cast pools of light here and there, illuminating warm wood furniture and piles of books. Just her kind of place.

"Nice," she said.

"Thanks," he said, but seemed distracted. "Why don't you have a seat? Here are some magazines in English. I have to run to make it to the Champ de Mars, but I'll be back right afterwards, and I'll take you home."

"And you'll call as soon as you know anything?"

"Definitely."

Joanna stood a bit uneasily. She'd barely been in the apartment two minutes, and he was dashing off again.

"I'll be back soon." He looked at her, then at his feet, then at her again. "When I return, I have something I need to tell you. I wish I had the time now, but I've got to run."

"Okay," she said.

As if on impulse, he leaned down to brush her lips with a kiss, then picked up his satchel and ran for the door.

"Lock up behind me."

Joanna stood for a moment, listening as the iron gates clanked shut behind him. She touched her still-tingling mouth with a finger. What the hell? She knew she was meant to be with Paul. When this was over, the first thing she'd do would be to call Paul and tell him how much he meant to her. Surely they could figure out how to settle their differences.

But, for the moment...

The armchair Luc had suggested she settle into might have been featured in the window of a store specializing in midcentury furniture, except that this one had been well-used, its wooden frame nicked and worn shiny at the arms, and the leather back and seat imprinted with Luc's lanky frame. A stack of *Economist* magazines rested on the ottoman.

She was too tense to settle in. She bolted the door as instructed, then turned to survey the apartment. She faced a large room—the living room—with French doors onto a side yard. Directly to her left was a kitchen. Letting off the main room to her right was a bathroom and bedroom.

She poked her head into the bathroom. A bottle of Eau Sauvage sat above the sink. Christophe would have ticked this as a point in Luc's favor. A towel sat crooked near the shower, and a pair of slippers was toppled near the door.

Joanna hesitated at the bedroom's entrance but peeked in, anyway. The bed was rumpled. Of course, Luc hadn't known he'd have guests. She remembered the women he'd greeted and the warm looks in their eyes. She turned away.

Was she comparing Luc and Paul in her mind? Luc wouldn't pressure her to have children—she felt sure of that. He wouldn't expect much of her at all, she thought. She could live her own life, do her own thing. Live it in Paris, even. Maybe Ruth would let her run Parfum d'Antan. She probably wouldn't take much convincing, as long as Joanna could show a profit.

But, Paul. Over the past two years, she'd learned she liked to be responsible for someone and to have him be responsible for her. She loved to come home to him. She loved being able to talk things through with him. She loved him. How could he ask her to give up such a large part of her life by having children? In the back of her mind, she suspected that even without the children, Paul would still hold her back.

Joanna wandered back to the living room. In the corner, near the French doors, was a desk with an adjoining table set at ninety degrees. Both surfaces were covered with papers. Here, Joanna felt comfortable snooping. She pressed a floor switch to turn on the lamp over the desk. It made sense that he'd have papers around. He was a professor. He was probably neck-deep in research.

She tipped a double-spaced manuscript. Funny, it didn't look like a history paper. "Notes on the Ernest Beaulieu reliquary," it said. Joanna dropped the stack straight away. What was this? His laptop sat open, its screen dark. She pressed the space bar and the screen sprang to life. The desktop image was an old-fashioned typewriter, and the screen was full of file folders with different titles, all in French. One looked to involve the secretary of commerce. Another seemed to point to an oil company.

She looked over her shoulder as if anyone were around to see her, then opened a file. Luc's name and contact info were in the document's corner, but it didn't look like a research project. Slowly, she stood straight. It was a draft of an article.

Joanna scanned the bookshelf. It was full of magazines grouped in cardboard sleeves. She yanked a holder from the shelf and grabbed the nearest issue of a news weekly and flipped through it. There it was, an article with the byline of Luc Cazaubon. She opened another magazine, then another. They all had his articles in them. She shoved the holders back into the shelf.

Luc wasn't a professor after all. He was a journalist. He'd written articles—lots of them—for France's most popular newspapers and magazines. He'd lied to her.

The fact took a moment to sink in. Joanna cursed under her breath and slammed the laptop shut. What else had he lied to her about?

She walked to the French doors and folded her arms. She had no idea who he really was.

Then she remembered Christophe's expression when she'd told him she was spending the evening with Luc Cazaubon, and her fingers tightened. Christophe hadn't recognized him as a professor at the Sorbonne, but he'd known him all right. Everyone knew Luc. He'd even asked a few questions to be sure it was Luc the journalist, not a professor.

Yet he had said nothing.

Her blood ran as cold as marble. Christophe knew Luc was after a story and had lied to her to keep the information flowing. The only possible reason Christophe had not clued her in to Luc's identity was because he was the person who had stolen the bottle of Lys Bleu, and he knew Luc was waiting for him on the Champ de Mars at that very moment.

From the stirring in her gut, Joanna knew this was true. The pieces had clicked perfectly into place. It was Christophe.

She spun around, listening. All was quiet on this side street. The French doors seemed unusually exposed without curtains, despite the deserted courtyard outside.

Christophe had access to Parfum d'Antan's books. He could have easily uncovered Elise's skimming. He would have known about her extra bills. Maybe he'd even suggested it to her. Joanna could almost hear him say, "Pearl will never notice. It's only a little bit. You'll pay it back."

As for the waiter, if the poor man had come forward about seeing Elise push Pearl into traffic, Elise might have told the police she'd been blackmailed. Eventually, Christophe's name would have come up as a suspect.

It wouldn't be hard to learn where Luc lived. Christophe would guess that Luc wouldn't bring the only copy of the map to their meeting. He might not bring an accurate copy at all, in fact. Without knowing Luc's identity, Christophe would have had to chance the rendezvous. Not now. While Luc was across town, all the way near the Eiffel Tower, Christophe could break into his apartment and steal the original map. Now, thanks to her, he knew where it was.

Joanna inhaled sharply. He'd killed once already. What would he do if he found Joanna between him and the map he so desperately wanted? She could almost hear him picking the lock on the big iron gate and pacing toward Luc's apartment.

If Christophe found her, she was as good as dead.

⁎⁎

Joanna checked the laptop's clock. Quarter to ten. Christophe would know that Luc was on his way, if not already at the planned rendezvous site. A wave of heat, then cold, passed over her. Christophe might even have watched Luc leave, take the taxi. He might have seen her come in.

He might know she was here.

Joanna swallowed, her throat dry. Now what?

With sudden determination, she shut Luc's laptop and got out her phone. "Amandine?"

"Where have you been? The gardienne's nephew was—"

"I can't talk now. I need you to do something for me. Something very important."

A pause. "Yes?"

"Go upstairs and see if Madame Dédé is home. I'm in Belleville right now, and her friends live close by."

"Belleville? Why? I—"

"I'm at the Villa Castel. Write that down. There's a man in a dark green Citroën Deux Chevaux who will probably be here any minute." If he's not here right now. Her breath came faster. "I need Madame Dédé's friends to delay him. However they can. Right away. I know this sounds dramatic, but it's a case of life or death."

Amandine gasped. "You think the man in the green car killed Pearl?"

"Indirectly. He also killed the man we found at the shop. Will you call the police, too? Ask for Detective Batignolle. Tell them to meet me at this address." Joanna gave her an address on the other side of town.

"Are you sure?" she said.

"Definitely."

Amandine started to say something else before she cut it off and replied, "Got it."

"Listen, I can't stay on the phone any longer. Can you do this?"

"I'm going right now." The line went dead.

Joanna slipped her phone in her purse and took out the piece of paper that Monsieur Saunier had carefully browned and folded into eighths. She slid it under Luc's laptop. Then she let herself out the side door.

Chapter 37

From the taxi earlier, Joanna had seen a metro station not far away. That, she'd learned, was one of the benefits of Paris. You couldn't get lost. Sooner or later, you'd stumble upon a metro station.

She hurried down the main boulevard a few blocks away, past Chinese restaurants and homeless kids sitting on the sidewalk. The August night lifted the smell of garbage from the alleys, mixing it with the scent of baking bread. An Asian woman in heels and a low-cut knit top leaned against a closed grocer's shop. The woman lifted a cigarette to her lips as she watched Joanna dodge an African man on a motorized scooter and a white-haired woman leading a bulldog.

Here it was, the Belleville station. Joanna ran down the stairs to catch the train just pulling into the station. Catching her breath, she fell back into her seat.

Would her plan work? She didn't know. There was so much she couldn't control. The memory of Luc's kiss goodbye and then finding his byline in a stack of magazines filled her with a potent mix of grief and anger. He'd lied to her all along. To him, she was only a story. After the meeting tonight, she'd never have to see him again. Her chest tightened.

Stations passed seemingly in slow motion. République, Temple, Arts et Métiers. The train pulled into Châtelet, and Joanna bolted from her seat and hurried through the vast station's halls looking for her transfer. The strains of Vivaldi reverberated in the tunnel behind her. She waited a few minutes in the dull fluorescent lights for her connecting train. A woman with a full shopping bag nodded off on a plastic bench behind her.

At last, the train arrived, and, twenty minutes later, Joanna ran up the escalator at the Port Royal station just beyond the Luxembourg Gardens. The streets were quieter here, except for the steady hum of traffic on the boulevard Saint Michel.

After a few seconds to orient herself, Joanna turned up the boulevard de Port Royal, then into a narrow side street. No green car in sight. She prayed that Madame Dédé's plan—whatever it was—had worked.

Taking a deep breath, she raised a fist and knocked on a beat-up lavender door, its glass transom warm with light.

"*Mademoiselle?*" A six-foot blond man in a fishtailed silver sequined dress with a hairdo to make a Texan beauty queen jealous answered the door. Her pink-frosted lips curled into a smile.

She'd arrived at her destination, the X on the map she'd left at Luc's for Christophe to find, the map Monsieur Saunier had forged for her as a safety net, and, now, as a decoy. The map to the À la Folie drag club deep underneath the city.

*
**

"*Parlez-vous anglais?*" Joanna asked.

The drag queen's laugh chimed up the scale like a musician on a vibraphone. "Dancing queen," she said. "I will survive. Is that all there is. Take a chance on me." She flashed a wide smile of dazzling teeth. "*Mais, oui, je parle anglais.*" She swept Joanna inside, checking up and down the alley before closing the door behind them.

They were in a small room—or, at least, it felt small. The room's walls receded into shadows. Taper candles and a book of crossword puzzles sat on a table next to a hardback chair.

The drag queen lifted a handful of Joanna's hair and took in her sundress and cardigan. "*Oh là là.* Where are you from, my vintage princess?" she said in perfectly accented English.

"Portland." At the drag queen's blank look, she added, "Oregon." When that didn't elicit a reaction, she said, "The state above California?"

"Ah, California. Land of Hollywood."

"I own a vintage clothing boutique."

"And why are you here?" The candlelight shimmered all over the queen's evening gown.

Joanna drew a deep breath. "I'm meeting someone."

"Someone we know?" When Joanna didn't respond, she said, "I see. I'm afraid you'll have to leave." The drag queen rose to her full height, filling the space of an NFL linebacker.

She had to stay. She was expecting Christophe—and, if she'd played it right—the police. Joanna put on the smile she used for her most reluctant customers. "Lovely dress. Early Thierry Mugler?"

"An inexpensive reproduction—you can't tell in the candlelight. But candlelight does so much more for my complexion."

"I'd like to see you in Alaïa," she said.

"Ha! As if. What, do I look like Naomi Campbell?"

"More like Christy Turlington, actually. I know a tailor who specializes in larger-sized Alaïa styles that would suit you well." Thank goodness for her relationship with the queens down at Marquise's. "Black is awful on me. Takes the light right out of my skin. But on you? I see it. May I?" She reached into her bag.

"What are you doing?"

"Searching for a lipstick. The blue tones in Cherries in the Snow are perfect for you."

The queen flipped open a compact and lifted her chin to examine her moue. "Hmm. Maybe."

Joanna grabbed a candle in one hand and rummaged for a lipstick in her bag. The light illuminated a Grand Canyon of powdered lines on the queen's face. "Try this."

The drag queen reached for the tube, then withdrew her hand. "What's really going on with you? Why are you so eager to go downstairs?"

She couldn't exactly tell her it was to meet a murderer. "I like to dance." She smiled as convincingly as she could.

The door opened to three men dressed in zoot suits and fedoras. The drag queen's lips widened into a smile. "Ah! At last!" Then, to Joanna, "Fine. Through there." She pointed to a staircase behind her.

Joanna took this chance to get in. She'd have to rely on Christophe's greed to get him past this sentry. On the other hand, he might already be below, waiting.

She grasped the cold iron handrail and went down two flights of stone steps, then a narrow spiral staircase. As she descended, music, driven by a throbbing bass, grew louder. Shouldn't the police be there by now?

She arrived in a wide room carved from limestone and thick with the warm scent of bodies, liquor, and beeswax candles. Candles burned everywhere, from niches in the walls to a string of iron chandeliers suspended from the ceiling. A bar stretched along the wall opposite the staircase. To her left was a stage with a short runway where drag queens vogued while the music pounded.

Joanna stood, mouth agape, staring at the crazy scene. A man in a suit, less buff than the queen upstairs but still built to take care of business, pulled her arm and ushered her into the crowd. He wore an earpiece. As rustic as operations upstairs seemed, the queen at the door must have sent word down that she was okay.

Joanna found she was grasping her purse so tightly that her hands had spasmed shut. She stretched her fingers and looked for a place to settle and watch the staircase. A quick glance had assured her there weren't any other exits to be found easily.

"Have a seat here," a voice drawled into her ear.

She turned to find a lanky black drag queen in a green marabou bikini. The queen led her to a small table near the bar on the other side of the room.

"I'll get you something to drink."

Joanna watched her saunter to the bar and lean over to whisper to the bartender. She pointed to Joanna. The queen's shapely legs begged for a pantyhose commercial. She returned with a martini glass holding a milky white liquid with a vivid red cherry.

"We're calling this Cherries in the Snow, just for you," the queen said. She had to press close to Joanna to be heard. "Compliments of Raison Delectra upstairs. Vodka, maraschino liqueur, and a cherry, of course."

"Thank you." Joanna left it untouched on the table as she kept her gaze on the entrance. The pounding music made listening impossible, but above the crowd she could see who came down the stairwell.

And come they did. Most of the arrivals wore stiletto heels, and Joanna could rule them out as soon as their ankles came into view. A few polished loafers descended, as well. Once they reached the dance floor, they disappeared into the crowd.

The driving bass reverberating in her gut was beginning to nauseate her. Joanna had no idea what Madame Gadio had cooked up to delay Christophe, but surely he'd be there by now. If he were coming at all, that is. She'd left the map in a fairly obvious place. Could he have missed it? Or could she have misread the situation completely? Maybe the murderer had shown up in the Champ de Mars after all, and Luc was trying to call her at that very moment.

She glanced at her phone. No service, not this far down. Luc wouldn't care about calling, anyway. Her stomach curdled, and she pushed away the cocktail. He'd gotten what he wanted. He had his story. Maybe she should call it a night and go home.

The next set of feet that descended was clad in Converse tennis shoes. Joanna's breath froze. Jeans. Then a polo shirt with a backpack. Christophe. Joanna shrank toward the bar. Through the undulating satin and sequins, she couldn't see what happened with the doorman, but this new guest did not return up the stairs.

Christophe was here. She had been right. He'd found the map and come to get the Beaulieu family's reliquary.

She almost laughed, from both hilarity and fear. What did he think now?

But, more importantly, where were the police?

Chapter 38

"You did this!"

Joanna lifted her head to see Christophe standing so close to the table she feared it would tip.

"You have the real map." His words were barely audible above the pulsing music, but Joanna could read his lips.

Joanna finally found the words to speak. "I don't know what you're talking about."

He leaned so close she could smell his breath. "You found the map, or you wouldn't have made this—this—phony one. Where is it? The real map?"

Joanna looked past him, desperately hoping to see police.

He reached across the table and shook her, jostling the table and tumbling the cocktail. Its cherry rolled to the floor. "Where is it?"

"Take it outside," a stern voice warned. Christophe suddenly jerked back, the doorman's hands on his torso.

Joanna relaxed and nearly closed her eyes in relief.

"You, too," the doorman said. "None of that down here. We don't need your trouble." He had one hand firmly on the scruff of Christophe's shirt, and the other hand was ready to manhandle Joanna, if necessary.

Joanna threw up her palms in surrender. "I don't want trouble, either. He's dangerous." How could she explain? "Call the police. Ask them."

That was all the doorman needed to hear. He yanked Christophe toward the staircase and gestured that Joanna should follow. What else could she do? She eyed Christophe's backpack. The Lys Bleu had to be in it. If she could just grab it and run ahead…

At that moment, Christophe yanked himself free of the doorman. Joanna plunged forward and reached for the backpack with both hands. The backpack slipped from Christophe's shoulders, but he spun and lashed out for its straps. The zippered compartment split apart. A package fell out.

Time stretched to slow motion for Joanna as she watched the paper-wrapped package tumble from Christophe's backpack to the stone floor. She yelled and stretched out her arms, but the package slipped through her fingers and shattered against the floor, soaking the paper surrounding it and filling the air with scent.

Joanna's hands flew to her mouth. The pounding music seemed to have vanished. The crowd of preening drag queens might have disappeared. All that mattered was the amber puddle spreading across the stone, and the monastic yet seductive fragrance of Lys Bleu.

She'd heard the fragrance compared to stained glass and cello music. She'd learned it was Beaulieu's greatest composition. She knew perfume fanatics would give their kidneys to smell it. But nothing had prepared her for its intimate yet orchestral aroma. It smelled truffled and personal, like the unwashed sheets of lovers, yet as full and radiant as a summer morning on the Mediterranean. She couldn't have told you its notes, only that she wanted to smell it again and again to plumb its story.

She watched in shock as Christophe dove into the broken bottle and rolled in the perfume.

The doorman pulled Christophe to his feet, and, pushing Joanna ahead, marched them to the stairwell. "*Allez-y.*"

Up they went. They had no choice. The bottle of Lys Bleu was lost to them now. Christophe's body trembled as if he were weeping. Joanna continued ahead, praying with every step that the police would be at the top.

When they emerged into the ground floor room, the drag queen had the front door already open and pushed them into the street. The alley was completely empty, quiet. Joanna glanced at Christophe and bolted for the boulevard de Port Royal, but Christophe grabbed her arm. His eyes were dry and his expression might have been etched in plaster.

"You're coming with me. You know where the map is."

"What does it matter now?" Joanna said. Where, oh where, were the police? "We don't have the key."

Christophe held out his fist and opened it. In his bloodied palm was the jagged neck of the Lys Bleu's crystal neck and bronze cap. The key.

"Where's the map—the real one?" Christophe backed her against the wall so that her arms grated against the building's stone.

She glanced down the alley again, but Christophe straightened her head with a hand. A strong hand. His love of discipline and the gym was evident.

"At home. The apartment."

He grabbed her arms and whirled them behind her back, holding her by her wrists and marching her forward, pushing her when she tried to slow for time. Her purse dangled from her shoulder. Her phone was in there, but useless to her now.

The green Citroën was half a block away. Christophe released one hand so he could unlock the passenger side door and duck her inside. She could scream, but who would hear? The quiet courtyard of the Val de Grâce stretched impassively along the boulevard.

Once Christophe was inside, he reached over and yanked off the door handle. No way she'd be getting out now. Without saying a word, he pulled into traffic. They weren't even to the stoplight when two police cars shrieked to the alley, blocking it off. Christophe looked at their flashing red lights in his rearview mirror and laughed.

"Nice try. I saw you trying to stall. It didn't work, did it? I would have been here sooner if some band of crazy African ladies hadn't circled my car waving banners of fabric."

Joanna dropped her head and rubbed her sore wrists. "Why? Why did you do it? Why did you blackmail Elise and kill the waiter?"

"You've been clever so far. Why don't you tell me?" His voice was calm. The flash of anger—and brutality—in the alley was now fully under control.

"You want the reliquary, of course." The police were far behind them now as Christophe's car edged up the boulevard du Montparnasse. "You must have learned about it when you were researching Beaulieu. You figured out that to get to the reliquary, you had to have the bottle of Lys Bleu."

She tilted her head toward Christophe. Streetlights through the trees moved over his face, but he didn't reply. She continued. "Working at Parfum d'Antan, you discovered Elise was taking a bit of money each month to pay for her father's medical care, so you blackmailed her anonymously. When she couldn't produce the bottle, you upped the stakes. You would have taken the bottle yourself, but you weren't able to get a copy of the key until you came back to help with inventory."

"Not bad," he said and jerked the car's stick shift to slow and change lanes. "Keep going."

"You didn't reckon that Elise would kill Pearl, or that the waiter across the intersection would see it happen. And you certainly didn't count on the waiter coming around with his own hush money scheme."

Christophe snorted. "Wrong. He had the idea of going to the police. The guy wasn't crooked at all. I told him I'd invite the police detective to the shop, as well as Elise, so the waiter could identify her."

"And you…"

"Killed him. Yes. I'm afraid that's what I'll have to do to you, too, once I get the map."

Joanna's throat closed up. Any further words would come out as a croak.

He glanced at her and returned his gaze to the road. "Don't worry. I'll make it quick and painless—as long as you come through with the map. I'll tell everyone you returned home early. Homesick."

She was sick all right, and it wasn't for home. The map wasn't at the apartment. The police had it. Christophe would find out soon enough, and then what?

Her phone buzzed. Before she could reach for it, Christophe had plunged a hand into her bag and grabbed it.

"Luc. The professor." Christophe's laughter was sudden and loud. "You are so stupid. Didn't you even check the Sorbonne faculty list to make sure he was who he said he was? Everyone knows Luc Cazaubon."

They were passing the Café de l'Espérance now. Only a few blocks until the apartment.

"Why are you so greedy?" Joanna said. "Aren't there easier ways to get money, like robbing a bank?"

Christophe pulled the car into a spot on the street and cut the engine. He ripped the parking brake. "You don't get it, do you? It's not about money."

"It has to be. What else? Otherwise, why—"

"I am Ernest Beaulieu's heir." Before Joanna could respond, he held up a hand. "His artistic heir. I will carry out his work. I can't let the accountants and millionaires at CosmeCorp destroy his fragrance, cheapen it so a bunch of Americans will buy out their malls. Perfume is sacred. It's art, for God's sake. Don't you understand?"

Joanna stared. Christophe had lost it. He'd gone crazy. Running and shouting would only make it worse. "I see," she said softly. "Like you've taught me."

He froze. He hadn't expected this response. But his anger didn't wane. "You're playing me, aren't you? Hoping I'll let you go."

"No. No, of course not."

"We're going in to get the map." Christophe got out of the car and looked up and down the quiet street. He opened her door. "Don't try anything. I warn you. I can get the map by myself, if I have to." He leaned toward her. "It only takes a moment to strangle a person."

She involuntarily shuddered. "Fine."

What she'd do when they got upstairs, she didn't know. She could try for her phone and call the police again. She might run for the kitchen door and dart down the stairs. And, of course, Monsieur Saunier would be home downstairs. She looked with hope to the windows below hers, but they were dark. She cursed silently. He would choose tonight to follow her advice and get out.

With Christophe's hand firmly in the small of her back, she punched the code to the front lobby, then the code to enter the stairwell. As they rounded the stairs to the third floor, Amandine,

Cassoulet beside her, sprang to her feet. She'd been sitting on the steps.

"Psst!" she said.

"*Bonsoir, madame*," Christophe said.

"What are you doing here so late? Why aren't you inside?" Joanna said. Christophe's hand pinched at her flesh.

Questions in her eyes, Amandine looked at both of them, then remembered her business. "Go back. You can't go upstairs, understand?"

"We have to go." Joanna's throat was as tight as if strapped with metal bands. Maybe she could turn around quickly and push Christophe down the stairs. But if she failed…

"No," Amandine said. "It would be much better if you don't. Truly. Much, much better." She lifted her eyes dramatically to the floor above and motioned as if chopping her neck. "Maybe you'd like to go out for a drink. The gardienne's nephew—"

"Excuse us, madame." Christophe pushed Joanna past Amandine, Cassoulet growling quietly.

As they turned the corner to the fourth floor, Joanna ripped herself away from Christophe and shouted, "Amandine, call the police! He wants to kill me!"

Two policemen seemed to come out of nowhere. One caught Joanna's wrists, and the other grabbed Christophe. Christophe struggled until the officer clipped his hands behind his back.

"What?" Joanna gasped.

"I understand you broke into the apartment across the street yesterday?"

Chapter 39

The next three days passed quickly. Joanna signed the documents the notaire required and said her goodbyes to Philippe and the neighbors.

Elise was in jail awaiting trial. Joanna hoped the justice system would be lenient, once they knew the facts.

Monsieur Saunier had agreed to take Jicky, and Joanna had even made friends with the gardienne across the street. The gardienne had kicked out her nephew when she'd heard what he'd been up to. One of the reasons he'd been booted from his hometown in Portugal was because of abusive behavior toward women. She'd declined to press charges against Joanna.

Jicky wound herself through Joanna's calves. Joanna couldn't bear to give her up just yet.

The newspapers were full of the story of Lys Bleu and the ancient reliquary. Each morning, Amandine brought Cassoulet and a copy of *Le Monde* to Joanna's apartment, and she read the stories to her over croissants and milky coffee. Cassoulet had a new haircut, and his silky fur smelled like roses. He was turning out to be a natural lap dog. In the newspaper, Joanna's name came up more than once, and each time, Amandine tapped the words as she pronounced "Joanna Hayworth." Joanna carefully folded them and slipped them in her luggage to show Paul.

Christophe was charged with homicide and attempted homicide, and the police, in searching his apartment, had found a key to a small perfume laboratory. There he had a decant of Lys Bleu perfume he'd taken from the bottle before he'd left home. From the look of the apartment, the police said it was likely he hadn't planned to return. His computer's history showed he'd been researching apartments in Cabris, Ernest Beaulieu's hometown. The police had promised the decant would go to the Osmothèque once it was no longer evidence.

This morning's paper featured photos of the reliquary, which was on its way to the Louvre. Even in the newspaper's grainy depiction, it was a majestic piece of art with filigreed lilies studded with blue sapphires, entwining a bone. Philippe had pulled one of his never-ending strings in government and arranged for a private showing.

And, yes, Luc had written many of the articles Amandine recited to Joanna so carefully. He'd also tried to call and text her, but she'd ignored him. Once, she'd found a bundle of iris stuffed in Parfum d'Antan's night gate. The card attached said, "This is as close as I could get to a blue lily. I'm sorry. I hope you'll forgive me. Love, Luc."

She'd held the thick vellum a moment and traced his signature with a finger. Then she dropped the card in the shop's wastepaper basket. Maybe, another time, things could have been different. She knew she wouldn't forget him for a long time.

The baron had found a way to turn a buck from the incident, too, and, according to Amandine, was making the rounds of daytime television touting his upcoming history on Lys Bleu.

But now she was going home. Her bags were packed, and in another hour a cab would arrive to shuttle her to the Charles de Gaulle airport. She wandered the apartment, touching Pearl's kimono and the evening dress she'd worn to visit Monsieur Saunier, smelling

Pearl's bottle of Bois de Violette, putting her hand into the fireplace cavity where she'd found the bottle of Lys Bleu, double-checking that Pearl's papers were bundled and labeled. Philippe had promised to mail them.

It was time to move on to the next phase of her life, whatever that would be.

Her conversations with Paul had skimmed the surface of her life in Paris and hadn't touched what Madame Gadio termed her essential nature. Joanna looked forward to home and Paul, but she dreaded the conversations they couldn't avoid any longer.

The buzzer sounded, telling her someone was in the lobby. She glanced at the mantel clock. It was too early to be the taxi.

"*Oui?* Yes?" she said into the security phone.

"Ruth Littlewood."

She pushed the button to release the door and, a moment later, the elevator's motor chugged into gear.

"Joanna?" she heard at least two floors away. No mistaking that voice—it was Pearl's mother, all right. "What a flight. How are you, honey?" Ruth pushed open the elevator door and rolled out her suitcase. Now, here she was, complete with a Sierra Club baseball cap and a T-shirt reading "Birders Do It in the Bush."

"Aren't you going to let me in?" She pushed past Joanna and paused in the hall, taking it all in. Joanna remembered her own first minutes two weeks ago, standing in the same spot. Two weeks that felt like months. A faint sound escaped Ruth's lips.

"Mrs. Littlewood. Why are you here?"

Ruth tossed her baseball cap on the dining room table and fluffed her hair. "That's what you wanted, wasn't it? When you mailed me that packet of letters?"

The letters. With everything that had happened, she'd almost forgotten she'd sent them. "You read them?"

"Finally did. Every word." Ruth made herself at home, rooting in the kitchen cabinets for a glass. "The water here any good?"

"A little hard, but not bad."

"I told you my best decisions have come from my gut, right?"

Joanna nodded.

"Opening the first letter wasn't easy, I admit. But once I began reading, I couldn't stop. I was up all night." She drained her tumbler of water in a gulp. "I'd been an idiot. An unconscionable idiot." She set down the glass and locked gazes with Joanna. "I knew I'd made the right choice with you."

"Thank you. That means a lot." Joanna steered Ruth to Pearl's reading chair. "Have a seat. I'll get you a refill." When Joanna returned, Ruth was staring out the window but not seeming to focus on anything in particular. "It doesn't do much good to beat yourself up over the past, not now," Joanna told her.

"I've always been a hardheaded businesswoman. There's no problem—no matter how sticky—I can't figure out eventually. But what did I do with Pearl? Nothing. It was as if my only options were to capitulate or cut her off. No in between."

Joanna sank to the couch across from her. "No in between."

"There's always another way. Always. When two people love each other like I loved Pearl, they can figure it out. I simply refused. And I missed so much." She wiped at an eye. "Sorry. Tired, that's all."

Joanna handed her a tissue. "What do you mean?"

"I mean not everything's black and white. My fear of losing Pearl turned into the instrument that drove her away and kept her there."

Ruth's words had opened a door in Joanna's mind. She still had a lot of thinking to do, but one thing she knew was that she loved Paul and he loved her. Maybe what she'd been seeing as a dealbreaker wasn't an impassable path. Or maybe it was. She wouldn't know until she explored it, as painful as it might be.

"Anyway, I have an offer," Ruth said.

"The taxi will be here soon to take me to the airport."

"Fine, fine. This won't take a minute. I've been thinking. Pearl put a lot of herself into the perfume shop. The more I contemplate it, the less I like the idea of a giant corporation taking it over."

"Parfum d'Antan," Joanna said. Perfume of Yesteryear. Nearly a sister shop to Tallulah's Closet.

"Yes, well, maybe it would be all right to see how it fares. You say it's been making a profit?"

Joanna nodded. "Pearl wasn't getting rich, but she was doing fine and putting a bit aside, besides."

"You've enjoyed yourself here, am I right?"

"Oh, yes. It's been…" she couldn't find the words. "Yes, I've loved it."

"Now, just listen. Think about what I'm going to say. You don't have to answer me right away. What do you say you go home, take care of business, then come back after a while and manage the perfume shop? Manage it for me, of course. Things start slipping, you go home. You can continue living here. The apartment is a good investment. I'll pay you a living wage with bonuses, if you work out."

If Joanna's emotions were a symphony, it would be that crazy time when the orchestra tunes up, but more and more loudly—until it crashes to a stop.

"I can't."

"No?"

"I—I have a few things to work out at home. I couldn't commit to returning." Saying each word was pulling a tooth, but she knew it was the right decision.

To Joanna's surprise, Ruth smiled. "Good, honey. You go do that. No running away. I don't need an answer from you today. I'm planning on staying in Paris a little while. Take some time to think about it."

Ruth's offer should have complicated Joanna's thinking and deepened her anxiety. Instead, she felt lighter. Emotion thickened in her throat. Ruth was giving her the luxury of time to work things out and a place to go if they didn't.

"I don't know how to thank you." She reached out and grasped Ruth's thin hand in hers. "I hope you discover more of Pearl while you're here. You might start with Jicky, her cat."

The cat stared at Ruth, not with malice, but with curiosity, as if she recognized some of Pearl in her.

The intercom buzzed again. Joanna looked out the French windows. This time it was the taxi. The driver saw her and honked.

"Hold your horses," Ruth shouted down.

Joanna hugged her. "Again, thank you so much, but I have to go now. Jicky doesn't like wet food, by the way. And make sure the kitchen door is locked. You know, you'd better just call me every night—that would be easiest." She pushed the suitcase into the hall. "Every night. Don't forget. You're not here to loaf around, you know."

Acknowledgements

A big thank you to Charlotte Rains Dixon, Jenni Gainsborough, and Debbie Guyol for their valuable comments. A huge thank you to Denyse Beaulieu and her cat Jicky for giving me encouragement and for many happy stays in an apartment suspiciously like Pearl's. Last, but certainly not least, the community of generous perfume enthusiasts at Now Smell This, where I've written for many years, continues to inspire me.

www.ingramcontent.com/pod-product-compliance
Lightning Source LLC
Chambersburg PA
CBHW050240110726
47898CB00007B/2217